The Oracle

Matthew Oakley

In loving memory of my Mom,
Thank you for always believing in me

The Oracle

Part 1 of the White Wolf Series

by

Matthew Oakley

Table of Contents

Chapter 1

Inhale…

Both the castle city of Torek, and the event taking place were not things that Keelin enjoyed. The castle itself was a dull grey slab. Nothing about it was particularly impressive, but that pretty much summed up Sabal as a whole. Being invited to a slave auction truly wasn't Keelin's idea of a good time, but he was there on business, and therefor had to play his part. The issue wasn't the slaves. He had owned a few himself, though he rarely used them for more than conversation. It was the buyers. The pompous, arrogant royalty that would think of this as nothing more than entertainment, and another excuse to get drunk.

The participants all gathered into a small room. Twelve in total. Several women wearing nothing but thin strips of fabric along with gold ankle and wrist shackles presented them with drinks and small snacks to tide them over. Most of the other bidders, Keelin noticed, brought guests, and that fact only added to his annoyance of the festivities.

As he took in the dreary halls of the castle, others began to take notice of him. Each uncomfortable shift and soft whisper brought a small smirk to his face. It helped with the wait, but after what seemed like an unnecessary length of time, King Malachi finally entered the room. He looked a little fatter than Keelin remembered. His beard was disheveled, with bits of grey showing. Maybe the rumors of his mental breakdown were true. He led the way past the others and into the twelve sided hall that would host the night's event without saying a word.

Keelin found his way to his seat, and began to take in the inner chamber. Tall metal dividers separated the bidders from one another, giving each a little privacy. It was fairly easy to see the people across from him still, but the dim lighting made it hard to make out much detail. Hanging from the ceiling was a brass horn that spiraled out towards his seat. Each room had one he noticed, and they led up to a smaller room on the floor above. In front of him, three buttons, reading out IN, PASS, and OUT in a number of languages.

The horn burst to life as a female voice echoed out through the chamber. "Welcome esteemed guests of King Malachi." Each visitor was then introduced one by one. Most were met with a cordial applause from the others. There was a Prince from somewhere in the Northern Glen, a few visitors from Anchala, a city in Western Coille, a pair of sister rulers from The Isle of Skye, and a few others who didn't particularly stand out. "And last but not least, Keelin, Alpha of the Wolves." Silence... Complete silence.

Exhale...

"The rules are as follows. A price will be named as the items are brought out for purchase. If you are interested, press in. If you are not interested, press pass. Once you press in, the price will continue to rise. When it becomes too much, press out. The last person in... wins the prize." The message was repeated several times in various dialects before moving on. "The price will be announced at every increase, and payment is expected before you leave the castle. Best of luck."

As Keelin thought about his fellow bidders, he knew they all had more than enough money to spend on a few new slaves. From the clothes, to the cocky grins, their indulgences of luxury were obvious. It only made him smile however as he thought of all the ways he had interrupted their posh lifestyles. They had money, but the Wolves had power. Real power.

The first woman made her way out, and the realism of the moment sunk in. The room fell to a mumble of anticipation. A tall, lanky blonde with pale skin made her way to the center. She had on a dazzling white sequined dress that frayed just past the hip. As the music started, she seemed hesitant to perform. She resisted doing much more than a little hip wiggle, her face showing her discomfort. It was intriguing at the least.

He leaned forward in his seat as the horn bellowed once again. "Bidding starts at 50 tyrs." Immediately a series of clicks and clanks rang out, which must've symbolized other bidders buying in. He thought about staying in for the fun of it, but eventually hit Pass.

A large, well-built man entered the room with her and began shouting. The aggression of his body language continued to grow, but she refused to move. He stood inches away from her, and yet there was no fear in her. There was a fire. Some boos rang out from the other boxes. Keelin closed his eyes. He knew what was coming.

Inhale…

The loud thud of her body hitting the ground confirmed it. He opened his eyes as the large man picked up the now docile blonde, slung her over his shoulder and carried her out. "Damn"… Keelin whispered under his breath.

Exhale…

The King quickly stood and shouted out to the room to try and calm everyone down. "My friends! I can assure you that our other items will be much more willing to earn your business. This was her first time. A little stage fright. That's all! Please, let us continue!"

The next woman was much more willing, but he could hardly focus. He wasn't here for this show. The sooner it was over, the better.

One by one the women entered, and the bidding continued to rise. It became clear that they were in order of what the King thought they could fetch. Keelin was almost glad to realize that he and the King seemed to have different tastes in their women, though none truly stood out.

The servers kept the drinks coming, which at least made the proceedings a little more bearable as the hours passed. He had lost all interest, sinking his head into his hands, begging for all of it to end, and then she entered...

Bell… Drum… Inhale… Bell… Exhale… Drum… Bell….

She was different. Her skin… her eyes… they spoke. She was wearing nothing more than a twisting red piece of fabric that wrapped around her body and clung to her curves. The color matched the long flowing hair on her head. The moment she entered the room, the atmosphere changed. He was transfixed on the simplistic beauty of her walk. It was effortless. He wasn't alone.

The noise in the room suddenly fell even quieter than when Keelin was introduced. "The bidding will start at 3,000 tyrs..." He had to have her. He immediately pressed IN, and sat on the edge of his seat as she began her performance.

A soft step forward with her right, *Boom...* Another step... *Boom...* Her hips swayed. The bells around her ankles began to chime to life in tune. A twist... a bow... a single bead of sweat rolled down and dove off the tip of her nose. It became a mantra of mind and body, a twirling, contorting vessel of energy focused completely on each sound, each movement, the music, and the dance. Nothing else was left... the dance... the music... the movement... the sound. Then nothing. Nothing but the pounding in her ears. The pounding of her own heart. "We are now at 4,000 Credit."

Inhale...

The vessel broke free, and the energy exploded outward. Her body was now separated from mind as the music picked up the pace, but she did not hear a single note. She felt them. She gazed off into the distance, entranced by something that wasn't there. Her lips parted as if she was in rapture, but she was numb. The drums continued to echo through the small chamber, and her solo in a way became a duet. A dance between beauty and chaos, and it was only now, that she was blind and deaf... that she was free. She was free because she could not see them. Their lustful, malicious gazes could not burn her flesh.

Exhale...

"5,000 tyrs. Five bidders remain." No girl had gone for more than 5,000 yet. It didn't matter. This one had secrets. There was something in her soul that immediately caused Keelin to experience things he never thought he could feel. Things that only stories spoke of. The kinds of things men bragged about when telling lies while trying to appear impressive. This was no lie. She was real. He would sell everything he owned if he needed to. She was going to be his. He had to know more.

The music slowed. This was her favorite part in the routine because it felt for a moment as if time decelerated as well. She dropped to her knees and threw her arms into the air, before slowly lowering her palms down to the cold sandstone floor of the palace. Her forehead kissed the tiles then she snapped back, flinging her head up until she was facing the ceiling. It sent a wave of billowing red locks spiraling around her. Her back arched as she continued to reach behind, twisting until her palms met the floor once more. The music stopped…

"7,000 tyrs."

Inhale...

Boom. The drums roared back to life. Cymbals crashed as she shifted her weight forward and up, her hips rose up level to her shoulders and then her toes reached out toward the ceiling. She held the handstand and waited for the next pause.

"8,000 tyrs, 3 bidders remain." Three? Who? Keelin began looking around the room. The King? The King must be a part of this. "The benevolent King Malachi, the High Priest Cadius, and the Alpha Wolf from Dachaigh are still in." He had no idea who this High Priest was, though the title was interesting. Sabal didn't have any particular ties to a deity that he knew of. Why did they need a priest?

He had to stop. If the King wanted her, he was paying himself. He could bet any amount. There's no way he could win. There had to be a reason he was betting on this one though. Why did the King want her so badly? Keelin was risking too much for a slave. His entire mission could be compromised.

Exhale…

Boom. The music began a spirited crescendo as the dancer sprung backwards from her hands to her feet, and with a slight spin revealed a tambourine from within the folds of her skirts. She began twisting and swaying her hips, banging the instrument with each outward movement in an aggressive fashion.

"10,000 tyrs, 2 bidders remain."

The music rounded out and headed for its conclusion. The dancer paused, ran, and gave a final leap, floating through the air before landing on her knees in front of the King's box, her head tossed back, and chest heaving with every breath. "We have a winner. 12,000 tyrs to the Alpha of the Wolves, Keelin." He won.

He won!? This was not going to help to negotiate with the King. Malachi gave a dismissive nod, and waved her away. Exhausted, she shakily rose to her feet. "You may claim your prize."

A woman walked out to the dancer, bound her wrists behind her back, and blindfolded her before leading her down to Keelin's area. It was the same procedure that had been done with all the girls so far, but he wasn't ready for such sudden interaction.

He figured the exchange would happen at the end of the day. There should have been paperwork to sign. He stood, straightening his deep purple robes and running a hand through his dark black hair, and then down to his chin. He was tall, but not a giant by any means. He had a solid frame, but not a typical warrior either. It was his cunning that got him where he was in life. His blue eyes pierced with the sharp intensity of his demeanor.

He began circling the magnificent dancer, who was now kneeling before him. He felt like an artist moving about his sculpture, inspecting it for flaws. He paused, placing a hand softly under her chin, lifting her face to the light as his other gently ran along her jaw line. There was an aura about her. A raw energy filled the small space. In that moment he wasn't sure if it was something to embrace, or to break. A slave who believed in herself was a dangerous thing.

He took a step forward, cupped her cheeks in his hands and pulled her in for a strong, passionate kiss. It was sloppy but forceful, meant to establish their roles and break some of that fight. Her body stiffened, but she leaned into it. He wasn't the first to take a kiss from her. She was used to this.

He ended, and pushed her away. "Follow" he barked out, and moved back to his seat. The rush of it all finally hit him. What the hell was he going to do with her now?

She didn't even fall when he pushed her, instead gracefully shifting her weight to the balls of her feet and standing in a fluid motion that seemed right out of her dance. Slowly she walked towards him. Still blindfolded, she was careful in her approach.

She obediently knelt before him once more. "Master." She said calmly, awaiting his next order. There was a slight accent, but Keelin couldn't quite place it. Somewhere beyond the Southern Pass perhaps.

"Sit here, in front of me." He spoke softly, no longer feeling the need to be aggressive. As she took her place between his legs, he undid her blindfold and her wrist restraints. A small noise behind him caused him to look back. A few of the other bidders had gathered to inspect his purchase, but with a slight wave, and a furious stare down, they were gone. She truly had everyone's curiosity peaked.

His focus shifted back to her. Everything she did had such intent, nothing was wasted. He was glad he didn't bid on anyone else. She was the only one worth coming after. Why was she so calm? How long had she been here? Had the King put her up before and just always bought her back? How cruel that tease of freedom must have been. That hair... He'd never seen anything like it.

His hand instinctively ran out and began playing with the fiery red locks. No reaction... Nothing. It almost frustrated him. He struck fear in Kings and merchants from coast to coast, and yet this girl seemed indifferent to his existence. She lived a sheltered life he thought. Maybe she just didn't know any better.

In reality, she was as excited as she had ever been. The King always bought her back. He never let someone else show him up like this. The nights that followed the auctions were normally terrifying, traumatic experiences. This new Wolf could be her ticket out of the castle forever. It was possible she was headed somewhere worse. It could prove true that this man was even more of a tyrant than her King, but it didn't matter. It wasn't here.

Her hand grazed along his thigh as she watched the next performers. It was odd seeing them from this side. Normally when the King bought her, she returned to the King's chambers, and waited for him to stumble in drunk, hours later.

"Face me..." The request caught her a bit off guard, but she turned. Her eyes looking up into his. "It's my belief that the eyes are the windows to the soul. I wonder what I can see through yours?" Within a matter of moments, he found himself lost in her gaze. They were a mesmerizing swirl of blues that he had only seen a few times in nature. He felt silly for the grip they had on him. Deeper down, there was confusion, hurt, pain, passion, energy, and so much more... all locked away behind layers of training and discipline.

He had to get a reaction out of her. He had to see more. His hand came down violently across the side of her face with a vicious slap that filled the chamber. She wasn't able to brace herself this time, and hit the ground hard. Her head bounced off the stone floor. Regret filled Keelin almost instantly, but her reaction was as unpredictable as the rest of her... she chuckled.

He wasn't sure what to feel as he looked down at her trying to hide a small laugh. She had read him. She knew what he was after. Almost impulsively, he returned the smile. He then reached forward, grabbed her under her arms and pulled her back up to her knees.

He reached out towards her, softly caressing the same cheek he had just smacked. His hand wandered up to the wound on her head. After inspecting the blood on his finger, he showed it to her, and then tasted it. "You may think you have been trained before. You will forget what you know. You will be retrained."

There was a bit of remorse and hesitation. He realized that this wasn't going to be easy for either of them. "In order to rebuild you, I must first break you. How long that takes is up to you." His gaze broke as he took a long sip of his drink, then spoke. "Your first true task is this. Sing."

"I'm sorry?" She replied as if she misheard him. Such a bizarre request. Just because she could dance didn't mean she could sing. They were nothing alike. It was the same as asking a cook to hunt. They were related, but not.

"Sing me a song. Anything. Sing of how much you hate me! Sing about this dreadful castle. It doesn't matter what the song is. Just... sing." He returned to his more relaxed posture in his chair, wondering what would come next. Again she let out a smile. He wasn't so different she thought. He was a fool if he believed she could be manipulated so easily. She spat a bit of blood out onto the floor from where her teeth had bit into her cheek, and then began her chosen song.

There was a girl made of sand,
She could break and she could bend.
She did not fear his cruel hand,
And her cracks he could not mend.
She bowed and obeyed his every command
She never wavered in his demands.
But he could not lift the stains from her heart
His will to break her was doomed for the start.

Her face turned a bit somber as the words struck her. Keelin laughed. A small chuckle at first that then rose to a boisterous sound straight from the depths of his soul. "Beautiful my dear. Beautiful. I wonder what possibly could have stained a heart such as yours. Or am I just being vain to think this song has to do with our current predicament?" Again he smiled and leaned forward so he could speak more softly.

"That couldn't possibly be me though. My hand isn't cruel, and you are clearly more than sand. There's so much sand out there. I've never seen anything like you. Do you know what happens to sand when it gets struck by lightning?" He paused, allowing the words to sink in and making sure he actually had her attention. "It turns to glass. Perhaps once you were sand, but you've been heated. You've been charged with... something so much more. It's made you special. Allow me to return the favor with a song of my own. A song of my people."

There once was a girl... A slave
Who was slave in name alone
For she knew she was destined for more
She could feel it in her bone
She had felt the pain of a thousand needles
She had burned under a thousand suns
She had learned to let her heart go numb

No matter where her mind did run
And so she went on searching
Lit by a passion for more
She could never escape her slavery
Its scars she always wore
A kind soul finally purchased her
And he gave something she didn't get often
He gave her a simple choice
Of how she'd be remembered in her coffin
By her movements he was simply entranced
It was not her body but her soul that danced
He knew he must take her, he knew he must break her
So that she could finally have a chance.
That choice he presented was simple
There were two options that he gave
The first was to keep on fighting
And wind up in an early grave
The second was harder to take
For there was no guarantee
But if she listened, and followed him
In due time he would set her free
He wanted nothing more than to release the soul
That captured his wandering heart
But he looked in her eyes
And to no one's surprise,
She thought he was doomed from the start...

"Too bad huh?" He let out a grin as he ran his hand through her hair once more. "Name woman? We have a long journey ahead, and you deserve at least that much." His expressions were fluid, intended to keep her guessing, but she never really wavered.

She had watched intently as he sang to her. This was new, but when he mentioned setting her free something in her hardened. She wouldn't fall for these tricks. Why would he buy her just to set her free? No. How cruel to even tease her with such a thing. She was a possession, and... "Possessions don't have names. They have nothing of their own."

Defiant to the very end. Nothing was going to come easy. "Such pride you have. Such a sense of righteousness." Keelin knew he'd have to choose his words carefully to get anywhere with her. "Why would I free you? I know you're asking yourself that." Her gaze broke as he somehow guessed correctly.

He lifted his cup and took a long sip, leaving her hanging on his words. "The answer is simple. I'm going to show you that I am the best possible thing that could ever happen to you. By the time I'm done with you… you won't want to go anywhere. You'll be better."

He stood, lifting her to her feet as well, with a bit of a grin on his face. "One way or another, I'm going to set your soul free. What your body looks like when that happens, well that's up to you." She hung on those last words. She didn't fear pain. But… there wasn't actually a way to avoid it. She knew what was coming. He wasn't any different. These were tricks. "Let's go." He barked.

She followed closely behind, but they barely made it out of their section before being cut off by King Malachi and two of his guard. "There you are! My friend from Dachaigh! The city in the mountain. I hope you enjoyed the auction." The King's words were full of false sincerity, but also clues for Nodiah. "Now just so you know, it is customary here in my palace that I get one last night alone with my property before she leaves." The dancer shivered at the thought, and looked up to her new Master. She hoped he was smart enough to know that wasn't the case, but worried that objecting could lead to her new Master being dead.

Keelin stepped towards the King and responded forcefully. "Look that's cute, but these 12,000 tyrs say she isn't yours anymore." Keelin presented a large pouch full of coins, and threw it at a guard, causing him to fall back a step. Malachi's jaw dropped. Nodiah tried to hide her happiness at the King's dumbfounded face.

"That doesn't bode well for our arrangement." The King smirked confidently, feeling as though he'd played his trump card. "What would your fellow Alphas say if they knew you threw this all away for some girl?"

Keelin stood his ground, unwavering in his resolve. The more the King pushed, the more certain he was that she was worth protecting. "Well then I guess our arrangement is off. Buy yourself a new arrangement. I'm sure you can get someone else to take on your little mission."

Keelin wasn't going to get one upped. He reached out, placing a hand on the back of her neck. He then proceeded to pull her in for another passionate, rough kiss, right in front of her former Master. As they broke, he pushed his new slave ahead of him, past Malachi.

Her eyes opened wide, surprised at the bold move. She couldn't help but let them flick over towards the King for just a moment. As they broke, she felt his hand push her forward. She smiled ever so slightly, and ducked her head during her walk. She thought about the price, 12,000 tyrs?! Who was this man that could afford to do all of this, and be so brazen in the face of the King?

She knew he was watching every intentional, purposeful step she took away from him. Her body didn't sway, it flowed. She knew the King was watching as much as Keelin was. Once they were out of view of the King, she felt just the slightest hint of something new. This was as close to free as she had ever been. "12,000 tyrs? Really?? I can't be worth that much. My name is Nodiah" That freedom faded quickly.

Keelin spun her around, and slammed her into the wall, pinning her with a forearm across her collarbone. "I won't tolerate any more lies. Understood Nodiah? Even dogs have names. You may not like me, you may not even be afraid of me. In the back of your mind, you may already have figured out how to kill me, and that's all fine. But you will respect me. I'm not one to use scare tactics and empty threats. I'd much rather we get along." His hand raised up to her head, pulling on her locks sharply. "Next time you lie I'm going to cut all that fire right off of your head."

He assumed her hair was a source of identity or pride at the least. It was one of many things that set her apart from any other slave, or person he had ever seen for that matter. He had no intention of actually going through with it, but it was obvious that physical punishment would have little to no effect on Nodiah unless it was taken to extremes. "Am I understood?" He asked sharply, releasing his hold on her.

Just like that, she was back to numb. She had already seen him for what he really was, and she was right. Shame on her for thinking for even a second that he could have been different. Just another predator.

Her chest puffed. Her hand twitched and clenched. It took everything in her not to swing. She knew he felt it, he saw it. It wasn't her hair, it was her name that was sacred. No one had known her name. Why did he care so much? She laughed again at the idea that he threatened to cut off her hair. It couldn't be that rare... could it? She finally responded... "Yes... Master... It won't happen again."

They made their way down the hall, and towards the main gate without another word. She was willing to put all of that interaction behind her. It didn't matter how cruel he was. Nodiah was finally getting the moment she had thought about for years. She was leaving Torek for good. At least she hoped.

Matthew Oakley

Chapter 2

"It's a full days ride. We don't have time to stop. You can sleep, but not for long. I expect you to help keep me entertained, and awake so we don't lose our way." Keelin's stiff commands had little effect on the fiery red-head. His threats were mere words at this point. He paid too much for her just to turn around and bury her now.

The sun began to rise, morning already. He led the way to a tall grey horse with long thin streaks of black running through its coat, and a long black mane down its back. He pulled out a couple of small goggles from the side bag, along with two lengthy pieces of fabric, one black and one white. Keelin wrapped the white one around her nose and mouth, tying it in the back, and then helped her up onto the horse. She found it odd that she was placed facing the rear of the equine, but quickly understood as he climbed on just in front of her, leaving them facing each other with her legs wrapping around him. She still was sitting on the saddle at least, though it was less than comfortable.

They finally began their journey. Nodiah watched the great palace of Torek get smaller and, smaller in the distance. The only home she ever knew was now fading away. She had no idea where they were going, and it was difficult to turn to see, but as long as it was away from Torek, it had to be better.

Her mind raced with thoughts. 12,000 tyrs… Who was this man from Dachaigh? She had to figure it out. She gazed into his eyes as if searching for more clues. "I will keep you entertained… but I don't want you to be distracted." Her words were without malice, instead testing just how much freedom she had.

He chuckled a bit as his hand ran along the curves of her legs. He was studying her. The amount of scars, bumps, and cuts was something that he hadn't really noticed before. He was impressed that she hadn't asked the usual questions, food... water... clothing... but there was still time.

His hand traced along her body up to her heart. "What wondrous stories you must have locked in her. I assure you my dear Nodi, there is nothing you can do that will distract me. Bore me maybe." It was meant to be a challenge. Another statement intended to create a reaction, but it didn't work.

The terrain in Sabal wasn't much different then the Outlands. The dividing line was only established based on the crumbling defense wall that stretched across the island. The terrain itself was barren and dry, with a few clumps of trees and the occasional city popping up here and there in the distance.

The horse picked up speed, breaking her concentration momentarily. She did her best to adjust to the horses pace, and find a comfortable spot, but it hurt. She could feel her skin breaking against the rough leather beneath her. She needed a distraction,

Her focus shifted to his body. She trailed the tip of her finger from the top of his robes, to his collarbone, and up to his neck. It was an absent-minded wander of her finger as her gaze remained on his eyes. They hid so much. Eventually, she buried her head into his shoulder, and decided to focus on other things. "Yes....I have stories..." She spoke in a near whisper. "But I am more interested in yours."

Hours passed, and she began to show the signs that her body wasn't used to the rough nature of the ride. He felt her weight press in, but assumed she was tired. He noticed her wincing, but barely. Reluctantly, he stopped and got off. Her entire body slumped as she let out long exaggerated breaths of relief.

Reaching into the saddlebags, he pulled out a long cream colored robe that was similar in shape to his own, and threw it to Nodiah, "You'll need this. Wind is picking up." It was hardly a breeze at the moment, but he felt it. "The weather out here changes in an instant." He pulled out his canteen, taking a long sip. Nodiah gulped loudly. She couldn't remember being more thirsty in her life.

He smiled, debating just how cruel he felt like being, but finally approached and offered her some. She did her best to remain calm, but immediately took in a mouthful, and attempted to swallow it down. Keelin thought about stopping her, but it was too late. Her eyes widened as the burn of the alcohol hit the back of her throat, but she didn't give him the pleasure of a full reaction. Instead, she stared at the canteen and smiled. "Sweet as mother's milk," she remarked, passing him back the container. She then stripped off the thin fabric and began to put on the new robe.

Keelin was surprised at the bleeding patches of skin that started to seep into the new fabric rather quickly. She was hurt. He had no idea how badly until now. She had never made a sound, not one complaint. Just a few winces. She had been taught that it wasn't okay to feel. He had to change that.

He spun her around, meeting her amazing blue eyes with his once more. "Just because you're a slave, you're my property, and I do fully intend to take advantage of that fact... That doesn't mean that you aren't human. You are allowed to feel. You are allowed to express what you feel. Pain, guilt, joy, happiness, all of it. Show me. As with all people of course there may be consequences to your actions, but that doesn't mean you hide them. If you're hurt, I need to know."

He got a closer look at her open blisters and let out a frustrating sigh. "Now that's just stupid... You'll be lucky if those don't get infected out here." She wouldn't make it all the way. They had to detour. "A little east of here there's a small town. We'll head there for the night and let you rest. Maybe get to share some stories. I'll let you sleep a couple hours and see if the storm passes. Then we go home."

Keelin surprised himself at his sympathy for the girl. He felt as though he wasn't running around with a dog on a leash. Nodiah was a tiger in a cage, just waiting to be let out. Keelin was left to train her so that when he did open it, she didn't pounce on him, but it was obvious she was hungry.

In her mind, the only thing that was stupid was him expecting her to confess weakness. That and his weather prediction. What storm? She opened her mouth to speak, but wasn't sure where to begin. He clearly had not had a slave before she thought. Slaves felt what they were told to feel. Admitting weakness, or even the ability to feel pain just gave the Master that much more control.

Her pain was the only thing that truly belonged to her. She was the only one that felt it, that understood it, and whether or not she chose to let it affect her was one of the only forms of control she had. Nodiah then made a rather reasonable request. "Perhaps if I sat side saddle, or behind you, then the saddle wouldn't hit me in the same places." She coiled, almost expecting anger in his reaction, but it didn't come.

Keelin smiled as she spoke. It was a start. He watched her retract, almost as if she was mad he made her speak her feelings. She must have been a slave since birth, he thought. She didn't know anything other than her role as slave.

"I don't know where you came from. I don't know where King Malachi found you, and I don't expect you to want to tell me just yet. I do know that the King needs to be taught some lessons on how to care for his things." He watched as Nodiah tried to process the words.

Everything about him was so perplexing. Couldn't he speak plainly? There was a compliment, and yet that word again. She was just a thing.

He mounted the horse and headed in her direction. He reached his hand down, and pulled her up behind him, allowing her to sit facing the side as she mentioned. He then continued his rant. "When you hold something so delicate, so beautiful in your hands, you should handle it with care. Too firm of a grasp, and you deny your possession the chance to shine. You suffocate it. Not enough grip, and you may drop it or, or it could get stolen. There has to be the just the right amount of touch to get the most out of it." Those words hung in the air as they rode out towards the sands.

Not long after, the small town known as Brade came into view. It was a welcome sight, but as they got closer, Keelin was overcome with an uneasy feeling. People were scrambling, a loud clanging bell rang out from a tower. Nodiah looked back, and suddenly was all too aware of what was happening. "Go... Go.... GO!" She screamed, somehow wondering if her journey out of the castle was going to end in her death a few hours later.

He looked back to see what had her attention, and realized that her fears were for good reason. A sandstorm. A giant wall of dust and sand was headed their direction, moving tremendously fast. It towered over everything, taking out and consuming the light from the sun. He choked up on the reins and kicked the horse into a full sprint. Outrunning the mountain like cloud was unlikely, but they had to try. "Hold on tight!" He yelled back.

He helped her re-position so that she could properly straddle the horse, and wrap her arms around him. The cloud caught them just as they hit the edge of town. It was hard to see anything other than the shadowy outlines of the buildings, but that was enough. The sand felt like tiny bee stings as it blasted into their bodies. Staying balanced and fighting the force of the wind was difficult, but they had to make their way inside.

Without really stopping Keelin dismounted, then helped her down, and the duo ran into the nearest building. Most of the people inside had hunched down and covered their ears from the howling storm. The noise was a constant roar, deep and menacing, combined with the creaking of old wood as it swayed and bent at the mercy of the winds.

Keelin didn't even bother hiding or crouching. He instead took off his goggles, and looked around. He was all too happy to see they had wandered into a bar. He walked behind the counter and grabbed a large spherical bottle. He took the bottle to a large round table, placing four glasses down in front of him. He then smiled in Nodiah's direction as he took a sniff of the liquor.

Now finally out of the elements, she chuckled. She walked over with her slow, intentional strut, and stood next to him. She watched on as the bottle appeared to be letting off a little bit of smoke from the top. "You weren't supposed to win, you know?" Her voice rose to top the storm. "The auctions are just a way for the King to show off his play things. He never loses. He just entices the would-be buyers in, and then, after they lose, he bribes them with favors from the girl. I don't know what was going on in his viewing room that made him lose, but I'm sure he's quite unhappy about it. You made a powerful enemy today." The main question she had, she couldn't ask… Why? She was waiting for permission to take a seat, but realized that maybe it wasn't needed.

Keelin began pouring the drink, filling two of the glasses, and then quickly flipping the other two glasses over on top. This trapped the smoke on top of the beverage. "This is Talon." Keelin yelled back, and pointed to the cup. "It goes down smooth, but it hits quick. Dangerous stuff." The King wasn't worth his attention at the moment. He was far more interested in her.

Cautiously, she pulled out the chair and sat next to him, staring at the liquor in front of her. She took off the top glass, and watched on as the tendrils of smoke drifted away. She raised the bottom glass, and took a small sip. The taste, infused with the smoke, was strong, but smooth. She shot Keelin a confident glance.

He watched intently as she tipped her head back, downed it, and put the glass back in one fluid motion. Everything she did was part of a dance it seemed. He was more of a sipper himself, especially when it came to Talon. It was meant to be enjoyed for its flavor, not just its side effects.

"So, do I ever get to know your name? Or do we stick with Master."

He chuckled a bit at the bold question. "Seems drinking gives you some liquid courage little Nodi." ....little... her face scrunched with displeasure at the word. The wind seemed to die down as if even the storm wanted to hear his response. "Most call me bastard... or ass... or murderer... thief... devil... animal... and those are the ones who like me." His eyes found hers, which were staring on with full intrigue. "To the rest of the world, I'm known as Keelin."

Their stare was broken by the sound of people shuffling away from them. As they did, a big man dressed in plain tan clothes moved towards them. He was sporting a large mustache, and a rather serious grimace on his face. Nodiah watched on intently, but nervously.

Keelin... She rolled the name around in her mind as if it was a memory she was trying to recall. She moved closer to him as the other man approached, and wondered just who Keelin was. He couldn't be as bad as he made it sound... could he?

Looming over Keelin, the man began to speak. "My apologies for interrupting, my name is Corrig," his voice boomed. "Did you say your name was Keelin? The... Keelin?" Keelin didn't bother looking up, instead quickly finishing his drink and wiping his mouth. His name often got him in trouble.

"Well, Corrig, it's not nice to eavesdrop on others' conversations there friend. We didn't come here for anything more than to get out of the storm. So why don't you go sit back down over there and let me buy you a drink alright?" His mouth was the other thing that got him in trouble.

Keelin could hear the man's knuckles crack as he clenched them tightly into fists. His own hand rested on a small dagger he keep pocketed near his right thigh just in case. This didn't feel like it was going to end well. The man had not moved. Keelin turned to Nodiah, and began to ignore him for the time being. "Another drink my dear?" he said with a bit of a chuckle.

"What is this? As if you being here isn't bad enough, bringing her kind here is trouble for all of us." The man refused to back down. Keelin watched on as her body cringed at the words "her kind." He wasn't even entirely sure what the man meant.

She waved off the drink, and Keelin stood, turning to face the man. She wasn't sure what he meant either. Were slaves not welcomed here? He looked up into the larger man's eyes, and with a surprisingly calm demeanor, addressed the situation.

"Now that was uncalled for. So I'll tell you what. Apologize to the woman." Keelin unfastened the button holding the dagger, and clutched the handle. The room gave the two men some space.

"She is no woman. She is your slave. On top of that, likely the last Sky Dancer after what the Kings did..." Keelin's patience had worn out. He didn't know if he believed the man or not, but he had heard enough. He grabbed the towering figure by the collar of his shirt and drove him back into the far wall. He then brought the dagger up to his throat as the room fell silent.

"Apologize, and buy her a drink, and you won't fall victim to the Wolves." His eyes spoke louder than his words. His thoughts wandered off however. Nodiah being a Sky Dancer hadn't crossed his mind. Corrig put up his hands, seemingly ready to cooperate.

As Keelin and the man returned to the table, Nodiah's thoughts were racing as well. Sky Dancer? She didn't know what that meant, or why it made this man so angry? It didn't feel like a compliment.

She wasn't surprised by Keelin's sudden outburst. He seemed to have a short fuse when it came to feeling disrespected. She reflexively curled back on her chair as the two men approached. Corrig knelt down before Nodiah, thanks to a stern push from Keelin.

"I... apologize for disrespecting you. Allow me to buy your drink, and your meal." He said reluctantly. He refused to make eye contact with her, but the words still escaped. Nodiah was shocked. This large man was kneeling before her. It was embarrassing at first, uncomfortable, but it quickly grew on her.

As she adjusted, her mind moved past the awkwardness. She wanted to see what it felt like. She needed to know. She reached out and grabbed his jaw, forcing him to make eye contact with her. Keelin dragged him away before she could do anything else.

In a rather loud voice, Keelin called out "If you find her kind to be trouble, well then this is going to bring all kinds of bad things your way isn't it?" Without hesitation or remorse, Keelin pulled Nodiah to her feet for another passionate kiss. There was no sloppiness to this one however. It was intentional, emotional, and aggressive. It was meant to prove a point. To the crowd... To Nodiah... to himself. The kiss broke, leaving them both taking a gasp to recollect their breath, and then sharing a collective smile for the first time. The man simply turned around, and made his way to the bar with his back to the pair.

Keelin's hand wandered to her heart. "My people believe in transferring energy. If you place your hand on someone's heart, it opens a connection. You can feel what the other person is feeling... and I'm wondering what that felt like. To have him kneeling before you. You made him look at you... Why?"

For Keelin, that was the most important question in the world at that moment. It was the exact opposite thinking a slave should have. They would never worry about why they did things. The answer was too simple... Because they were told. She chose to make him look at her. She acted on her own. The why, however, was far more important than the what.

Her own hand softly extended, gently finding its way to her heart as well. Something began stirring inside her. It was strange. All she wanted to do was fold into him and rest in his arms. She felt... protected. After a small shake, she brushed it off however. Another trick... it had to be.

"I..." she thought about her words carefully. "I wanted him to see me... Not some notion he already had in his mind. I have my own identity. My own name. I wanted him to see me." Her voice trailed off. She had so many questions of her own. Would he let her ask? One way to find out. "Keelin... Master... who are the Wolves? And what's a... Sky Dancer?"

Tension refilled the atmosphere between the pairing as Keelin considered the answers. He could tell her what he knew, but it wouldn't satisfy her curiosity. He wasn't entirely confident in his response on the latter question himself. As for the first… "Why tell you when I can show you? You'll meet the Wolves soon enough." He said with a slight smirk on his face.

Bringing her home was going to be met with resistance. She was different. He had to protect her, even from them. "Think you can make it the rest of the way?"

He didn't wait for an answer, instead finishing his drink and heading back out to the horse. Nodiah almost mentioned the fact they still hadn't eaten. She was a bit disappointed that Corrig was getting away without paying for their meal, but she didn't say a word. He had promised her sleep too.

Something changed. Why was he in such a hurry? They moved outside, and she shot the horse a scowl as if it were the beast's fault she was injured. The last thing she wanted to do was ride again.

Despite her hunger, pain, and exhaustion, she was excited. Maybe she could unlock some of the mysteries of her new master along the way. Then she remembered how the man inside cowered at the mention of the Wolves, how Keelin had drawn the knife, how he threatened to shave her head, and even promise an early death if she did not obey. Maybe she didn't want to know.

She wondered if he would be inclined to share his new possession with these 'Wolves', but she doubted it. She was his… He wanted to protect her. She felt it. So many questions, but so few answers.

The rest of the journey was rather quiet and uneventful. Keelin had no interest in getting caught in another storm. The faster he rode, the faster the wind blew, and the cooler the ride became. He glanced back towards her occasionally, just to make sure she wasn't wincing again.

He found himself completely engrossed with her touch. As she leaned against him, he felt the heaviness pressing into his back once more. This was only the first day. It was possible she wasn't as strong as he thought.

Within a couple of hours, they reached their destination. They approached the massive peak that served as the backdrop for Keelin's home. Nodiah's jaw dropped as she took in the landscape before her. A series of structures were carved deep into the base of the mountain. A giant overhang gave the entire town shade most of the day, and protection from the heat and the storms. The scale was the impressive part. It wasn't one building. It appeared to be an entire community nestled into this cave like crevice. She had never imagined such a thing was possible.

Before long, they were beneath the overhang and making their way down the strips of dirt that served as paths. They rode through rows of poorly constructed tents and huts, along with a few small buildings that seemed to be built from the dirt and clay of the mountain itself. At first guess, Nodiah estimated about 200 people, but it was hard to say for sure.

As they made it to an intersection, Keelin leaned back and let out a loud wolf howl. It echoed off the ceiling enough that Nodi covered her ears. The massive amounts of movement quickly took her attention from the noise. People came from every direction They all had the same symbol somewhere on their body. It was small, and seemed to come in a variety of different colors, but they all had it… A wolf.

He addressed them all as he dismounted, and then helped Nodiah down. "She belongs to me. That means she is one of us. No one is to touch her. No one is to help her. She is to be trained." A few chuckles and snickers rose up from the crowd that made Nodiah visibly uncomfortable. "This one will not be easy. No one is to mention what she may or may not be. Speculations and assumptions get people killed."

Keelin's eyes scanned the crowd. There were mixed reactions. Most were simply surprised, some angered. It wasn't enough to cause an issue however. She was safe for now. Keelin led the way towards the back of the town, where a seemingly impossible four-story building stood, made out of something as black as night. It was significantly out of place with the surroundings. So much so, that Nodiah thought she was imagining it, and began rubbing her eyes. She paused... staring... hypnotized by its darkness.

Keelin entered, looking back to Nodiah as she tried to take it all in. He knew she wouldn't be impressed by wealth, but that's not what the Den was about. "It's black for protection." He pointed to small troughs that ran along the ground all through the village, forming the borders of the paths. Then he pointed to tall, massive torches every so often that she had somehow missed thus far. "That's our lighting system. When night falls, this place disappears. It's our fallback. It also happens to serve as quarters for some of us." He wasn't sure why he was bothering explaining so much. He didn't owe her anything, but he wanted her to understand.

She followed him through the giant double doors, and began trying to make sense of the layout. The main floor of the building was one massive room. From the center one could stare all the way up to the ceiling, where glass panels lined up with a hole in the overhang, stretching up to the sky and letting in a little natural light. In the far corners, staircases led the way to balconies that jutted out from the upper floors, and beyond those were doors of various colors and sizes.

It felt a bit more like a museum than a palace Nodiah thought. In front of them, maps of all sorts of kingdoms were spread out on the wall. Ogla, Sabal, Coille, and even places beyond the Southern Pass were laid out in explicit detail, though Nodiah only knew most of the places from conversations with people visiting Torek. Some of the maps included star charts and others that didn't make any sense at first glance. A giant round table stood to the left, with another map of the Southern Pass laid out on it.

To the right, two people were cutting open and dissecting what looked to be a large boar. The tusks were longer than Nodiah had imagined, but she'd only seen the animals cooked on platters.

Other charts of all kinds of different anatomies, including humans, hung on the walls near the animal. In another section, a bookshelf with hundreds upon thousands of texts, scrolls, and books of all kinds. They must have had some kind of information on just about everything.

Keelin made his way to the center and then spun around to face her... "The entire mountain, we call Dachaigh. This building, we affectionately call the Den... Welcome home..." he said genuinely. He took a moment to appreciate the structure himself. It was unique. It was something to be proud of.

H... home... This wasn't her home. She waited to be taken to her chamber, or cell, or quarters where the slaves were kept. That must be where the other women were. She saw the people on the streets. They suffered while he lived in this palace of luxury? He truly was just another King. Fire swelled in her heart, and must have shown in her eyes. The pain of the ride, bruises, blisters, and cuts, all seemed to intensify but that only fueled her passion. She finally brought her eyes down to meet his.

Inhale... Exhale...

He saw it... "Is there something you wish to say Nodi? Or perhaps something you'd like to do? I'll give you a chance. You have freedom. Complete freedom. Do whatever you'd like." He turned his back to her, adding to the notion that she was truly free to do anything. "Scream, yell, run, attack... Whatever you'd like. Then we'll go eat and clean you up a bit." Keelin had no idea how she'd respond, but once again she had a choice.

Her eyes widened at the thought. That didn't make any sense. This had to be another test. As much as she wanted to attack, her body was in no condition. He didn't say he wouldn't respond. Her seemingly always graceful poise was gone. She was doing all she could just to stay on her feet. He expected rebellion, outburst, violence, but she wouldn't give him the pleasure.

She strode towards him, mustering up the energy she had left to take very meaningful, strong steps. She planted her toes in between his feet, rising up on them, pressing her entire body into his. Her hand slid gently over his heart as a tear rolled down her face. She placed her head on his shoulder, taking a moment to let her breath glide across his ear before finally, firmly stating her request. "I want you to tell me what a Sky Dancer is..."

His eyes turned blank. His face cold, emotionless. "Are you sure? How badly do you want to know?" He already knew the answer, but he felt her hand press in that much harder. She'd give her life to find out. He broke her grip, and moved back a step with a bit of a smile on his face.

"You could do anything you want. You could run away, you could hit me, you could say all the things you want to say. Instead, you choose to ask a question." He nodded his head, deep in thought. "Maybe there's hope for you after all... Come with me."

He led the way towards the bookshelf, and quickly grabbed a thick white book. He then led the way to one of the staircases, and started his way up. "Let's take care of those wounds first, and while we do that I'll tell you a story."

For a moment, Nodiah felt more like a daughter than a slave. He wanted to take care of her. In many ways they were one and the same if you took the physical nature of it all away. That was very hard to separate though, and the thought fled as quickly as it came.

Nodiah seemed genuinely confused. He was really going to tell her just like that? "What would I have gained from attacking you? There's no way I could actually harm you, and you know that." She stammered on, regaining some of her confidence as she made her way up the stairs, one painful step at a time. "Run away? Run into that pack of Wolves you have out there. I'd never make it." She smiled a little at her play on words, but kept following. Information was powerful. Information was the most valuable thing she could have.

She shed her robe intuitively, dropping it on the stairs and continuing behind him naked. Her steps left a small trail of blood from her sores. Each step, a little mark of her ascension.

He led the way higher as Nodiah kept her eyes peeled for other slaves and where their quarters may be. She wasn't quite sure whether to expect the silk beds and pillows King Malachi had provided, or a cold cell block with a dirt floor.

She wanted to ask his plans for her, and what she was being trained for. She already knew how to be obedient. She scratched at her head, and found her hand tangled in the matted knot of blood from where she had struck the ground back at the palace. She was thankful in that moment there weren't many mirrors.

Keelin led the way through another set of double doors, with an intricate carving of a staff on the outside. Twisted around the staff were two snakes that rose up and faced each other. Inside was a fairly small man, wearing a wolf's pelt, scurrying about mixing ingredients in a large cauldron. The creature's jowl rested on his head as a hat which Nodiah found a bit odd, but she said nothing. "Leyos we need a session." Keelin barked abruptly, barely making eye contact with the man. Leyos approached, circling Nodiah with a bit of wonderment in his eyes.

"Is she...?" Before he could even finish the question, Keelin cut him off.

"People keep saying that, but I'm not sure." Keelin said, less than happy at the continued theory. "Now please, can we get on with this." Leyos smiled, and led the way back through another set of doors. The room was extremely hot and humid. Moisture hung in the air in stark contrast to the arid Outlands they had just ridden through. She began sweating almost immediately upon entry.

Built into the floor of the room were three square pits that served as baths of some kind. The first seemed to be crystal clear water. The second had a thick, grayish substance in it. The final looked black as night. Keelin wasn't about to explain the process. This was a test of Nodiah's trust.

Leyos took Nodiah's hand and began to examine her more closely. "What did you do to her? It's like you made her ride back from King Malachi's naked or something." Keelin's face transformed with a guilty smile as Leyos rolled his eyes at the thought. "Of course you did."

He led Nodiah into the first pool. Warm water overtook her senses. It stung, but it also refreshed as her muscles surprisingly began to loosen and relax a bit. She could tell it wasn't just water, but had no guesses as to what it actually was.

Keelin sat near the edge and opened the book. "Once you know, you can't unknow. Are you sure?" His eyes showed genuine concern. If this turned out to be the truth, none of this would be easy to hear.

She narrowed her eyes and let out a sharp exhale with a tinge of frustration. "You know I am. Do whatever you want to me, but please don't placate me." Her tone wasn't scathing, or rude, but honest. Keelin couldn't help but feel a bit bad as he saw the amount of blood that began swirling around the bath. Leyos walked by, pouring various jars into the water. Keelin never bothered asking what they were. He just knew they worked. His eyes went back to the book, and he began reading the story aloud.

"In the time before time, the Creators grew bored of the neverending sea, and made an island. On that island that planted the Great Tree, and that tree gave birth to everything else. The tree blossomed, and those flowers spread their pollen, giving birth to the many flowers and plants of the world. From the bark, the first man and woman were carved, as well as the other animals. It's said that all living things first were carved into the tree and breathed into life.

Danu, Morrigan, Brigid, and Eiocha created Man not for a grand purpose, but for entertainment. They were bored with the darkness of the world and its simplicity. For thousands of years that was enough as Man and Woman learned about their world, and did everything they could to appease their Masters.

Everyone was the same however. They were the same color, had the same features. They all spoke the same language even. Eventually that got boring, and so the Creators decided to divide the people. They started with simple things like colors, heights, and passions.

This worked for a while, but eventually the Creators saw the limitations of people. They needed a push to reach their full potential. Something that allowed them to truly create masterpieces. So they gave gifts to the ones who had been the most loyal, and the most obedient. With the introduction of passion, people began obtaining skills on their own, but these gifts were beyond anything a normal person could reach."

Mankind as a whole was nothing more than a slave system she thought. Her eyes focused on the small tendrils of blood that came off in the water. It didn't mix with the other liquid, instead spinning and dancing its way away from her towards the far side of the bath, and disappearing through small cracks in the far wall. She ran her hands over her legs to help speed the process, noticing that the throbbing was beginning to subside.

"Of those were the Fire Breathers, the Water Walkers, the Earth Sculptors, and the Sky Dancers. Of course they have other names for the people, but those words aren't possible for us to speak. The Creators gave these people gifts, and left them to discover their intended purpose. They promised each that eventually they would return and teach each to use their gifts to their fullest, but only after they felt the people had gone as far as they could on their own.

The Fire Breathers got their name for their admiration of dragons. It's said that the Creators would come to them on the back of a two-headed dragon that would represent the balance of dark and light." Why were there no rumors of her being one of those, with her red hair she wondered.

"Think of the duality of fire. Think of all the things that can only be made if you have it. Foods, art, tools, weapons. It is both a creative, and destructive force. They focus on both. They not only have no fear of fire, some live up to their name." There was a discomfort at this description. His body tightened, he looked away from her, there was more to this story.

"The Earth Sculptors built the world's great wonders. They built statues, monuments, and pyramids all to give thanks to the Creators and keep their favor. They were given an understanding of numbers, angles, and mathematics that most others simply can't begin to computate. Most of the great works of architecture in this world are from Earth Sculptors.

It's their belief that the Creators will return in the form of a gopher, and will dig a tunnel that will lead them to an eternal paradise that exists below our feet." Nodiah looked down with a sense of wonder, but then closed her eyes as he continued. "The myths say they could move huge amounts of earth and rock just by placing a hand on it." Nodiah instantly wondered if Dachaigh was carved by Earth Sculptors. Was he one of them?

"The Water Walkers ruled the seas. They took an interest in all things ocean. They were a tribe that very much lived in the moment. Like the tides roll in and out, so do seasons in our lives. They have a vast curiosity that has made them great inventors, explorers, and philosophers. They see the flow and the connection in everything. They tend do whatever it takes to explore the world around them. Particularly the oceans." Nodiah became distracted as she stared at the water surrounding her.

"They believe that the Creators will show themselves in the form of a great whale when the time comes. Then they'll ride that whale to an island of paradise that isn't on any map." This was the silliest so far, but then again she had never really seen the ocean up close, let along sailed on one. What was so special about it?

"The rumors say they carried jugs of water that never ran dry, and could sail any ocean safely because they could feel the energy of the water itself." Water having its own energy was a fascinating trail of thought for Nodiah. She would love to have a conversation with a Water Walker some-time. Though she expected them to be able to literally walk on water, so it was a bit of a let down.

"Then there are the Sky Dancers. Everything they did was with purpose. Every move they made was done with the path of least resistance in mind. It was because they felt the aura of the air around them. They didn't move through the air, they moved with it. The leaders were said to be able to manipulate the air itself. They could control temperature in that fashion. They could carry words to others on little wisps, and could send whispers miles away."

"Let me guess, the Creators would return as a giant bird of some kind?" Nodiah's words rang with sarcasm, but the story had her full attention. She was still pulling out the clues of what this all had to do with her.

"A phoenix, risen from the ashes. It's also said that the Creators gave the Sky Dancers each a tiny piece of their heart, with which came great understanding of people. It created distinguishing features such as brightly colored hair, eyes, or distinct birth marks. It made them easy to identify." Things started to connect for Nodiah.

"That made the others jealous. Some tried to fake themselves as Sky Dancers, coloring their hair. Most of the common people were turned off by the favoritism towards them. Instead of being revered, they were out-cast. They retreated high into the mountains, and built a temple to protect themselves. As settlements became villages, and eventually kingdoms, the eight Great Kings decided to wage war against all four of the Creator's Chosen.

Against the Fire Breathers, their armies were burned. Against the Earth Movers they were buried. Against the Water Walkers, their ships were sunk.... but against the Sky Dancers they were relentless. They charged up the mountains with ease.

It was almost too easy. It turned out they had made alliances. The Earth Movers built them a staircase up the mountain. The Fire Breathers joined the charge, crafting weapons and armor. They broke their way into the tem-ple, and they slaughtered everyone that resisted.

Then the Kings took the children, and divided them up. They decided that they would make a bold statement to the Creators. They lashed out in defiance in an attempt to show that man would no longer be ruled by the Creators. So they made all the children their slaves. If the Creators favorites were the slaves of Kings, then the Creators themselves were as well. They took the final four kids, and put them on boats, and the Water Walkers scattered them to the corners of the world, spreading the stories of the Kings who conquered the Creators."

Keelin watched her eyes. He wondered how the emotion would manifest itself. Anger? Confusion? Frustration? Disbelief? Motivation? "The old tales were never told. The books were burned. The mention of the Creators Chosen is outlawed. For if the Sky Dancers were to realize just who they were, they could rise up. They could reach out to the Creators once more. For the Creators live inside them. They have a piece of their heart. In that, is true power. It's all a great tale isn't it?"

Matthew Oakley

Chapter 3

That's what all of this was about? Just some myth? She inspected him as he looked back at her, gauging to see if he really believed any of this nonsense. His face was unreadable, but the others she had come across, even Leyos, seemed to believe every word this man said. Keelin let a small grin cross his face. He took her hand, leading her out of the first tub, and into the second. "Yes, it is interesting at the least. Tell me something though. Do you fancy yourself above Creators and Kings then?" She shot him a stern look, before making her way down into the second pool.

The thick waxy substance immediately gravitated towards her, sticking to her skin, and coating her all the way up to her neck. It clung to her tightly, creating a mold around her body which built up an immense amount of pressure and heaviness. It caused a good deal of pain from her bruises and wounds as it hardened and caked to her skin.

He took a moment, and then let out a laugh at the ridiculous notion. "Depends on your definition of fancy I suppose. I wouldn't want to be them. I wouldn't want to hold that weight. That responsibility. At least not that of a King. The good ones don't last long. They get taken out by the corrupt ones, and the corrupt ones usually get taken out by someone even more corrupt. It's a vicious cycle.

The only reason I went to see your former King was business. He wanted a job done, and he was going to pay us to do it." He looked down at the floor as he debated how to answer the other part of the question. What was she trying to get out of him.

"As for the Creators, they have to be real. I say my prayers, I repent my sins, I give my offering. I don't really know if they are around or not I suppose. I can't imagine this tree that has existed forever, and no one has ever found it... I'd rather believe it's real... that they're real and find out I'm wrong, than not believe and be wrong. We had to come from somewhere right?" He was rambling. He had a stronger belief in the way the universe worked, but he wasn't ready to share that just yet.

Nodiah grimaced a bit, and took in his words. "Was? I take it you messed that up when you wouldn't give him his way?" She smiled, remembering the King's face as she left. It was a sight she would never forget.

"I suppose it's easier to believe in Creator's when you have actual power though. I don't even own my own body, so why would I give my soul away too?" It was a legitimate question. One that struck Keelin rather profoundly.

She continued before he had time to respond however. "So you've no desire to be King, and you revere the Creators... Why purchase a possible Sky Dancer then? Do you really believe that I could be one of them? Am I a trophy for you to show off in your display?" She grimaced a bit, trying her best not to get caught up in the fantasy. She always had to remember her place.

Keelin was clearly angered by her continued resistance. He lifted her out of the tub forcefully, the grey waxy substance clinging to her body. He grabbed her by the forearm making sure he had her full attention. "You are no trophy. I hadn't even thought of the Sky Dancers until Corrig said it. You just deserved to be in better hands than the King."

The tension was once again palpable as her body pulled away from his subconsciously. "I didn't buy you because of what you may or may not be, I bought you because I see what you could become." His hand found her hip and began moving up her side slowly, but with intent. "What you can be defies Sky Dancer, or Earth Sculptor, or Master or slave. Let me ask you a simple question Nodiah. Do you trust me?" A smile took over his face as he moved his arms up to her shoulders and held her square to him. She took in the question, and thought about it intently.

Inhale…

What she could be…
She is to be trained….
Do not help her…
Sky Dancer…. Possession…

She may be punished, but she had to tell the truth. "No." He gave a small nod of approval. Much to her surprise, he then led the way to the third tub, helping her in. He watched on, mesmerized as the black inky water pulled at the wax on her body, breaking it off into large pieces. This was always the most fascinating part of the process to him. He had no idea how it worked, and he never asked. Some things were better off as a mystery.

His mind wandered to several things. The King, the Creators, the story, until finally his thought landed on destiny. Why now? What was the reason that Nodiah had made it here? What was he meant to do with her? He thought he knew, but if he was wrong their story would not end well. Finally he responded with a loud voice.

"Good!" Keelin paced, again catching himself deep in thought. In this moment he was envious of Nodiah's very intentional approach to life. He wished it came as easily to him. Some of his biggest successes were by accident.

"Why should you?" He said forcefully. "It's not smart, not yet, but you will. You'll come to know what to expect. You'll realize that I'm not the monster that people make me out to be." He knelt down beside the tub and made sure he had her full attention. "I am searching for purpose in this world… just like you."

After just a few minutes in the final bath, Keelin motioned for her to get out, and helped her do so. He grabbed a towel, and began slowly wiping away the blackness left behind. His eyes studied every inch of her body as he went; every curve, every hair. Kneeling down at times, he took note of all the gashes from the ride, freshly healed by the treatment. They were obviously still sore, but he was happy with the progress.

What truly surprised him were the scars. They were in all shapes and sizes, and had he not been looking so closely, he would have missed half of them. One deep mark on the lower part of her back stood out. It was several inches long, right along her spine. It was truly unique, even amongst the dozens in front of him, as it seemed like it never actually healed. "Who would ever want to cause so much pain? I'm guessing the man that did this one enjoyed it." He traced his finger along the ridge, anticipating a reaction.

All Nodiah could do was stiffen. No one had taken any interest in her marks before. No one else would ever know what it felt like to get them. She earned them in a way. Each scar was something that she survived... Someone... Each one made her stronger.

This man was clearly crazy. He was unstable, inconsistent, dangerous. He knew his way around words but that was all the more reason to be cautious. She again wouldn't give him the satisfaction of a response. As hard as she tried to fight it, his next few words caused a reaction.

"I need you at full strength. Tomorrow we go back and talk to your former King." Keelin continued to examine the effects of the baths, but at these words Nodiah instinctively jumped away from him.

"Go back?" She tried to hide the panic from her voice. Her gaze turned to the wall before her as she nervously brought a fingernail up to her lips. Why on earth would they go back?! He had just taken her out! He truly was insane. What would the King do? After the way they left? It couldn't happen. "Keelin..." She turned her head slightly, speaking over her shoulder. "I don't want to go back."

For the first time, Keelin saw Nodiah truly resist his wishes. Up until now, her submission was an obligation. There was no question, following was a part of her being. Now it felt as though she was pleading... begging not to be forced to return to her former prison. He was torn. "I think you misunderstand Nodi. I'm not taking you back to hand you off. You're a Wolf now. You run with us." This clearly did little to comfort her. "Come on..." He said with a bit of a smile. He had an idea.

After a loud whistle, two men made their way into the room. Ryker, who was a tall, lanky man with arms that seemed unusually long even for his tall frame. He had scruffy facial hair and cold, dark eyes. Thorin was a solid brick of a man, barrel chested and thick throughout. He was quite a bit shorter than Ryker and Keelin, but twice as wide. "Get her some clothes and then bring her down for a meal. Leyos go with. No one lays a finger on her, understood?" Keelin looked to all three men for affirmation, and in turn they nodded. He then turned his attention back to Nodi. "You'll be safe with them. I'll explain more when you come to eat." He flashed a genuine smile, and then made his way out of the room.

Nodiah forced what she considered to be a smile at his reassurance, though it did not reach her eyes, or even her cheeks really. She felt the slight twitch of muscle under her skin, and for a moment she allowed herself to once again believe Keelin. Maybe she really was precious to him… important… and in that, she had an insight to one of Keelin's weaknesses. This thought process brought some energy back to her body, as she rose to her feet like the dancer she was.

She walked past the two men indifferently. She did wonder just how loyal these men were, and if she could give herself even more of an advantage with the Wolves. They moved their way down to the second level, and through another door into a square room. She wandered her way to the center, and then spun back around. "So what is it I am supposed to wear?" She inquired, finally turning some attention back to the two new men. Leyos had wandered off somewhere.

Ryker nervously made his way over to a large dresser. He pulled open drawers one by one, and came back with an outfit not unlike what most of the Wolves were wearing. There was a long grey dark grey robe, with a circle on the back. Inside the circle was the symbol of the wolves, all in a lighter grey. Various swirls and patterns also ran through in the lighter grey color. It was long, but narrow, meant to fit the body.

Next was a pair of thin black pants with some added padding on various critical parts, and a pair of lightweight boots that Ryker had guessed the size on. "There's other clothes back there. We keep all the lady clothing in those.

" pointing towards a couple other dressers in the corner of the room and a small door that led to a closet. "This is what you wear tomorrow, but as for tonight you can take your pick," he said with a coy smile.

Nodiah cringed a bit at the idea of wearing garments used by other women. Even at the palace as a slave, she had her own wardrobe. At least here, she got to make the choice. That felt amazing! She approached the dressers, slowly and methodically going through each drawer. She touched all of the fabrics, inspected lengths, and tried to find the exact right outfit. Finally she disappeared into the closet.

Hanging to her right was a solid piece of thin linen. It was a bright white, which stood out against most of the other things in the Wolves Den. She draped it over her shoulders and let it hang like a scarf down to her hips. She then crisscrossed it, and tied it up behind her neck to create a top. After a little more digging, she found another cloth was adorned with several bells, and small golden disks not unlike the cymbals of a tambourine. She tied that on her hip like a skirt, fixed her hair, and stepped out of the closet.

Thorin's mouth dropped, which gave Nodiah a bit of a smile. He was clearly overwhelmed at her choice of attire, but Ryker was quick to get him back in line. "Thorin you oaf. You're here drooling over her like a steak. She's not food, she's one of us! Keelin would cut out your tongue if he saw that." With a quick smack on the back of the head, the duo motioned to escort Nodiah let out a bit of a disappointed sigh. "What gentlemen... too bad," she said with a flirtatious wink and a smile.

She pulled her hair into a loose braid that curled over her shoulder. The white linen and gold disks seemed to glow as they fell against her skin. Slowly she moved towards Ryker, with a confident grin. She leaned up and gave him a soft peck on the cheek. "Alright then... Let's go..." There was a hint of hesitation in Ryker's eyes. Maybe he wasn't off the hook just yet. She swayed her hips just enough to make the bells ring.

"G...Go? I mean... Are you sure you're ready? Thorin, go find Leyos. If we don't all come back together, Keelin will ask questions." *Smart boy*, Nodiah thought. She smiled as Thorin begrudgingly disappeared out the door.

As Nodiah stood before Ryker smiling, she could see him struggling for words. "I... you belong to Keelin. Don't you feel any loyalty to him temptress? You know I can't... I can't touch you." His honesty was a bit refreshing. It was a question that actually paused Nodiah for a second, but his eyes never found hers. They seemed a bit distracted.

"I've yet to decide where my loyalties lie to be honest. I belong to him sure, but loyalty. That's a choice. It's not bought or paid for." She slid her body against his in a snakelike fashion, and in an instant was breathing directly into his ear. "But of course I will be loyal to my Master." She turned, slowly pacing away.

"Keelin, however, is boring. Wouldn't it be fun to know that all the while he's standing on his pedestal barking order, my mind is purely... on... you..." Her gaze turned seductive. She made sure she had his eyes this time. After a moment of surveying the room, Ryker grabbed her by the hand and pulled her into the small closet she had changed in. His eagerness getting the better of him, Nodiah couldn't help but smile.

"I... I can't do this..."

"Shh... Of course you can." Her lips pressed against his neck, and then moved towards his chest. She laughed as his breathing increased. Her body started to lower... and he ran. He broke out of the closet doors with force and stumbled into the middle of the room. *Almost...* She turned, chasing after him. As she got to him however, the others appeared in the doorway. She trailed a finger across his chest and mouthed to him "Tonight... To be continued..." and then made her way out. This wasn't over.

Keelin entered the dining area and surveyed the scene. Long tables ran parallel with the four walls, leaving enough space to walk on all sides. At the far left, a serving window that connected to the rudimentary kitchen and food storage area behind it. In the far right corner, a small doorway that led to a more private room. Keelin made his way through the Wolves, engaging in some playful banter along the way, and approached the food.

The spread was quite impressive Keelin thought. Hunting must've been good the last couple days. Lots of exotic meats, smothered in some rather thick sauces and gravies, sat on large silver serving trays that seemed more fitting for a palace than the Den. He filled his plate with a fair assortment and then made his way into the small side room. Inside was a round table, with four chairs. Lanterns hung on the wall providing a bit of extra light. He took his seat, opposite the door, and awaited Nodiah's entrance.

Inhale...

She made her way through the Wolves, her earlier ferocity gone. She kept her eyes to the ground, her body language noticeably calm and still. She passed through the hall, finally raising her gaze to meet his. This moment felt... important... defining... How he treated her in front of his men would let her know what to expect. She wouldn't begin to fall for his attempts at camaraderie anymore. You're one of us now... What an awful lie. She was an item, not a person, and he was figuring out how to use her. She passed through the entrance and stopped just in front of the table, crossing her wrists behind her. She gave him an inquisitive look, with an arched brow and a half smile. It was his move.

He took a moment to take her in. The outfit was stunning. Even though she tried to suppress it, every step still had such purpose. As she put her hands behind her back, he smirked a little. It was evident her training was so deeply ingrained in her core, that it was nearly impossible for her not to follow it.

A few awkward moments passed before Keelin quickly realized she was waiting for his orders. "You look wonderful but, aren't you going to eat?" He motioned to the door, and the long table of food that was just beyond it.

This was a genuine display of kindness, but also a test. What she chose, and how much, would tell Keelin about her judgment, and her motivations. What was she trying to prove to him? To herself?

She stood for a moment, but the aromas got the better of her. She couldn't remember the last thing she actually ate. The auction felt years ago, and Keelin had let Corrig off the hook. Doubt crossed her face as she processed what he asked. "You wish me... to dine... with you?" She cocked her head to the side, not bothering to hide her surprise.

After being reassured that was exactly what he meant, she stepped back out towards the food. It wasn't the level of elegance usually presented in the meals at the palace, but there was something about the look and the smell that made it simply salivating. It took her a while to choose, but she finally determined she should make the most of the moment. Who knew how long the kindness would last?

She began to pick out the best cuts of meat she should find. Not too much fat, lean and tender. She also nabbed a few of the more decadent looking side dishes, and a delicious swirl of chocolate and something orange for dessert. It appeared baked, but she couldn't tell much about it.

She returned to her spot, standing at the doorway, and waited for permission to take her seat. As she paused once more, Keelin had a flood of thoughts rush into his mind. Nodiah's submission was her safe place. It was her comfort. This kind of behavior truly was all she knew. Maybe too much freedom too fast would be overwhelming.

He had to keep feeding into that familiar comfort, but it wasn't slavery to him, it was training. Training her for something better. It was hard for him to even imagine the life she was living just a day ago. This woman before him was not meant to be a slave. She could be an Alpha.

He finally waved her in to sit across from him, and watched as she entered. She set her plate down, and he inspected carefully. It wasn't a large amount of food, but he was sure there was a reason why she picked each item. "I didn't see you as the kind to eat duck," he remarked. "It's a little gamy, but it has a lot of juice."

He took a bite of his food, and continued to make small talk. "We don't have much in the way of spices out here, so we make due with what we have." He shot her a friendly smile, taking in her outfit some more as he did. Finally he stabbed his fork into a bright orange leafy looking object on his plate, and extended it towards Nodiah. "Here, try this," he encouraged.

She let out a bit of a relaxed smile, and then leaned forward taking a bite of the orange plant. It somehow managed to be sweet and salty and tangy and full of flavor, but she wouldn't give him the pleasure of a reaction. "Interesting..." she replied calmly, "around Torek they don't have much in the way of plants, but there is no end to the spices." She quipped. Everything was different about this place it seemed.

She began picking through her own food, taking small delicate bites and trying to truly explore all of the unique flavors. She never let on to the ravenous hunger consuming her stomach. She wanted to throw manners aside and devour the plate, but she couldn't show need.

His eyes rarely left her... and she liked that. "Keelin..." she began softly. "I notice that no men dine with you... or women... You seem to want to make me a part of this... of your... pack." She slowed down, confirming in herself she wanted to actually ask this question. "Can you tell me what my role is to be here? At the palace I was nothing more than a toy. I was used as entertainment... A trophy... What is it you plan to display me as?"

He felt her walls go up. The mention of Torek seemed to bring back the toughness and training that she could hide behind. He couldn't help but laugh, knowing that wouldn't make her happy either.

She couldn't get past the idea of a trophy, but he had never thought of it that way. She was never to be a display for him. "Display you? My beautiful Nodi, I have no intention of displaying you. The pack knows that you are mine, but that's mostly for your safety." He took a long sip of his drink, letting those words hang in the air. "There are some among us, whom I fear are not loyal to the cause, but wouldn't survive without us. Then there are others like Thorin and Ryker, good honest men... True friends."

Nodiah did all she could to stop from choking on her own drink. She muffled a cough into the fabric wrapped around her, and tried to hide the reaction. Her nerves rose a bit though. If he knew they weren't loyal, then this was sarcasm… and a set up… If he didn't… she just felt bad for him.

"That's why I trusted them to watch after you. I told you before, you my dear are no trophy. You will become a symbol against corruption, against tyranny, and against everything King Malachi and those other bumbling, stumbling dictators believe matters." The only thing that she knew mattered to the King was his image. Admittedly, Keelin had done a number on it by purchasing her out from under him, but how could she be a symbol for anything?

"Look if I'm being honest, I don't know exactly where your place in the Wolves will be. So for now, you are a Grey. That's what everyone starts as. You are one of us. You fight for us. You always do what's best for the pack. You do what the Alphas tell you. In particular, as I tell you."

She did her best not to roll her eyes. These were the words that she was used to. Suddenly reality came crashing back in. "When away from the others, the rules will be a bit more relaxed. Nodiah, I didn't purchase you to prove that I was better than anyone. I purchased you with the intention of bringing out the best in you." He caught his own eyes wandering, and chuckled a bit. "Although if you keep dressing like that, I'll be sure to have some fun along the way!" The laughter was meant to take the intensity out of the statement, but it wasn't a total lie.

Her mind tried to process it all as his words continued to ring through her head. Most everyone had to take orders at one point or another, but for a slave it was different. There was no cause, no motivation, no belonging. What he was describing wasn't slavery at all. It was something more. Did he mean it? Or were these the false promises of a boy who wanted to play with his toys before he discarded them?

A shiver raced up her spine. She really didn't know anything about him still. She needed to refocus. "Why are we going back to see the King?" she finally responded. Her fire was back. She had been in survival mode for so long, never really thinking that leaving Torek would be a possibility. Going back could mean forever. Was that his plan all the time? Maybe this was all just foreplay. He had business with the King and now he had a bargaining piece… That was it. She was his leverage.

"Nodiah…" He moved next to her, placing a hand on her left cheek, just barely touching her. He wondered if she was ready. If she could handle what came next. Could he make her go through with it? He wanted to see this reaction in her eyes... In her soul... "Isn't it obvious?" Keelin smiled... "To kill him... You... are going to kill him." His eyes matched her fire. This was no joke... There was no sarcasm... This was the plan.

Matthew Oakley

Chapter 4

"KEELIN!" She flung his name as a curse... an accusation. Her eyes widened as she dealt with a moment of catatonia. He had suggested both her greatest hope, and her worst nightmare. Kill the King? Until just a day ago she had belonged to him. She couldn't remember a life before him. She had spent most of that time, thinking of his death, along with a few other choice individuals... and yet... How could she? It went against every fiber of her being, every lesson she had been taught. It wasn't possible.

She violently pushed against him, breaking herself away from his body... from his orders... and suddenly found herself on her feet moving back. She was gone. She ran to the one place she knew in the Den, the closet, and slumped to the floor bringing her knees to her chest. Her breathing was a harsh, sporadic gasp. For the first time she could remember, she was panicking. He was a King... she was just a slave. How could she? How could she?!... She couldn't... Could she?

Keelin gathered himself and then formulated his next move. "RYKER!" He hollered out. The man quickly responded, though visibly nervous.

"Yes Keelin?" He kept his distance.

"Find her, and just make sure she's ok will you? I have a fear she may try and run, but we can't lose her." Ryker did his best to hide his happiness. It had made his plans for the night that much easier. It was his duty to find her, so he would.

"Of course." Ryker immediately started his search.

She just wanted to sleep. She had hoped she was sleeping, and at any moment her eyes would open from the dream that she was in. She felt as if she may just be able to drift away when another presence made their way into the room. "I wonder where she went? This room seems empty!" Ryker...

She didn't want to perform for this idiot, and yet if she wanted to escape, she didn't have a choice. Part of her, deep down, wished Keelin had come himself. "I'm not going to run," she called out softly. "If... If I could just have some time..." She weakened her voice. Maybe he was a man who would be turned off by a weepy woman and would leave her alone.

"Ya know... I don't know what Keelin's asked you to do, but he often asks more of us than we think we can do. If you are never pushed... How will you ever know what you're capable of?" She took in his words with a grain of salt. This wasn't a man that respected Keelin right? He wouldn't be here if he did. Asked... right... She had never been asked to do anything.

The silence was broken as she heard the man stomping with heavy footsteps, that then grew softer but clearly came from the same place. She couldn't help but laugh a bit as he tried his little marching trick. She was a dancer... It didn't work. She listened intently as he approached the outside of the closet. "And what has he pushed you to do?" She whispered softly.

It was truly satisfying to hear Ryker nearly jump out of his skin, both at the ghostly nature of her voice, and the fact he hadn't fooled her at all! She listened to him slow his breathing as she sat back, and he began his tale.

"When I showed up at his door, I was found wanting. I wanted things on my time. I complained a lot. About being hungry, being thirsty, being hot, being tired... My needs... My selfish needs. One day Keelin caught me complaining, and he called me out in the middle of the hall. He challenged me."

There was no doubt in Nodiah's mind he was telling the truth. There was something to the tone of his voice that lent itself to empathy. "He said if I could go without food, water, or sleep longer than he could, that he would allow me to eat, drink, and sleep whenever I wanted. Sounded like a good deal to me. There's no way little Keelin could outlast me. I was strong, in great shape. I never stopped to consider that meant my body actually needed more of those things."

Nodiah smiled a bit at the conclusion in his information. Going without was something she was used to, but she also understood how difficult it was. She moved closer to the door and listened in to the rest.

"Day one was easy, relatively. Hours twenty-four to thirty-six were hell. The pain got worse. Everytime I even closed my eyes, he'd hit me to wake me up. By forty-eight hours, I quit. I told him he won. He said I could pick one of the three, and I chose water. That's the one that would kill me first if I didn't have it right? We went another day before the lack of sleep was too much. I begged him to let me sleep... and he did. Four hours of the best sleep you could ever imagine.

Day four, he walked me out of the room, led me down to the hall, and we ate together. I devoured everything in front of me. I couldn't get enough. He took a small piece of bread, and some water, and nothing else. We talked about it all. He finally turned to me and said 'Now you know what it is to truly want. Don't let me hear you complain again. I haven't let you starve, and I don't intend to'" Those words hung in the air a bit as Ryker fought back honest emotion.

"It was about a year after that, we were out in the desert, just him and I. A big storm came up. Out of nowhere, this amazing beast of sand and wind just rose up growling at us. We had no choice but to push through. No food... no water... no sleep... three days... And I didn't complain once. Sometimes life isn't always about having what you want. It's just about wanting what you have."

Ryker couldn't help but smile as he realized just how fond he was of the memory. Nodiah added the story to the list of things she knew about Keelin, but it was still remarkably short. He spoke of him with such reverence, but it made her wonder that much more about who he was.

"You make him sound like a hero..." The door slid open, and Nodiah made her way out. Her hair had fallen from its braid, now wrapping itself around her. She slid her palm to Ryker's cheek, an imitation of the touch Keelin had shown her.

"What would your hero do to me if he thought I was no longer his though?" She smiled. "What would he do to you?" She slid her hand down his neck, trailing along his collar bone. Her fiery gaze filled with a resigned softness. Then she stepped away. She would have a bit more fun, but this new-found side of Ryker she could at least respect.

Keeping her back to him, she pulled the knots holding up her skirt, then her top, and they fell to the floor with a light ringing of the bells and a flutter of the fabric. She reached out and instead pulled the Grey Wolf robe up over her head, then bent to retrieve her pants. She moved to examine herself in the mirror, her back turned to Ryker the whole time. Once dressed, she playfully glanced over her shoulder and laughed at the overwhelmed look on the man's face.

The tight, dark clothes clung to her figure and seemed to sharpen her features rather than diminish them. Her red locks were luminescent against the grey, her bright blue eyes pierced that much more. In a quick move, she turned on her heels and left him to regain himself. She made her way back to the dining hall, and to the doorway, waiting at the threshold. Keelin wasn't alone.

Keelin had settled in to finish his meal, determined not to let Nodi's disappearance bother him. He couldn't let the others see it effected him either. He continued eating, but was soon interrupted by a large mountain of a man taking up the entire doorway. Standing easily seven feet tall, and 300 pounds, the man spoke in a deep aggressive growl. "Your plaything run away then?"

Keelin was in no mood. "Excuse me Strom?" He shot back.

"That new toy of yours scurried out of here in quite the hurry. Seems you made her upset. You having trouble controlling your slave?" Keelin threw down his silverware, and eyed the large man, visibly frustrated.

"Is there a point to this?"

"How do you expect to keep control of all of this... When you can't even control what's yours?" Strom asked with the intention to provoke. It worked. Keelin stood.

"All of this... is mine. Damn you Strom, I don't know who sent you in here, but if they have words for me, they know where to find me. Let me ask you something. Don't you ever get tired of letting them take advantage of you? Don't you ever get angry that people use you to do the things they have no courage to do themselves? Why don't you wander on back to whoever sent you, and tell them that if they wish to challenge me there's a procedure to doing so, and it will be followed." His words were emphatic and forceful. There had to be an order to things.

Challenges for the title of Alpha were nothing new. Strom seemed to take particular offense to his words anyways. He huffed, and stormed out, nearly running over Nodiah in the process.

Keelin calmed himself, took in her change of attire, and smiled. "Sit..." He welcomed her back in, pointing to the seat next to him. She hesitated for a moment, but it wasn't long before inspiration struck. Maybe dissent was her ticket out. Loyalty was something that only ran robe deep around this place. Everyone had their doubts in Keelin it seemed. Maybe there was a piece of the puzzle she was missing, but with the right pushes she could see the Wolves tearing each other apart, and all she'd have to do is step lightly over the bodies towards freedom.

She didn't bother looking in Strom's direction, instead focusing intently on Keelin. Much to her surprise, he seemed genuinely glad to see her. Did she really want to see this man fall? He saw something in her. Something beyond servitude and helplessness. Something beyond control, power, or pleasure. He saw more than beauty and lust. She wished she knew what it was.

She realized the moment had become awkward as she continued to stand in the doorway. Quietly, she moved her way to the chair next to him. Decisions had to be made. He could destroy her... He could free her... He could train her, whatever that meant... Could she trust him? She stayed quiet, ignoring the half-eaten food on her plate. From the corner of her eyes, she couldn't help but notice his gaze hadn't left her. His stare dominated her, and in a way made her feel safe. She hated him for it.

Finally a thin wisp of a smile crossed her face. She planted her palms on her chair, puffing her chest slightly. The wolf's crest was on full display as she confidently posed. "How do I look?" Her body language was playful, but her voice came out with an unexpected intensity... A dare... a challenge...

Keelin let out a small chuckle behind a smile from ear to ear. Her display of confidence was unexpected, but she looked fantastic. The outfit seemed like it was made for her. It caught her body in all the right places. She looked strong, yet beautiful. He controlled himself for the moment, and turned the conversation. "You should eat. You'll need your strength." His smile faded as his mind wandered off to the events that lay ahead. "We can... play... later, but I wouldn't recommend it."

Initiation... It wasn't to be taken lightly. He reminisced of his own. It was an experience that forever scarred him, mentally and physically, but it was also necessary in order to become a Wolf. "It would be best to save your energy." He didn't tell her anything more. No need to scare her.

Instead he moved closer, putting an arm around her shoulders and pulling her bright red locks towards his cheek. "You look incredible. Best looking Wolf in the whole Den." He finally mustered out softly. His thoughts still carried through his voice. He almost wished he had a distraction. She had a way of breaking him down so quickly. She affected him in more ways than he was comfortable with. Being the Master she needed would be more difficult than he thought, but he knew he had to. The time for pleasantries was fading.

Hunger and curiosity got the best of Nodiah as she reached for a succulent looking piece of pink fruit, bringing it slowly to her mouth. She pressed it against her puckered lips, inhaling the sweet scent. It was an explosion of tart and sweet that was unexpectedly pleasant. Finally she took a bite. A thin stream of juice rolled down her chin, but she didn't care. She quickly popped the rest in her mouth, and then let out a breath.

Exhale...

"Okay," she acquiesced, moving towards her own plate. She began nibbling on what was left, and the conversation stopped as Keelin watched on. Once most of the plate was finished, she turned back to him. "I would like to see more of your..." she hesitated before forcing out a correction... "Our... home... Before we leave again."

The idea of home brought thoughts of the castle flooding back, but she forced them away for the moment. "Maybe tonight you could just show me one thing. Where is your favorite place here?" She had a genuine excitement in her voice. "I'd like to see you in your element..." a small flirtatious grin pulled at the corner of her mouth. "It'll tell me something about you..." Her eyes looked down, fawning a bit of shyness.

"In my element? Heh." Keelin scoffed. He was always in his element. He had to be. The only thing that had made him uncomfortable in a long, long time was her. The only way to thrive as an Alpha in this pack was to adapt.

His brain wandered through all of the places he could take her, until finally inspiration struck. He hadn't been there in a long time, but it would create a fantastic opportunity. "Alright Nodiah, I have the perfect place. A place of both spiritual and historical importance... But... let's not rush." He said with a soft smile. He took a small bite out of a piece of bread on the table, and then proceeded with his mouth half full. "There is someone I'd like you to meet first."

A sharp yell broke the moment before she could think about it for too long. Nodiah jumped at the unexpected shout. "Roland!... Get Tracer for me..." A man nearby stood with a bit of a coy grin, and then disappeared into the halls. Keelin turned his attention back to Nodiah. "You can learn a lot from Tracer I think." He hoped at least. They had a bit of a kindred spirit.

She wasn't as eager. Another person. She considered a witty retort, but was too exhausted. Her life had changed so dramatically in the past hours. At this point whatever mind games he was playing were beyond her. She wanted to know more about him. Knowledge was the only weapon she seemed to have, considering seduction appeared to be beyond Keelin. Well... maybe not entirely.

She stretched, running her hands through her hair. A small flinch came when she reached the wound on her scalp. She trailed down towards her own cheek, which was still the slightest bit tender from his slap. It was a quick reminder that this man was trying to break her. She couldn't forget that. Her wits were back.

"Tracer?" she asked curiously, but it was more out of manors than interest. Her heart wasn't in it. She just wanted to have more alone time with him. Maybe she could be the one who would do the breaking. "Who could possibly teach me more than you?" she inquired, trying and failing to bite back the sarcasm in her tone.

Her comment was subconscious, almost a reflex Keelin thought. It was a great reminder that as captivating and intriguing as she was, she had a long way to go. "That's good... very good... You're lucky we are where we are. You're lucky she's coming. I won't forget that comment though..." He responded in a hushed, controlled tone. The tension was broken by a rustling near the entrance.

There stood Roland, a long leather leash wrapped around his wrist. On the other end, a huge, stunning wolf. Streaks of grey and white swirled through its fur. It approached the pair cautiously, sniffing everything as it went. As it looked up at Keelin, he knew Nodi would see her left eye. It had been lost, leaving a long scar, but most of the area had regrown with fur just making it look as if its eye was shut. "This is Tracer... And she is coming with us." Nodiah's feelings were mixed. The first female she'd met in this place was on a leash. She knew the feeling.

Pity overwhelmed her as she took in the wolf's missing eye. She wondered if Keelin was responsible. She rose from her seat, and knelt before the massive wolf, though it stood well beyond her hips on its own. She let Tracer sniff her for a moment, and she studied her patterns. "You poor thing..." she murmured, ignoring Keelin completely as her hand stroked the side of the wolf's head, muttering and cooing softly. Finally she looked up at Keelin. "What happened to her?"

"Follow" ... The command was cold... Meant for Tracer, but Keelin was pleasantly surprised as Nodiah responded appropriately as well. He led the way out of the room, through the kitchen, and out of the back of the large building. They continued in silence down a dark alley in the shadows of the Den. Finally, he led the way through a small crack in the mountain wall. He struggled to squeeze through, but Nodiah had no issues manipulating her body to do the same.

As the space opened up, he began climbing up a large carved stone staircase in front of them. Not once did he look back. Nodiah couldn't help but feel the thrill of the unexpected. Palace life had been the same every day. Different faces, different countries, same dance... Always. This was new. It could be a place of beauty, or sacrifice, or fire, or... Who knew?

All of her thoughts disappeared as she made her way up the first few steps. Suddenly the sky above opened up to the most spectacular display of stars she had ever seen. They were everywhere. She nearly stumbled over a step, because she was so caught up in them.

They eventually emerged on top of the cliff, and a small level plateau opened. Nodiah knew they weren't directly over the Den, but couldn't quite get her bearings. She was too busy looking up at the amazing sky.

Keelin still didn't bother turning around. Instead, he led the way forward to a small statue on the very edge of the cliff. It was a tree that stood about four feet in height. All along the trunk, and the branches were tiny carvings of animals of all kinds, extending right out to the leaves. Each branch seemed a little different. There were flowers of all kinds, and fruits hanging as well.

As Nodiah's eyes moved from the stars to the statue, she began to ask... "Is that the tree from..."

"Ashtu thrian oh tak leoh pan tat thole... Reshan tel a li ko rosu kalo...Nodiah... Bal ran... To...

This... This is my element..." As he began to speak, she finally brought her eyes back to him. The force of his words put her on high alert. A shiver ran down her spine as she approached him. There was something about his form... She could only make out his silhouette against the backdrop of starlight. She gently cupped her fingers around his shoulder. "It's beautiful," she spoke softly in his ear as they stared out towards the infinite space. "What... What does it mean?"

He smiled. For once things were going according to plan. "I introduced you to the Creators. The weavers of fate. I have a feeling they already know who you are. But I swore I would protect you." His energy faded, and eventually he sat as Tracer approached them.

"Tracer lost her eye protecting Ryker. He was wandering the Outlands, and a scout got the drop on him. Shot an arrow... Tracer blocked it... with her face... She gave everything." He paused, scratching behind the wolf's ears. "Our healer was able to save her. She went through the same bath process you did, but we couldn't save the eye.

I've learned a lot from Tracer since then. She trusts herself... Her senses. Since that incident her tracking ability is unmatched. It seems she can not only smell flesh, but intention... heart... instincts. That's something you've had taken from you." He made his way to the farthest extending point of the cliff and stared off in the distance. "Now... Do you trust yourself?" It was an odd question, but it was intended to invoke pride.

He waited... Tears welled in her eyes. She wasn't sure if it was the emotion of this place, or exhaustion. She pulled her knees to her chest, resting her chin on top. She wasn't sure whether to throw herself at his feet, or off this cliff and end it. Maybe that was why he chose here. She felt lost.

"I don't even know myself. I have no sense of self. I am like a frightened animal... Looking for somewhere safe, but ready to run... and I have trust for no one." They both were surprised at her honesty. It was something about the stars. Everything else seemed so insignificant. Nothing mattered but right here, and in a way that made her feel free.

"STAND THEN!" His shout echoed through the open sky. "If you do not know yourself, then you do not know what you fight for. So perhaps a fight will reveal your purpose." Fight? She could barely walk. Was he insane? "Stand and fight me Nodiah... And if you win... I will set you free." Those words echoed for an eternity against the stars. Her eyes widened. He couldn't be serious. It was a trick she thought. She closed her eyes, sealing them shut...

"No."

He was insulted. Angered. She had to. "No?" He charged at her and sprung into the air. His forearm smashed down on her shoulder with a heavy thud. Before she could respond, he picked her up around the waist and threw her away from the cliff. Regret instantly swelled in his body.

She felt her shoulder dislocate, separating from its joint. A sharp bolt of pain followed by an alarming numbness left her arm hanging dead. The impact with the ground reopened the wound on her head. She lay there, shocked, as the blood pooled around her face. Then something in her snapped, as if waking up from a slumber.

She pushed herself up on one elbow, feeling the blood run across her nose, gathering in the corners of her mouth. "There is no such thing as FREEDOM!" She screamed at him. Hatred filled her veins. "If you wanted to free me you would let me go. You wouldn't try to break me. Fighting is letting you win. And I won't. So come on damnit. Break me. Here in front of your Creators, beat me. I won't become the monster you want me to be!"

Her heart was beating wildly in her chest. She wanted nothing more than to pounce... to attack him more viciously than any wolf. But she wouldn't. It was what he wanted... and he would have to break every last one of her bones before he would break her will. "COME ON THEN!" She screamed once more.

It was his eyes that filled with tears this time. "Don't make me do this!" He yelled back. He expected a fight. This... was foolish. "There is no freedom if you aren't willing to fight for it." He made his approach. "Your stubbornness isn't brave. I'm giving you a chance!" His elbow snapped into her jaw with a quick strike. His hand then swiftly clawed down, ripping the collar of her shirt as she fell back. "You want this? FINE." He approached again...

As more blood filled her mouth, she could feel her teeth tear into her cheek. A moment later, she spit out a collection of red, and then much to his surprise, she let out a low growl of a laugh. "You.... want this..." She snarled, something in her, giving way. She did not cower or guard or hide. Neither did she rise. She knelt before him, and began to sing...

There was a girl made of sand
She could break and she could bend
She did not fear his cruel hand
And her cracks he could not mend
She bowed and obeyed his commands
She never wavered in his demands
But he could not lift the stains from her heart
His will to break her was doomed from the start...

Inhale...

Any sense of compassion or sympathy he had for her was gone. Maybe she wasn't who he thought she was. Maybe this was all a waste. "You're wrong... You choose to rest on your songs... your fairy tales? This is your weakness... You lost the will to fight!" As she finished the song, an open-handed blow struck her face. A kick planted squarely in her chest, driving her to her back. He ran after, his hands grasped down on her throat, choking what little life was left away. "Your problem isn't that you don't embrace freedom Nodiah. You don't want it. You're scared of it!"

Finally... A low snarl caught his attention. Suddenly, he felt as though a boulder had rammed him in his side as he was flung off of her. He looked up at the clearly angered Tracer. Her teeth glistened in the starlight as she kept him pinned down with a massive paw pressing into each shoulder. He looked into her eye, startled, betrayed, unsure of what was to happen next.

Nodiah's vision flickered as her loud gasps brought life back into her body. Slowly, tenderly, she brought herself back to the sitting position. Her eyes searched for her attacker, and she couldn't help but smile when she found him.

Every bone in her body ached. The dark wolf shirt was slick with blood and sweat, torn at the collar. Finally, she forced herself to her feet, staring down at him with a strange, hungry look. He had tried to kill her. He had purchased her. He owned her. She was just property after all. "How does it feel Keelin, when your pets won't listen to you? When they turn against you?" Savagely, she spat a mouthful of blood onto the ground once more.

She turned from him, walking towards the statue on the edge of the cliff, and staring out to the horizon. "You told them you would protect me! You are protecting nothing but your own sense of power and imperviousness. You want to talk about my fairy tales? You only believe in the Sky Dancers and Creators to give you a sense of purpose. You really think the Sky Dancers were the favorites of the Creators?"

She let out a loud howl, tears running down her face. Nodiah wasn't quite sure why, but she then charged the statue, ramming it with her shoulder. A loud shriek of pain escaped as her already dislocated shoulder hit, but her rage fueled her on as she pushed... and the statue gave. Keelin watched on in horror as it tumbled over the cliff's edge. Her voice dropped to a whisper as she fell to her knees. "You think I could be the favorite of anyone?" Those were the last words that escaped before she collapsed.

Chapter 5

Keelin smiled. Tracer moved away from him and towards her. She stood over her body, snarling in his direction. He spoke to Nodiah, knowing she couldn't hear. "The Sky Dancers were their favorite, and you are my favorite." He took a moment to look over where the statue once stood, mourning its loss. It was one of the few things from the Isle of Skye that existed in the Den. He always thought it may hold some clue to the location of the tree, but never found anything concrete.

He calmly extended a hand towards Tracer, low to the ground, symbolizing that he meant no harm. Cautiously, the wolf moved away. He picked up Nodiah's body, immediately taking her down the steps, through the crack in the mountain, and back to the Den. He quickly took her up the stairs and returned her to the healer, Leyos. Her body was led through the same three pool process as before. It didn't wake her, but he did see improvements. She was alive, and that was enough.

As he picked her up from the last pool, he carried her on to his personal chambers. He gently laid her down on his bed, pulled up the covers, and then scooted a chair to the side of the bed. There he sat, and watched on as Tracer came and rested at her feet. All he could do was wait and wonder if he had made a mistake. Hours passed. He couldn't pull his eyes off of her. He watched her body inflate with every inhale, sometimes doubting the next would come.

Finally... "Keelin..." It came out as a croak, her throat straining against the bruises left by his hands. She tried again, "Keelin..." her eyes made their way around the room. The site of Tracer let her smile just a bit. Maybe she could learn from the wolf after all. Then she saw him, and the smile faded.

"Well good morning sunshine..." He said with a bit of sarcasm. He approached the edge of the bed, gently gliding his fingers along her cheek. Tracer lightly growled. "Easy girl... It's over..." He smiled as her eyes found his. He wanted her to know she was safe. "I'm glad you're awake... And I'm sorry for what I did." He lowered his head for a moment, with a sincere sense of guilt. "I wish I could say it was going to get easier, but I can't promise you that." Again remorse fluttered through his tone. He physically shook away the thoughts that followed.

She ran her fingers over the back of his hand as he cupped her face, but averted her eyes at his apology. No one had ever said sorry to her before the man at the bar, and that felt like a lifetime ago. That wasn't of his own volition either. She was struggling to reconcile the intensity of the emotion of the night before, with the feelings that poured through her this morning.

"I've delayed it for a couple hours, but today... today you earn your colors." The thought was exciting. The tests were grueling. They were mental challenges as much as they were physical. Keelin knew she'd find a way though. He had never met anyone who thought or moved like her. "For now, take your time and gather yourself." With that he leaned in and gave her a warm hug, gently pressing into her stiff body. It felt good to have a somewhat normal exchange.

His embrace was just as conflicting for her. The physical marks wouldn't let her forget what he had done. She resisted for a moment before finally burying herself in his chest. Her hand rested along his collar bone. She allowed her body to surrender to him while her mind raced... Her colors... The castle... The Wolves... The taste of blood still fresh in her mouth.... Keelin....

"Do I kill him today?" She asked in a surprisingly numb tone.
She remembered. Good. "Yes... in time. But first, you earn your place in the pack." He could feel the exhausted sigh against his chest. "I know, I know, you don't owe them anything. Your status means little to you. You belong to me, but..." He was still being very selective with his words. "Your role in the pack is important to me." It was a genuine chance to test her as well. He could push her even farther.

"These tests are not just physical. They are designed to judge all aspects of character. There are three, and I cannot help you." He gently kissed her on the forehead and gave her one last assuring look. "Your first test will come to you." And with that, he walked out, taking Tracer with him. Any feeling of safety she had, left the room when he did.

A few minutes passed before the giant man she saw harassing Keelin earlier, made his way into the room. Emerging from his shadow was another person, a woman. She had long flowing white hair that extended to the back of her thighs. Her body was thick, curvy, voluptuous. Her skin was perfect. Her bright blue eyes shined against the dullness of the room.

She approached Nodiah with little hesitation, humming a song to herself. "Well well... Don't you look tasty? This should be fun." Her smile was devilish, laced with actual enjoyment. She methodically moved closer to Nodiah, one step at a time while Strom guarded the door. "Tell me my dear. Wasn't life easier over there? At the King's feet? You knew your place. You could dance. You had nothing to actually fear." She continued her approach, now within arms reach.

This woman... If Nodiah had been an animal, her hackles would have been raised. As it were, her teeth were bared with a snarl. This woman was not her master in any sense. She threw the blanket draped over her to the side, and coiled back like a snake ready to strike. As the woman moved within range, she leapt, driving the woman down to her back. Nodiah felt absolutely savage. She wanted nothing more than to rip the woman's throat out. Something animalistic had awoken inside of her, some archaic survival instinct she had never felt before, but she liked it.

The woman wasn't entirely surprised. She smiled in Nodiah's face, knowing it would only make her that much more angry. "Easy girl, I'm not here to hurt you." This stranger talked to Nodiah as if she was an animal. Could she sense it too? "I am Saoirse, the temptress." She kept her poise, focusing on her breath throughout. Nodiah could both feel and hear the rhythm.

She reached a hand up, gliding it playfully along Nodi's cheek, and then against the back of her neck. She pulled her in, and planted a light, fun kiss on her lips while her hand ran through her locks. "So let's figure out what it is you want huh?" Saoirse laid back with a smile.

Nodiah snarled as the kiss was taken from her, letting out a spiteful laugh. She slapped the woman across the face, hard. This... Saoirse... thought she could tempt her? A woman who had been the object of temptation her whole life? Who was an expert in the art of manipulation and seduction? She had been trained her entire life to resist what she wanted. How could a slave be tempted?

A slave.... Exhale...

"Why... Why did they send you?" She huffed in the woman's face. Her breath still tinged with the coppery scent of her own blood. Saoirse took a moment to take Nodiah in.

She seemed to thrive off the energy coming from Nodiah as she continued. "Oh my dear, your body is in pieces. Strom over there could snap you in half on a bad day. Do you really think you're in position to fight? Although... It is fascinating you refused to fight Keelin, but you're so willing to kill me."

How did she know so much? Nodiah was taken back for a moment. When did Keelin have time to tell her? Nodiah and Saoirse both slowed their breathing. It seemed each was re-evaluating the current situation.

Behind Saoirse's eyes, Nodiah read a bit of envy... jealousy... Which only made her that much more interesting. The energy that Saoirse brought forth was a facade. She was miserable. Her thoughts were broken by Saoirse's voice.

"I am your first test. You see the Wolves are split into six colors, each with their own... benefits as it were. The Greys are the new recruits. Those who have been captured, bought, recruited, or otherwise taken in. We all start as Greys, though normally you have to be a Grey for a year before you're allowed to go to trial. Proof of your commitment. Since Keelin bought you however, I'm sure he has no fear of your allegiance."

Nodiah wondered if this was true. Would her being sped through to the trials bring more trouble than it was worth? For him, or her? Why was she so special? Why was she even being added to the Wolves? There had to be other slaves in the pack. These Wolves seemed to have little interest in women otherwise.

Nodiah moved to the foot of the bed, and continued to listen. "The Blues are mystics. They are spiritual, or magical in nature. There is a pure connection with the arcane, or so they believe. They are curious, fascinated by the unexplored, and usually quite intelligent. Leyos the healer is a Blue.

Then there are the Greens. In tune with nature, always aware of their surroundings, skilled climbers, and able to live in any environment. They are taught survival to the extreme. There is no condition they don't feel comfortable in." Saoirse laid down, letting her hair flow out above her, and stretching her arms out.

"Then we get to the upper classes. The Reds are passion filled fighters. Full of pride, purpose, instinct, and emotion. They unlock their power from their cause. Like Strom. A true warrior.

The Blacks, powerful and cunning. They have shown promise in multiple skills. They are guardians. Normally each Alpha has a personal Black to protect them. Someone they trust They are the protectors of our way of life, and yet pride often blinds them. They are the ones who challenge the Alphas the most. They believe they have all the skill to rule, and don't always get the recognition. If they give in to those thoughts, division follows."

She sat up, locking eyes with Nodiah. She knew this was what Nodiah was waiting to hear. "Finally, there are the Alphas. Keelin, Fulgrim, and Rowan. They are the leaders. The decision makers. Usually they wear purple, but they have their choice. Skilled in all of our ways... No real weakness." That caused Nodiah to scowl. Everyone has a weakness.

"They have been tested... challenged... tried... and found to be the strongest. They are able to be challenged at any time, and yet they rarely are. Fail a challenge, and you can be returned to Grey status, or worse... banished. Each of the Alphas are very unique. They have their own background. Their own story. It is their differences that make us strong. They balance."

Saoirse couldn't help but smile. She crawled towards Nodiah on her knees as she continued. "Today, you get your colors, and this is your first test. So why don't you relax, and tell me what it is your mind wants right now?" She looked up inquisitively. Her breath grew deep and slow as she focused on Nodiah's eyes, prying to get at the truth.

"What's on my mind" she spat, eyeing Saoirse with distaste, "is why they would send one such as you to test me. We are one in the same, or..." she thought to the previous night. To the animalistic nature that was now present in her. "Or we were..."

She leaned forward, her fingertips grazing Saoirse's jaw. "So... What are they testing in me? My cruelty? Shall I try to kill you as Keelin tried to kill me hm?" Saoirse's eyes widened. The energy had shifted. "My kindness? Should I consider you my friend? My patience?" She leaned in closer, now just inches from her face. "Shall I ignore you completely? Or..." She leaned in, and got a little payback for the earlier kiss. She took it from her. There was no fun in this. It was purely about power and control. She did it because she could.

For once Saoirse was speechless. She tried to regain herself, but it was clear to Nodiah she was lost. Nodiah chuckled. "I... I ... grr..." a low frustrated growl escaped. "So you think highly of yourself huh? Even when you don't want to admit it. You're just looking for the same thing you always have. Comfort... security... An advantage."

Saoirse composed herself, twirling to her feet in a rather graceful move. She pulled out a necklace from beneath her shirt, a silver wolf head emblazoned on a blue background. She continued her slow, methodical approach. "And your heart... It wants... Vengeance no? It wants to make others feel what you've felt. That leads down a very dark road Nodiah." Her eyes never left Nodi's. The true test had begun.

Nodiah laughed confidently. She had played with Kings and royalty. This was nothing. "How could you possibly know what's in my heart?" she growled, striding towards Saoirse. She snaked her hand around, grasping the white locks in her hand. In a violent jerk, she pulled her head to the side exposing her neck, and bit down. Shortly after, the taste of blood was fresh in Nodiah's mouth once more, but it wasn't hers.

"Ah... AH... OW!" She was completely surprised. Strom moved in, but Saoirse waved him off. The pain was a rush. "I..." her mind was perplexed. Her thoughts were gone. Strom again seemed ready to intervene, but a quick glance from Nodiah froze him in place. Finally her teeth retracted from Saoirse's neck, as a creepy smile crossed her face. "Say it. Tell me you want more." Nodiah's tone was flat... calm... in control. She pulled Saoirse's head back, forcing her to look her in the eyes. The fear and hesitation only fueled Nodiah's power.

"I... want more... I'll do whatever you want..." Saoirse couldn't believe what she was saying. Temptress no longer.

It was at this moment, Keelin returned. He was in shock as he tried to read the room. He stood in the entryway watching on for a few moments before making his presence known. "Excuse me..." He saw the blood on her lips, and the control Nodiah had taken.

Saoirse's eyes popped open. Her hands pulled up to Nodiah's face, forcing their eyes to meet. "Who cares about him. Don't leave me. Please... Don't stop..." She was begging. For the first time in a long time, Saoirse was feeling something genuine. This was a feeling Nodiah sympathized with all too much. She considered going in for another bite, but Keelin stopped her short.

"Impressive." It was all he could manage to say. He did his best not to show his hand, but he failed.

Nodiah's eyes roamed over Saoirse's gasping form. This feeling was intoxicating. Power... control... It was so strong that when Keelin entered the room, she smiled. As Saoirse's pleas became even more desperate, Nodiah let out a laugh, dropping Saoirse back to the ground. "No..."

Keelin watched as real enjoyment spread over Nodiah's face. As she approached him, she finally had her sway back. She was dancing again. Only now, was she starting to see what she was capable of. It was a bit much, even for him to handle. She stopped no more than six inches from his face, pulled the back of her hand across her lips, wiping the remaining blood, and aggressively spoke to him. "I'm finished."

Saoirse's face turned from desperation to anger. "I'll get my hands on you. You're still nothing but a slave!" Refusing to back down, Keelin stayed where he was, just calling over Nodiah's shoulder instead. "You'll be dealt with later Saoirse."

Raw defiance emanated from Nodiah. For a moment it felt as if she was saying she was done with all of it. The trials, the Wolves, and even him. That wasn't a choice she had the privilege to make. Keelin needed to regain control. "Are you ready for your next test?" Before she could respond, he turned and led the way out of the door.

Nodiah didn't bother looking back. Her body was buzzing with the newfound power, but something about it went against the grain. She knew something unique had happened. "What will happen to her?" She inquired, only mildly interested in the answer. Truly she hadn't thought much of

Saoirse. She lacked control, discipline. Nodiah couldn't imagine how she achieved such a position, but maybe female Blues were a rarity.

"We have to figure out what you did to her first. She's never struggled to interrogate anyone. Many have resisted her, but to leave her like that." The realization finally hit. She broke Saoirse.

"She was meant to interrogate me?" Nodiah was amused, almost whispering the words to herself. It was a joke. Why send a woman to interrogate her, when even their Alpha Keelin, hadn't been able to pull out her secrets?

Keelin had little emotion in his response. In reality, he was disappointed. Both in Saoirse's lack of success, and her future outlook. "She will go through the trials again. Then you decide her fate." Keelin wasn't sure how Nodiah would react to having another dose of power, but none of that really mattered. Much harder tests loomed.

He led the rest of the way in silence, finally opening a large wooden door leading into a round room. In the middle, three chairs formed a triangle, all facing inward. Two of the chairs were already occupied. One, by a very tall man with a wide frame. He wasn't quite as big as Strom, but every bit as muscular. He was bald, with tattoos covering most of his skull. What truly stood out was that his eyes were almost completely black.

The other chair was filled by a much older man, late in his years, with long grey hair. He sat back patiently with a kind smile on his face as he stroked his beard. Keelin led Nodiah to the center of the chairs, and then took his own seat.

"Fulgrim... Rowan... This is the candidate. She has left Saoirse broken, and now stands before us for evaluation." His eyes moved to Nodiah's. "All you have to do is answer. Nothing more. Just be honest." He nodded, and then turned to the older man. "Fulgrim. I believe the first question is yours."

Nodiah felt a bit like a cornered animal. She was poised to attack if she needed. In front of these Alphas, she truly felt insignificant once more. There was something about them being together. These are the Alpha Wolves. These men... They struck fear into Kings. They led the pack. The energy was palpable. She had to shake it off.

Inhale...

The old man stood, leaning forward on an intricately carved wooden cane. "Hello my dear, tell me. Why are you here?" The man began to pace. Keelin was visibly nervous. These questions were never what they seemed.

A chorus of answers sang inside her mind. She tried her best to converge them into one answer. What did they want her to say? No... it didn't matter. Be honest. "I am here because I have never belonged to myself. I was born into the King's harem, hammered and crafted into a polished statue. They would not give me a name, nor the right to an identity, save for the one scripted to me." Each word was heavy. Each sentence felt like another punch to the gut. These were not easy things for her to say.

"I was trained to serve, to entertain, to manipulate. For pleasure. For power. For profit. Most recently, a token of a power struggle between an overly mighty King, and an overly confident mercenary." She glanced Keelin's way, but he didn't react.

"A mockery of an olive branch that became a red flag of war. I am here because I was bought and paid for. Because I am... owned.... Because I am a reminder of those who carry the sin of envy. I am a reminder of what it means to be cherished... favored." Her fingers sought the bruised skin of her throat as she remembered Keelin's story, and his following actions.

"To be precious to the Creators... and those who serve them." She could feel Keelin's gaze burning into her. It reinvigorated her to continue. "I am a reminder that there is a price to be paid for such favor. There is always a cost." She paused for a moment, taking in each of the three men in turn.

They were indeed different, unique, balanced. "I am here to be tested; to be changed again, to be trained to be something more. I am here to be smelted down and refined into something more beautiful than I am now. I am here to come into my own. To take charge of who I am, and I am here to make you question yourselves. To make you ask yourself... Why are you... here?"

It started small, but Fulgrims laughter eventually grew into a roar echoing through the chamber. His attention turned to Keelin. "Does she always make things so complicated? Amusing at the least!" His enthusiasm was genuine. Keelin's nerves grew. His frustration at his property grew. He could sense her anger towards his laughter. He dug his fingers into the wood of his chair. Even when she was right, she had to make a statement. Apparently Fulgrim sensed it too.

"It's quite alright Keelin. She is unique. That's why you brought her, no?" He turned his attention back to Nodiah. "Now tell me, do you believe you are favored? That you have a destiny? A purpose? Or are you just the play thing of an over confident mercenary?" He leaned forward on his staff, and awaited patiently.

She took a moment, calming herself. Her emotions towards Keelin were still anything but clear. She couldn't comprehend how at the same time, he was the only thing that made her feel safe, and the one she feared most. She wanted to make him proud. She didn't want to fail him. "It doesn't matter if I believe it or not. Those around me do, and it shapes what happens to me... but that is something I hope to change. To take charge of my own destiny." She offered him a smile, the last statement a bit of an epiphany for herself.

Fulgrim smiled back. "Awareness of the now, you excel at, but you fail to see potential... expectation... awareness of what the future could be. You still hold yourself back. Very interesting..." How could she explain to him that the ability to see past the now wasn't something she could even comprehend? How could she examine her potential when she had no idea what was expected of her? Fulgrim locked eyes with Nodiah one last time, before being interrupted.

"Quit wasting time with your riddles old man. Just because this is Keelin's new dog, doesn't mean we are giving her the golden pass just yet." Rowan stood, making his towering height even more prominent. He stopped just one pace away from Nodiah, looming over her like a bear. It was clear he wouldn't be easy to impress. "Tell me Dog... Slave... What is true power? Where does it come from?" He began circling her, pacing like a lion, ready to pounce on her first sign of weakness.

She tensed as the second man spoke, keeping her eyes on Keelin's as Rowan circled. This was the kind of man that she was used to. It sent a cold chill up her spine. "True power is... power over self. Power and control over anything else is just an illusion. Something those who believe they are in control... use to convince themselves that they rule supreme."

Rowan's response wasn't as kind as Fulgrims. It was fueled by sarcasm and ridicule. "Of course the slave thinks power comes from being one's own Master. Pathetic really. There is an illusion to power my dear, but you're missing who is getting fooled." His pacing stopped right in front of her as he looked down with an intimidating glare and continued. "Us Alphas only have power, because the Wolves believe we do. We are no different than them. Strom could crush us, Leyos could make us fall sick with a single prick, and Saoirse... Well Saoirse showed you how far power over self can go. Eventually, it runs into someone stronger… and is broken."

He backed up ever so slightly and his tone changed. His role turned from lecturer to educator, a bit softer. "You said it yourself. True power comes from the faith of those around you. What they, and you, choose to believe. You decide what is worth fighting for, worth dying for. If I told a story about a pearl in the middle of the desert that granted everlasting life, half the pack would scurry out there. Not only because of my power, but because their belief of a power in something that doesn't even exist. You must not only believe yourself, you must be willing to do whatever it takes to make others believe." He approached again, his glance much more inquisitive than intimidating this time.

"You have made believers out of many Our concern with you, is that you don't even realize what you already have. You are untamed. That can be a positive though. The decision to make is where are you at your best?" He nodded, and then retreated, giving the floor to Keelin.

He approached without hesitation, placing his hands on Nodiah's shoulders. His touch was enough to bring back a bit of confidence in her body language. "Nodiah, knowing the colors as Saoirse described, what color do you believe you deserve?" There was no right answer. It was a trick in every sense. Keelin awaited anxiously, knowing he had just set her up. "Choose wise…"

"Don't coach your little whore... Let her answer." Rowan shouted out. All three seemed on edge awaiting her answer.

"I…" She took in Keelin's eyes. She knew him best, so why was he the hardest to answer? "I want to be all of them." She finally let out softly. "I was sought after, and looking for a place to belong like all the Greys… and when I dance, I connect with the spiritual like the Blues. Nature brings me peace, and if I had not learned how to survive like the Greens, I would have died long ago. The past days have unleashed in me the passion of the

Reds. A passion unlike any I have felt before. I want to push and challenge you all like the Blacks. And I..."

Exhale...

I want to be by your side... She almost said it, but did she mean it? Did she really? "I, like you, want to have the power to really control what happens next. I want to be an Alpha. You tell me I don't know my own potential, well let me say that I refuse to have my potential limited by these boundaries. I want to be all of them. I want to be none of them. I want the freedom to become who I can, without forcing myself into one of your molds!" Her answer was spirited, honest, but clearly not what any of them were expecting.

Rowan scoffed, and stood angrily. "You have no aim! You are but a child, because you have never been forced to be more!"

"Enough Rowan." Keelin came to her defense.

"Unsure she is... Wild... hmm. Perhaps she is best kept wild. When you let a wild animal off their leash, you cannot expect it not to run." Fulgrim piped in.

Keelin came to her defense. "Isn't that what we all do? Isn't that why we are here? We have structure under the illusion of power, but ultimately we have sought after, and fought for the freedom to run. I will not let that be held against her." His head sank. He didn't have ground to stand on, and he knew it. "However, without purpose... cause..."

Rowan interjected "She can not begin to know how to fight." His attention turned back to her. "These are not molds, child! We do not turn you into anything. We help you embrace what you already are."

"And what she is, is a Sky Dancer!" Keelin called out, firm in his belief. "I have every intention of breaking her. She will not be given anything. She, like all of us, will earn her place." He approached Rowan, looking up at the much taller man. "She will learn power, she will fight for truth, but she can be so much more!" His tone was unwavering. Every word came from his full heart.

"Fairy tales. Why? Because of her hair? I'd just as soon cut out her tongue and shut her up for good," Rowan scoffed. The anger in Keelin exploded, he was on the brink of the unthinkable.

She couldn't let him throw everything away. Not for her. Just yesterday this was the moment she was hoping for. Total dissent among the Alphas. She could let them tear each other apart, or step in and save him. She gently placed her fingers on Keelin's heart, forcing her emotions into him, and then moved forward towards Rowan.

She knelt down before him. "What's it going to take?" She looked up calmly, much to his surprise. Keelin fought every instinct to act. Rowan was a Red before he was an Alpha. Violence was his calling card. The tension didn't disappear, but he held his ground.

"Take? Take? Is this how easily your allegiance to Keelin can be broken? You grovel at my feet?" Rowan laughed a bit uncomfortably. It was clear he wasn't sure how to respond, but finally inspiration struck. "I'm coming with you on your last trial." His composure relaxed a bit. "I want to see your confrontation with the King."

Nodiah smiled a bit to herself. *Guess that means I passed the second trial*, she thought to herself. Keelin looked furious, and tense. Was she really in danger? There's no way Fulgrim would stand for it. She had to be safe.

"I actually would quite like to see how you handle your past as well," Fulgrim chimed in, still smiling. "Then we will make your judgment."

Keelin searched for a reason to protest. "The three of us in one place is not wise." He begged to be the voice of reason.

"We are all here now are we not?" Fulgrim replied whimsically.

"Yes, but here isn't an enemy castle!" Keelin's frustrations were evident.

He took a sharp breath. He believed in her. She could do this. He had to believe in who she was. It was everything. "Fine…"

"To the castle then, and once the King is dead, you will be judged." Rowan's words were heavy, meant to last. They did in Keelin's mind as he forcefully led her out of the room. As much as he hated the philosophy of the other Alphas, he knew the Wolves ran best with all three of them alive. This became a much more complicated process with this final test.

His frustration at Rowan's brashness was justified. A war between the Alphas would be unheard of, but Keelin would have to teach Rowan about true power soon enough. Though that was no easy task. Rowan had a band of followers among the Reds that were fiercely loyal.

Nodiah tried her best to read Keelin's emotions. Obviously, he was not happy. He looked furious. It seemed everyone she came into contact with was subject to Keelin's wrath, except Ryker... She wanted to say something. She wanted him to say something to her. It was still unclear whether he was ready to throw her off the cliff, or congratulate her. Neither yet, they had to go back... but after getting a taste of her own power, she was no longer afraid.

As the duo put some distance between themselves and the room, Keelin took a sharp left down a narrow hall, and stopped and turned. Nodiah followed and jumped a little as suddenly they were face to face. "I don't know where all of these ideas come from, but I'd like to hear more sometime." Keelin's words were sharp and poignant, fueled by the adrenaline of the moment. "Of how you believe the world should work. It sounds like a fantastic place."

His first intention was to calm her nerves, distracting her of what was to come. His second intention was sincerity. She spoke of power and passion and desire in a way that he couldn't begin to grasp. He didn't like anything he didn't understand, so he had to know more.

He let a hand float up to her cheek, and along the back of her neck. "I'm sure you're conflicted. Your opinion of me will not get any easier, but you can do this." It was hardly reassuring. He knew how horrible it made him sound.

Nodiah bit down a response. He had to be the most impossible man to please. It didn't matter if she was strong, weak, dominant, submissive, selfish, or selfless. He seemed completely frustrated with her no matter what she did. She wondered if this just meant she was getting under his skin. Maybe he knew she was actually a weakness.

He didn't dwell on the moment for long, instead leading the way through a plain looking door. Inside was a surprisingly large room. The entire space was lined with rack after rack of various weapons. Swords and shields, mauls, daggers, maces, bows, and others that all had a distinct Wolves quality to them. They came in all sorts of sizes and colors, some clearly taken from other places, while others seemed to be carved from the same material as the Den. "Choose..." He said calmly, allowing her to take in the room. "Choose the weapon that will destroy your past, and decide your future."

He sat in the corner, focusing on her form as she inspected the room. This was the most important decision Nodiah had to make so far, and yet he couldn't help but think that even in her broken down state, she was the most beautiful woman he had ever seen. Her movements were so light. She hardly made a sound. How did she do it?

She methodically moved along the racks, tracing her hands against a few as she went. Weapons were something she'd never been allowed to touch. She had no training. It seemed like a hopeless cause to try to choose one now. She began to think about the skills she did have, and the props she had used in her dances. Staffs, rings of fire, aerial hoops, and chains all came to mind. Finally, her eyes found a pair of metallic fans that had a sharpened edge. She cocked her head to one side, full of intrigue as she examined them closer. She had danced with a veiled fan since she was a child, and as she took these in her hands they felt like a natural extension of her being.

She turned to face him, a fan in each hand. She held one level with her shoulders, pointed upwards. The other was held level with her hips, pointing downward. It felt providential in a way. She would dance for King Malachi one last time.

A smile crossed her face as she paced towards him, with all of the intentionality and purpose she had when they first met. "I can see that you really do believe... in me. And that you will protect me." She swallowed roughly, a moment of fear from the night before showing in her eyes. He was so explosive. This entire place seemed like a powder keg waiting to be lit. She let out a slow breath. "Thank you" she whispered, pushing herself up on her toes and pressing her lips to his cheek.

He felt the smile come over his face as he wrapped his arms around her waist. This moment was so simple. He wished he could hang on to this forever. There were no Alphas, no King, no confusion. Just the two of them. "Y... You're welcome..." he said, trying his best not to laugh.

An icy fire spread through her veins at his touch. His smile caused one of her own to blossom as she could feel it tugging at her lips. When she saw his face, she broke into a laugh herself. "What?" she forced out between the giggles. Her hands crossed behind his neck. She then moved her head back to his shoulder. "What about any of this makes you smile?" She asked with a bit of genuine confusion.

He considered his response for a moment as he tried to regain his thoughts. "What? The smile? I mean... Look at you!?" He took a step back, twirling her around in his hand, and then pulling her back in close. "You are mine... What man wouldn't smile at that." He said it playfully, hoping it wouldn't break the mood. "Together, we can set the world on fire. There will be plenty of moments for you to hate me soon enough. I just want to enjoy you... Not for what anyone thinks you are, but for what you actually are." No matter how things ended, chaos was a catalyst for change, and she had shown a gift of getting out of tough situations. He looked forward to seeing her do it once more.

Her mood wasn't broken, on the contrary his words seemed to put a spell on her. There was no going back to her life before. There never could be. The past was just that... The past... In that there was freedom! She knew in the future that she would pay for her actions today. He was still planning to break her. He would abuse her again, but say it was for her own good. Right now, in this moment, she was truly his.

For the first time, she craved him. Her free hand crept under the hem of his shirt. She wanted to crawl into his arms and just be held once more. She wanted to be protected. In this moment, before she faced her greatest foe, the great Master that had constantly ruled her life, she was happy to belong to him.

The moment didn't last though. Keelin knew if Fulgrim or Rowan walked through the door, it would weaken his position. It would create problems. Part of him didn't care. As her fingers found his flesh, he couldn't help but close his eyes. He couldn't break the smile on his face... but he knew what he had to do. "Patience my dear. You kill the King, and then we celebrate." It was harsh. He wanted to give in. This was a moment, days in the making, and he was just as frustrated as she was. In fact, he knew she could use this against him. If she could turn Saoirse into a gibbering pool of lust and jealousy, what could she do to him? He had to end this.

Inhale...

With a long breath, the passion left. The tension evacuated her muscles as she replaced her feet on the ground. She grazed his ear with her teeth, drawing her lips down across the hollow of his neck before pulling herself away. She stared up at him once more, her eyes round, bright, and cold. She wanted to yell at him. His self-control came at the strangest of times! Never before had she truly wanted to belong to someone, and there was no guarantee she would still want to when this was over. If they survived. "When are we leaving?" Her words were full of ice. Her hands tightened on the grips of the fans, and she began walking away before he could answer.

It instantly felt that whatever they gained from that moment was gone. He had meant to use all of it to encourage her, and yet it seemed it would become a moment of resentment. For the first time, he felt like he owed her. He had to make it up to her. "Our plan is simple. We bring you back as a peace offering. An apology for my... choice... words... The King loves a good stroke of his... ego. From there the plan is yours. If it's ever too much, you howl, and we take you out."

"Howl? Like a dog?" She knew the significance, but it felt odd. He ignored it.

"When you do it, how you do it, that's up to you. But Rowan will want to hear every bloody detail. We leave when you decide." His words were empty, distracted, but maybe it was better this way. He was too attached.

With a forceful sigh his eyes found hers. "Trust yourself. You wanted power over self, now you have it. What you do with it is up to you." She still needed more details. She needed to know why.

She began stretching and rolling her shoulders around. "But why Keelin? Why do the Wolves want him dead? I know it's not just because of me." Again she approached, looking up to him with her eyes shining as bright as ever. "And what will happen to me? What happens if I fail?" Would he still be proud to call her his if she had to be pulled out? What if she made a fool of him? Being discarded was a fear worse than death.

She hadn't said his name many times. It spoke to their bond, and in a way he found a strange comfort in that. "We want him dead because..." At that moment they were interrupted. Rowan marched his way into the room.

"Because Keelin lost track of his mission. The night he brought you home, he was there to accept a mission from the King." Rowan's arrogance was clear. "Since Keelin decided to do things his way, we never learned what the mission was however. He was going to send us to retrieve something. Whatever that something is, it's clearly valuable. We can't risk that information falling into someone else's hand. So we must silence the King." Rowan inspected Nodiah and her fans. "Small weapons for a small girl, but maybe you can make them work," he snickered.

"That's… mostly right." Keelin quipped.

"You ready yet?" Rowan responded with a bit of tease in his voice.

Nodiah felt her nostrils flare, and her body stiffen as Rowan barged into the room. Suddenly all of the aches and pains came rushing back. If all went well, and she became a higher ranking Wolf, he would have to be dealt with. He seemed all too eager to challenge and criticize Keelin at any opportunity.

"I can make them work," she assured her, baring her teeth slightly. "I'm just an obedient slave to him, a pretty bit of ribbon or a bauble to keep as a souvenir. You will see for yourself what happens when someone underestimates me." She backed a few steps from Keelin, before springing into a back tuck, her fans brandishing in fluid, almost invisible motions. She twisted in the air and landed just in front of Rowan, poised on the balls of her feet. She closed the fans with a snap in front of his face. "Besides, he won't even realize these are weapons until he's dead. No one will."

Keelin couldn't help but smile as Rowan rocked back on his feet. She glanced over her shoulder at Keelin, glad to turn attention away from Rowan. "It's not complicated. The King expressed his wishes very clearly yesterday. You will have to offer him more though or we will be lost before we've ever started. All I need is enough time for a private dance. You three will have to keep us alive until then." Her look was serious. If it was her position on the line, then she was taking command of the situation.

At this point, Fulgrim made his presence known from the doorway. "If this King truly enjoys his harems, perhaps the answer isn't something more, but someone more" he pondered. Keelin smiled, immediately getting what the kook was suggesting, and he enjoyed the thought. "Prepare her. We will head for the stables and get a start." Keelin smiled, and then turned his attention back to Nodiah.

"I'll need some clothes," she told them, ignoring whatever they were talking about for the moment. Keelin led the way back to the closet where she had been a few times before. "This is the last time I will be dressed as a prize," she said into the darkness. A few moments later, she was dressed. Bright red fabric that nearly matched her hair swung around her shoulders, and then around her chest and waist and draped down in a form of makeshift robe.

As she reappeared Keelin couldn't find the words, so they simply headed for the horses. As they approached, much to her surprise Keelin's horse had a double saddle on it this time. She took a moment to appreciate the gesture. Every new symbol of equality bestowed on her lightened her. With every new privilege, she felt herself becoming more free. The look on her face was excited. He helped her into her saddle before mounting up himself, and within a few moments they were riding. They were headed back to erase her past.

Matthew Oakley

Chapter 6

The hours stretched and contracted as they sped across the desert sands. When her fear ruled her mind, the miles seemed to pass in seconds. When she found her confidence, time crawled to a halt. She watched the sun sink below the horizon, giving way to darkness, but they didn't stop. At some point, she must have fallen asleep, because when she next opened her eyes, the sun had returned.

Finally, they approached her old home, Torek. "Keelin," she growled into his ear. "I.. I don't know what is going to happen when you... offer me... to him... but if you want me to succeed, to pass this trial, you have to control yourself." She reflected on his anger towards Rowan and even Corrig. Could he really hold himself back if the worst should happen? "You have to trust me." Her plea was genuine, but possibly in vain.

He couldn't promise that. In some ways he wished he could kill the King himself. Malachi didn't deserve to see her again. "Alright..." he muscled out. "But you know what to do if it becomes too much. There is no shame in staying alive." This scenario had no room for pride. They approached the gate, and waited for the others to catch up. It seemed Keelin must have outpaced them a bit.

Finally, Rowan, Fulgrim, and his passenger Saoirse caught up. She was hardly wearing anything. Small strips of blue cloth covered her essentials, and a small pouch hung at her hip. She did not look happy about it. Her hands were shackled and connected to her ankles by a long chain. Nodiah's mouth dropped.

She had a conflict of emotions. Seeing her like that was a bit too familiar for her. This woman had sworn vengeance on Nodiah, and yet now they were including her? She could ruin everything. This was an unexpected complication at the least. "We can't bring her. I can do this on my own."

"The King will want a better offer," Rowan said coldly.

"I understand that, but why her? Isn't she worth more to you?"

"She can handle herself. Besides, she failed. This is her trial as well. She has a role to play" There was no arguing. Nodiah had broken the temptress. Once Nodiah finished with the King, she would be dealt with.

"Shall we?" Rowan led the way towards the door, being stopped by a guard just outside. Nodiah watched as Saoirse moved to the side, and placed a small blue stone from her pouch down in the sand.

"You have a lot of nerve coming uninvited.." The guard forced out, trying to sound as intimidating as he could.

Keelin stepped forward, "I have something that belongs to the King. I believe I may have insulted him, and I'd like to make amends." The guard looked the group up and down, and then nodded and moved out of the way.

As they entered the castle, more guards, more explaining, until finally they made their way through a pair of steel doors emblazoned with King Malachi's seal. They entered the throne room, where the King was already standing and awaiting their arrival. Keelin expected a bit of hesitation in Nodiah, but she stood boldly alongside him. This was no longer her home.

The King moved in for a closer inspection. "She has been damaged. What have you done with her?" He circled around Saoirse first, and then paused in front of Nodiah. "Why is the other one shackled?"

Rowan moved in to explain. "She can be a bit wild. It is for your safety." The King nodded, his poor attempt at a poker face unable to hide the excitement in his eyes. His attention then turned back to Nodiah.

"And tell me my dear. Why shouldn't I just kill you all? Hmm?" He took her red locks gently in his hand, and inhaled her scent. Keelin's fists clenched as he watched on. His eyes were purely on the King, waiting for the first reason to get involved.

She dipped her eyes to the floor, and spoke softly. "It is only your desire I am here to focus on. I do apologize for the events that took place... and I am quite disappointed that I was forced to deprive you of your right as Lord. This man has seen his errors, and he is here to make peace. As for myself, I just want to do a private dance for my King one last time before you decide what to do." Her eyes glanced towards Saoirse, trying to hide her apprehension. What would Saoirse do? Would she try and save herself? "Please, sire. Let me dance for you."

As her eyes rose to meet his, it almost felt as though she was asking Keelin rather than the King. He had to remember her words. He had to trust her. He inhaled sharply, relaxed his fists, and awaited the King's response. Rowan seemed to be just as on edge as he was.

"Why private? You can entertain us all I'm sure!" The King touted loudly, then he made his move. He grabbed Saoirse's chains, and pulled her towards Nodiah. Without hesitation, he grabbed Nodiah's hand and twirled her around. As her back turned to him, his arm lowered across her throat while his other hand began roaming across her body. Fists were clenched once more.

His arm began to squeeze just a bit, and it must have brought some light to Saoirse's eyes. "Do you enjoy this?" He asked her playfully. He began swaying against Nodiah in a surprisingly nonrhythmic fashion, which made the entire situation even more awkward. "Well I don't want to leave you disappointed. We could all have twice the fun." Saoirse couldn't help but smile at the thought. Keelin hated the idea of the three of them alone. All eyes fell back to Nodiah.

She thought of killing Saoirse right then and there, but she couldn't. They were far too outnumbered, and that wasn't the plan. She looked all around the room, eyes falling on everything and everyone except Keelin. She did not resist the Kings attempts at dancing, and even gave her hips a little twist herself. She gracefully extended a finger, and waved Saoirse to approach. Perhaps the woman could still be some sort of use to her after all. She needed the distraction.

Saoirse approached with a savage glint in her eyes. Her hand reached over Nodiah's shoulder and stroked the King's beard. "Forgive me my Lord, I'm just a little shy. But maybe..." She knelt before the King, looking up with her big round eyes, knowing that given what she was wearing he had full view of the rest of her as well. "Maybe a private dance isn't a bad idea. I'm sure I could get more… comfortable," Her hand grabbed onto his thigh as he continued to stare up at her.

The King took a quick audible gasp as he considered the requests. "Neither of you better be wasting my time. Lives are at stake." The King could barely speak. He wasn't as calm under pressure as Keelin was. It made Keelin smile a bit, as he wondered how a man like this became King. Then he remembered… The Wolves had killed his father.

Malachi took Saoirse's chains, and Nodiah's hair and forcibly pulled them into a private room. Playtime was over. The door slammed behind them as he flung them both to the floor inside. He made his way over to a giant pillow, longer than him and several feet high. As he laid down, it gave and slanted propping him up just enough. He pulled Saoirse towards him, and allowed her to join him on the massive pillow. "Alright... dance..." The King licked his lips and rubbed his palms together in anticipation.

Nodiah was more worried about Saoirse than him now. She shook out her red locks, pushing her shoulders back as she drew herself up to her full height. Her eyes scanned the room as if musicians would suddenly pop up from the shadows, as they often did in Torek. Sure enough, from the darkness came the sound of a single flute.

Slowly, she made her way to the center of the room, her back to them both. The flute started off with a slow, smooth rhythm. Her hips became fluid, liquid, dropping and swaying along with every note. The red fabric began to cling to her tightly.

Her whole body started to come alive as she slowly raised her arms straight out, extended at a perfect ninety degrees from her body. They moved with such fluidity that they seemed to be riding on the sound waves. The light jingling of a tambourine joined the tune as the flute's melody picked up pace. She snapped her fingers. The fans opened gracefully into her hands, and she turned to face them both.

At first, the King was wrapped up in Saoirse's playfulness. He closed his eyes and allowed her soft white hair to lay across his face. Something about Nodiah though, he couldn't keep his eyes off for long. Even Saoirse seemed encapsulated by her performance. She had begun to slide up the King's shirt, but whatever she was doing was lost as she laid her head on his chest, and just watched Nodiah move. Those familiar feelings of lust, and envy ran through her veins, but she couldn't help but just be in awe as well.

As Nodiah turned to face them, the King stood, leaving Saoirse clinging around his leg. Nodiah locked eyes with the King, taking in the scene of Saoirse on her knees before him, while she danced. That power was the boost she needed. She held the fans out level with the ground, and launched herself into a cartwheel. Her red locks whipped around as she lowered back to the ground. She came to a stop about ten feet in front of them, breathing heavily from the adrenaline that now filled the moment.

She slid her thumbs into the holes on the end of the grips of the fans, and began spinning each of them clockwise around her digit. She opened the fans wide, and moved her arms in a counter-clockwise fashion. The result was a pattern of a four petaled flower, becoming more and more detailed as the speed of her movements and spins increased. Then finally, in one swift jerk, she crossed her arms, dragging the blades across the fabric which dropped to the floor.

Nodiah smiled as Saoirse's jaw dropped, and the King could no longer contain himself. He pushed Saoirse back into the pillow and approached. "I hope you understand now my dear. There is no escaping me. Your friend.. Keelin. He will die for his disrespect. But you. I will keep you." He stopped about two feet from her, as he noticed her fans start spinning once more. "Come.. kneel…" The smile faded from Nodiah's face. Men just couldn't stop thinking about control. A point had to be made... but not by him.

She slowly moved her head from side to side, cracking her neck, then brought the blades back in front of her, still spinning in a frenzy. She leaned back, ever so slightly, and closed her eyes, and took in the moment. Once more, she was a trophy being displayed in front of this weak, lustful, pathetic example of a man, and a King. She let the adrenaline carry her forward. Now just inches between them, the blades being the only thing separating them, she smiled. She thought back to Keelin's description of the Sky Dancers. They move with the air, along the path of least resistance... She wanted them to see this. She wanted them to believe.

"AAWWUUUOOOOOOOO…"

The noise echoed through the cavernous halls of the castle. Keelin and Rowan sprung to action, running full speed towards the door. A cold chill crawled up Keelin's spine. He would never forgive himself if something had happened. He should have never let her go in alone.

The King smiled at her bizarre act, clueless as to what was coming. The door opened. The King's eyes widened, but he had no time to react. She reached a hand forward and down, blades still spinning around her thumb. As she shifted the angle she could feel the satisfying squish of blade on flesh.

Surprisingly there wasn't much resistance. She looked down to where the blade had gone, and let out a small squeal of unexpected joy. The King had been physically emasculated.

With a quick spin, she thrust the other blade cleanly across Malachi's throat. Nodiah flinched at the sudden spurt of blood that hit her in the face, but was overcome with the rush that came with it. A truly animalistic growl escaped her lungs. She brought the blade down into the now lifeless chest of the prone body, and let out one last howl amidst laughter.

As the other three surveyed the scene, Rowan bent over, ran to a nearby plant, and lost the contents of his stomach. Fulgrim stayed silent and observant as he always seemed to be. Saoirse approached Nodiah from behind, laughing herself, and wrapping her hands around Nodiah's shoulders. An admittedly risky move given her current state.

Keelin wasn't sure what to feel. The... being... in front of him was hardly human. The look in her eyes was untamed... crazed... savage. It both exhilarated him, and made him fearful. Was this her trap? Was he next? She had all three Alphas in front of her. He shook off the thought, and regained his composure as he walked towards her. "Well gentlemen, if she doesn't belong as a Wolf, I don't know who does. Her skills have been proven. She is still wild though."

He paused for a moment. Saoirse's advances had left them both streaked with the King's blood. Nodiah still seemed oblivious to it all. Rowan couldn't manage to look at any of it, but he did speak. "Red.. She is as passionate as they come. I vote red." He mustered out.

Keelin immediately objected. "But she is cunning, strong, and my protector. She should be a Black." He shot her an approving smile with an accompanying wink.

Fulgrim made his way up to Nodiah, locking eyes with her and staring on for a moment before finally breaking the silence. "There is... another option." The mere suggestion seemed to bother Rowan.

"Not this bullshit again! We are a group who wrote our own rules, and we live by them. We aren't some lost ancient religion. You can't really believe..."

Keelin saw an opportunity. "You said it yourself Rowan. We give the prophecy its power. Imagine what we could do if the people believed. Do you know what this means?!" Keelin's excitement was unable to be contained. He had thrown Rowan's own words back at him, and in that saw an opportunity that was just too good to let go.

He picked up her makeshift attire from the floor, and began to cover her up once more. "It would forever change our reputation. We would no longer have the same respect." Rowan continued to run through the thoughts from his own perspective.

Fulgrim's mind was made up however. "My dear. We believe you to be the White Wolf." He smiled his normal smile, and produced a white chalky substance. He dabbed his thumb into it firmly, and then placed the dot on her forehead.

White? Nodiah's confusion was obvious. Saoirse hadn't talked about White. No one had. It seemed to snap her back to reality a bit though. Her eyes refocused, and then searched for Keelin for some sort of understanding. "It isn't official yet. I'll explain later. For now, I'd like a moment." The tone Keelin chose let everyone know he was quite serious. Rowan and Saoirse paused, but Fulgrim nodded them along as they began to barricade the door. "Are you ok?" He asked calmly.

Inhale…

Nodiah seemed to wake up as the question was asked. She was aware of her state for the first time as she looked down at her hands, stained with blood, still clutching her weapons tightly. Slowly she raised her gaze to meet Keelin's. She saw his hesitation, and maybe fear? She dropped the fans to the ground with a loud clang. Her fingers drug across her chest, she was soaked. Slowly, she used her fabric to wipe her face, neck, and arms clean.

Finally she looked towards her once proud Master, the dead King. Her lip curled. "I am fine.." she replied softly. The realization came over her. "He is gone… He's really gone." She stepped towards Keelin. "He can never control me again." She tilted her head from side to side as if looking for Keelin for the first time. She then brought her hands to her head, and ran them through her locks. This was real. He was gone.

She shuffled closer to him until her cheek was pressed up against his chest. "I'm ok." She mustered a small chuckle remembering what she had done to him. "And he is not…" She said with a bit of a giggle. "I am ready to go home now."

She touched her fingers to her forehead, and was perplexed for a moment when they came away white. *I am the White Wolf…* she thought to herself. Her voice gathered strength as she pulled her cheek away. "Keelin, let's go home." He squeezed his arms around her. There was genuine relief. Finally, Keelin too was ready. "Want to take that," motioning towards a part of the King that was once attached. "with us? As a trophy? It'll keep Rowan away from you." He laughed heartily as they made their way towards the others.

"Saoirse, it's time." The group formed a circle, with Saoirse in the middle. She pulled an elegant blue crystal from the pouch on her hip. "Make sure you're touching her." Keelin called out. They all placed a hand on her, and she began.

"Ahk to navis tal a niv reya se no lok ti" Nodiah was mesmerized as the stone began to glow and let off a soft humming noise. Suddenly a massive amount of force seemed to pull on her body. She shut her eyes, trying not to scream. A moment later, it was all over. She opened her eyes, and found herself outside the castle gate. Right where Saoirse planted the first stone. Suddenly Nodiah was extremely greatful they brought the Blue temptress along.

They quickly mounted the horses, and started the journey back before most of Torek knew what had happened. She did it.

Exhale…

Chapter 7

The ride back was fairly quiet. He allowed Nodiah to take the front spot, his arms wrapping around her body. The only comment he made was playful. "You know... you're in a lot of trouble when I get you back." He lightly kissed her cheek to ensure she knew he wasn't trying to be menacing. He felt her lean back into his body, as she seemed to relax at the thought.

"You really know how to talk to a girl." She replied playfully. The hours stretched, and Nodiah took in some of the others in the entourage. She admired their endurance. This ride wasn't easy, and yet it seemed stopping never came to anyone's mind. They were tired, and hungry. She could see it on their faces, but no one said anything.

As they made their way into to the stables, Rowan ran off to tell everyone he could find the King was in fact dead. The Wolves smiled and seemed genuinely happy at the news. It truly lightened Nodiah's heart to realize this King was resented by others as well. She had done a good thing.

A thousand thoughts flooded her mind, and a few times she opened her mouth to speak, but nothing came out. Keelin didn't seem like he was in the mood for conversation. She wasn't ready to start chatting up the rest of the Wolves just yet. So she remained silent.

They made their way back into the large black building. She pulled Keelin along eagerly, her fingers finding grip in the folds of his robes. "Please, take me to the baths, showers, anything. I am covered with the stench of death and the taste of blood." She arched a brow at him mischievously. "Unless, of course you are in a hurry to punish me. I understand I'm in trouble? Committing murder will bring that out in a girl though." She raised a finger to her mouth, and bit the tip playfully. It was his move.

Keelin weighed his options carefully, pacing with his hands behind his back. "There are a lot of things that you need to answer for. I mean, I know the King was far from a perfect human being, but it's not ok to separate a man from his... scepter... as it were."

The day had enough serious moments. All of this banter stayed light and playful. It wasn't the same unbridled joy or enthusiasm as in the armory however. This was relief. The kind of feeling that comes from returning home after lots of travel. "And blood is a good look for you. On the other hand, you definitely do smell."

He hardly started to chuckle before she ran at him and shoved him away. The smile on her face showed her intentions. "Alright alright... come..." He led the way back to his own room once more. The sheets had been changed from the earlier exchange.

As soon as they were both inside, Keelin closed and locked the door. Finally, they were alone. No trials, no games, no missions, no interruptions. Just the two of them. He knew it wasn't the moment she was expecting, but the warmth, and comfort, and safety of that place... to be worry free for a few hours... that was exactly what he needed.

They entered the showers, giving Keelin another chance to take in her body. He took his time looking over every curve, every scar, continuing to map out her body with his touch. Finally, he exhaled deeply as if he was pushing out all of the emotion and the stress from the day. Under his breath he spoke. "I trusted you today, but I won't risk you again..."

It was so honest, and real. There was no reason for him to hold back any longer. She closed her eyes, letting the water wash away the day. *Then don't...* she didn't say it. There would be more days like today, and she knew it. For now, she twisted in his arms, her fingers running through his locks. She leaned up, and kissed him, trying to convey that, at least for now, she forgave him. Everything was okay, and they were safe.

What followed was a release of tension and frustration that was days, if not years in the making. They decided to make a game of it. The first to push the other past the brink, would get one request. One undeniable, inescapable order to be cashed in at any time. She wanted the prize, but for the first time in her life, Nodiah's pleasure came first. He won easily.

There were few words shared, but the looks, touches, and energy were enough. They continued until their bodies gave out, and finally Keelin drifted to sleep. Nodiah pulled the covers over them both, and nuzzled her head beneath her chin, trying to gather what just happened. This night is what she had to hold on to. This moment. He cared. "My Alpha... I'll protect you..." escaped her lips, as she too drifted off.

When he awoke, the sun was still down, the room was clung with darkness. He quietly made his way out of the bed, allowing his eyes to adjust to the surrounding blackness. He moved to the door, creaking it open and moving down to the central room of the Den. It was there that he met Fulgrim, who seemed to be waiting for him, but Keelin wasn't surprised.

In Fulgrims hands, a long white one-piece garment with flowing designs running throughout. There was a bit of padding in certain places as well. The entire thing had a bit of shine, almost like armor. Beneath the outer white, was a thin black layer that would cover the wearers body more thoroughly. The robe looked completely untouched, unworn. Keelin took it, and paused for a moment. "What if we're wrong Fulgrim? What if she isn't the one?"

Fulgrim seemed to sober up at the thought. He considered it carefully. "Do you believe she is?"

Keelin's heart raced as he thought of all the things he thought about her. "Yes... I do..."

"And does the pack believe in you?" Fulgrim asked more confidently

"All the ones that matter."

"Then she is. Have her ready at first light." Fulgrim smiled. Happy with his logic. Without another word, he turned and shuffled his way back into the darkness. Keelin was left chuckling to himself at the old man's wisdom. There was something to the way he thought. Maybe they had been waiting too long. Waiting for someone to be dropped in their laps. Maybe it wasn't for the Creators to decide, but them.

He lazily made his way back to the room, hanging the robe on the back of the door. He lit a couple candles, and then pulled another solid black shirt from a chest nearby, placing it on the bed. He paused, looking at her sleeping. It was possibly the least graceful he had seen her, but at least she was at rest. With that thought, he retreated to the bathroom to prepare for the day to come.

Nodiah had one of the best sleeps of her life. She didn't even remember her dreams if she had any. She was awoken to the sound of the shower once more, a smile crossing her face as she reflected on the night that was. She gave a long stretch, reaching her arms out, and arching her back up off the bed, before slowly rolling onto her side.

The running water grabbed her attention first. Promptly she put on the black shirt from the end of the bed, and made her way towards the shower on silent feet. Her forearm wiped the mirror clean of condensation, so that she could take a better look at her own body. She ached, and was stiff, but it wasn't too bad. She felt as one did after a day of dancing, or exercising, or fighting she imagined. Most of her wounds had closed, but the bruises showed better than ever. She moved her hands up her waist from her hips, tracing the patterns on her body, and feeling bits where dried blood had gathered. She wrinkled her nose and looked towards the shower for the first time.

There was a moment of hesitation, Nodiah feeling like an intruder, like she was out of place. But she pushed past it. She tiptoed to the shower, and peered in, feeling foolish as a laugh began to bubble up in her. It left her quickly as she took him in. Her eyes roamed over her Masters body, taking in every inch as she had felt him do so many times. This... was Keelin. Finally, she gave up her presence. "Good morning," she voiced loudly. She did her best to give an innocent smile, but it came out sultry despite her efforts.

Her entrance scared him more than anything else. He assumed she'd sleep much longer. She had to be exhausted. It startled him enough that he jumped, losing his footing and crashing into the wall in front of him. His pride hurt more than his body, but he turned and tried to recover. ".... Hi... Good Morning... Hi... I hope you slept alright. In my clothes I see." He pointed to the golden wolf that was emblazoned on the sleeve. Your wardrobe for the day is actually hanging near the door." His speech came out robotic, and official, but it was only to hide the embarrassment of his lack of grace and balance. She never had that issue he imagined.

Her smile widened. She ducked her head down and bit her lip hard to avoid giggling. Her body started to turn as he mentioned her wardrobe. She had been trained to read statements like that as a dismissal, but she stopped herself.

After a moment, she peeled off the black shirt and stepped in under the water. "Actually... I just needed to..." she trailed off, still unsure of what exactly she was doing. She had to get the rest of the blood off, but she could have fun in the process.

Keelin pressed his back against the shower wall once more, taken off guard at her sudden advance. He closed his eyes, and tried to focus. "We have to get you ready, sun is coming fast." His duty found his way in front of his pleasure. He needed a distraction. His mind focused on what she had done to the King, and he quickly regained his composure as he escaped the shower, and put on the black shirt himself.

She shrugged, still smiling playfully as she centered herself under the water, allowing it to stream through her hair. After a few moments, she stepped out, noticing how her now wet locks instantly coiled in the warm morning air. She took another glance in the mirror, noting that she looked much better without the dried smatters of blood.

As she thought about all that had happened with the trials, curiosity overcame her. "Keelin, you said Saoirse was supposed to interrogate me..." she began slowly. "What is the usual outcome?" she inquired, running her fingers through her hair doing her best to tame it. It was an odd question Keelin thought, but a fair one.

As Keelin searched for the rest of his clothes, he began to answer. "Saoirse's a Blue. Her promiscuity is normally just a tool. She normally uses a bit of her magic, and her intelligence to get into the candidates mind.

The show is a distraction, but her real goal is to ask three questions." He paused for a moment, and then turned and made his way closer to her. "All having to do with what tempts you. What does your mind want? What does your heart want? What does your spirit want? The sexual nature is just her truth serum. She breaks them down, stops them from overthinking, and then exposes the truth. Once spoken, facing the realizations of the answers is often enough to break a man. They realize they're so far away from what they really want." He leaned against the door frame, averting his eyes towards the rest of the room.

"It's even harder when what they want, they can't have. So we judge them in two ways, their answers, and their emotional state. In your case, you were found to not truly want anything in that moment You very much live in the present... In the now. As for your emotional state, you turned the entire situation on her. No one has ever done that... ever." It was meant as a compliment. An implication as to one of multiple reasons why so many seemed to see something special in her. "Needless to say, now we need a new temptress," he said with a bit of a chuckle.

For a moment Nodiah wondered about Saoirse's magic. She saw her use the stones to help the group escape, but anyone could have done that right? Did she have real magic? If so, why hadn't she used it? Maybe she did.

As she weighed Keelin's assessment of the woman, she took into account her own judgments. She had found Saoirse to be incompetent and petty at best. She was jealous. Jealousy was a weakness. Turning the situation on Saoirse had been easy, because she never established herself as an authority. To Nodiah, she was just another slave, and there was no fear in refusing to submit. "Didn't you say that her fate was for me to decide?" she asked with a slight smirk, already knowing the answer. She finally stepped away from the mirror, and back out into the bedroom.

Keelin had almost forgotten that Nodiah now held Saoirse's fate. "That's right. You broke her... You decide." There was a bit too much power in Nodiah's voice. She had already chosen. That carnal, primal edge of hers seemed to poke through once more. In some ways it excited Keelin, but he genuinely was intimidated by it as well. Her decision would have to wait for a bit. They were both surprised by a small tapping on the door.

Keelin unlocked it and swung it open. There stood Ryker. As his eye caught Nodiah, there was a palpable wave of discomfort. "Something wrong friend?" Keelin could feel the tension. Nodiah gave Ryker a demure, innocent glance from under her lashes. "N...no... Fulgrim is ready for you. Everything is in place."

Keelin looked into Ryker's eyes, and then back to Nodiah, trying to figure out exactly what he was missing. "You've never been one to shy away at a woman Ryker, but I appreciate your... respect..." It was his best guess. "We will walk back with you in fact." Keelin pulled the white robe off the door, and moved towards Nodiah. Holding them in his hands with the utmost care and respect, he presented them to her on a bent knee. "This is for you."

Her breath paused in her chest as she took Keelin in, kneeling before her. The robes... The White Wolf... What did any of it mean? What was it that brought this sort of reverence out of the man who owned her? She cupped the back of his hand with hers as she took the robes. Another turning point.

She felt herself hesitate, looking into his eyes. She could see just how much this meant to him. She put on the clothes with excitement, and confidence, running her hands along her body to smooth out the fabric. Her skin glowed against the white, her vibrant hair cascading down her back, curled yet soft. Her ice blue eyes had a new fire within. She reached her hand out towards his. She was as ready as she could be.

Keelin stood, smiling as he locked his fingers around hers. He looked back to Ryker who's mouth had dropped in the moment. Keelin played naive, but saw the look in his eyes. "Taking in the history my friend?" He said with an enthusiastic smile.

He pulled Nodiah by the hand, gently, and led the way. "Let's go see your destiny." Instead of moving out the front of the Den, Keelin headed for the stairs. They climbed up the four flights, and then a few more stairs that led to a door. It was here that Keelin let go of her hand, motioning for her to go first. As she passed he playfully smacked her behind just to lighten her nerves. She smiled back at him, and then froze in the doorway.

The ceiling of the mountain overhang that extended over the entire Wolves home was clearly visible as she stepped out onto the roof of the Den. At the very back were dozens of giant murals. Before her, a black carpet lined a walkway. On both sides, the Wolves, all of them. It pleased Nodiah to see there were in fact some women in the ranks, though not many, and all the ones she could see were Greys, minus Saoirse.

At the front, twelve actual wolves, including Tracer. Seeing her let Nodiah smile for a moment, but there was still so much to take in. The animals were all equal in size except for two. In the middle of that pack, a stark white wolf who was a bit leaner than the others. Its fur was the color of fresh snow, and seemed to shine against the dull backdrops surrounding them. Immediately Nodiah felt a connection. There was more than symbolism here.

Opposite that one, was a wolf as black as night. It was easily the largest, even with its head slightly hunched. One glance showed the hunger in its eyes. There was a connection with this one as well, but it wasn't the same. There was a desperation, and an unpredictability, like they were counters.

Her concentration broke as Fulgrim stepped between these two wolves, and began to address the crowd in a surprisingly booming loud voice. "Long ago, the first Alphas were led to this mountain, where a pair of Earth Sculptors were given the plans to carve out our home. This mountain provides not only protection, but also our destiny.

They were given a great story. One that the Sky Dancers chose to record on the ceiling of our home, for a day such as today." All eyes moved towards the massive pictures above. A general hush fell throughout the crowd.

"The story tells of a time of great need. A world divided. People no longer live together, but are spread out in the vast spaces of a Creatorless world. It is then that one will descend upon us. Just as when all colors blend together, they form white. This descender will be our White Wolf. They will have an inherent ability to tap into, and understand all colors. A gift from the Creators, but she will come naive to the world around her. She needs balance. She needs her Black.

It is the duty of her Black, the one who found her, to show her the harsh reality of this world. To push her to her limits, and beyond. Her Black must physically and mentally prepare her for an encounter with the Creators themselves." Nodiah closed her eyes and fought off a memory from her past. Nothing would ruin this moment.

"This pair must leave Dachaigh, one in search of the Creators, the other meant to learn about themselves. Neither to return without the Creators permission. A clear sign of what they wish us to do next."

The black wolf snarled unceremoniously, stealing Nodi's attention. It hunched its spine, ready to pounce. Keelin approached, grabbing it by the scruff on the back of its neck and attempted to calm it down. "Today we have found them! Keelin the Black... Nodiah the White... Your time has come. Is there anything you wish to say?"

Fulgrim moved aside, allowing them the floor. It was too much for her to process. They had to leave? Keelin was giving up the Wolves? For her? What if it wasn't true? Others doubted them. She wasn't ready to believe it herself. Her destiny was to commune with Creators? She was a slave dancer for a want to be King. She couldn't...

Then she watched as Keelin took the black wolf. The strength he had. He believed in this. He believed in her. Even if they went out alone together, wasn't that better than being here? He would protect her. She made her decision.

"My fellow Wolves…" She felt a tingle in the base of her spine as she addressed them. She had passed the trials. She was one of them. She didn't belong to them, she belonged with them. "I have completed the trials. I refused the temptation of the first test, and wielded it as a weapon myself. When questioned by the Alphas I did not give them the answers they wanted to hear. I am not a Grey, or Red, or Green, or Blue. I am not Black, the absence of light. The shadow that dominates us all. I want to be all of them." She paused, looking to Keelin once more.

She walked towards where the Alphas stood, and continued. "I broke my shackles of servitude, and killed my former master with my own hands. I have not, and will not, shirk my responsibilities to you… to MY pack." She looked out over the crowd, no longer concerned with their approval. "Do you accept me?!" she thundered out towards the sky. It was directed more at the Creators themselves than her fellow Wolves. If they existed, they had a lot to explain to her.

Keelin read the crowd. There was tension, and jealousy, and those who thought Keelin had handpicked his chosen. The Black Wolf responded to her question, standing at attention. He snapped back at Keelin's hand, and broke free from his grasp. "Nodiah!" He tried to warn her. The wolf charged Nodiah full sprint. She was frozen, but she did not flinch. In response, the white moved to block his path. She felt the white's resolve, ready to stand her ground but not trying to attack.

The black snarled and growled, looking for an opening as the white remained calm. Much to the surprise of even the Alphas, Tracer came to Nodiah's side. She rubbed against her leg, providing assurance that she was in fact safe. A small roar of cheers lifted up from somewhere in the crowd. "If she's good enough for Tracer, she's good enough for me!" The cheers built into an echoing applause throughout the cave.

Keelin, now unsure of what to make of the wolf's display, approached. As if connected to the black however, he felt its anger… hostility. His energy became aggressive. Though he stood face to face with Nodiah, his voice screamed to life! "MY PACK!" *Not hers… mine…* "My Family… I WILL NOT LET HER FAIL!" His shouts raised above the crowd. There was a true anger in his yell that they rarely saw. The crowd grew quiet quickly. "MAKE NO MISTAKES! NO MATTER HOW GIFTED OR CUNNING OR DECEPTIVE... I WILL NOT FAIL HER...AS HER BLACK" his tone lowered, now speaking to her directly. "I will break her. Sky Dancer, White Wolf, Kingslayer. All of these put a target on your head. I told you from the beginning that everything I put you through will be for your own good."

Nodiah looked straight into his eyes as he yelled in her face. He was a ball of raw emotion. She had not seen him so out of control of himself. She wondered if the way they had connected was finally bringing this out of him. Maybe this was all a horrible mistake. She was not here to bring glory to Keelin, or the Wolves. She would be their downfall. Keelin seemed to be at a breaking point, and this, more than anything, scared her. There were those words again. For her own good.

Breathe Keelin, what the hell are you doing? His thoughts became conflicted. Finally realizing that these emotions weren't fully his own, he managed to break their hold. His eyes softened as he looked to her once more. "But I will protect you."

Fulgrim piped in, "As is your duty. Though you may put her through a great deal, your heart must never give in to the Black, or you both will fail. This is just as much a test of you Keelin as it is her." Keelin's eyes shot wide. He had never heard of, or even thought of his side of things. He needed control. He needed discipline... balance... Finally he took a big step back, letting Nodiah have her moment once more. The black wolf turned and walked away as well, laying at Keelin's side.

"You both leave at sundown," Rowan reminded him. He seemed a bit too happy to see Keelin leaving. "Which means you need to name an interim Alpha. There must be at least 3." Great, something else for Keelin to try to figure out. He just wanted one day of normal. He had a feeling normal was a luxury he wouldn't have any time soon.

She crossed her wrists behind her back, having nothing left to say, and looked out among the Wolves. This collection of people from all over the world, all walks of life now accepted her as some kind of prophetic savior. She lifted her head up to the pictures one last time, burning their shapes into her mind.

Nodiah then closed her eyes and let out a howl that bounced off the cave walls, and reverberated out into the Outlands. It didn't take long until the howl was joined by others. Even Tracer and her kin joined. Eventually it built to such a volume it felt as if they'd trigger a rock slide, or the whole overhang would come crashing down. Keelin thought maybe this was the reason for this place. Built in a way that when they howled, even the Creators would hear. He wondered what it sounded like on top of the cliff.

Before it ended, he retreated. He was frustrated at himself for losing control. He began to think about where they would begin, and who would take his place. That had to be the next order of business. He made his way to the main room and laid down, staring up at the rows of balconies and doors, moving from door to door, and considering if the person who resided within could be Alpha.

It was an impossible choice. Thorin... Or Saoirse... But that would be Nodiah's choice. Maybe Strom. He was strong… secure… How could he choose? He let out an exasperated sigh, and closed his eyes. For the first time in a long time he thought about his own ascent to Alpha. A challenge… an open challenge… it could work.

The returning howls nearly moved Nodiah to tears, but as her eyes lowered she felt a shadow fall across her heart. Keelin had left without a single word. That was unlike him. She respectfully bowed to Fulgrim, and went searching. She felt quite forgotten as she traced his steps. Her approach was quiet. She watched on from the shadows as he contemplated his choice. Keelin had seemed to be a creature of instinct. This thoughtful side was actually nice to see.

As he closed his eyes, she approached, quietly placing her palm on his chest. Her expression was kind, concerned. She tried to convey with her emotion her desire to understand him, to help where she could, to support him when she could not. She ran a thumb along his jawline, conveying all she could with a simple touch. *Tell me your secrets you silly man…* With a word, she broke the spell. "Keelin?" Her voice soft, but her expression was piercing, powerful, excited, and so much more.

He had faintly heard her footsteps coming. Based on their delicacy he knew it was her. The touch surprised him however… genuine concern. Her eyes looked inquisitive, like they were searching for something within him. He closed his eyes once more, and began.

Inhale...

Matthew Oakley

Chapter 8

"At the age of 16, I met Geniveve. I was training to become a soldier, and she was the daughter of a baker in my village." The emotion in his voice was evident from the start. This was a place in his mind he seldom went. Her touch, her gaze, made him want to share it with her. "Fair skinned, long black hair, black as night. She was beautiful in all the right ways." He felt Nodiah settle in against his body, and it seemed to help him keep some control of his own emotion.

"She worked hard, and I always treated her with respect. Others often threw themselves at her feet and tried to woo her over with gifts, flowers, candies, tricks, or jokes. Whatever they had to offer. I kept my distance. One day, she called me out on it. She asked, 'I see you watch me, and yet you act as though I'm not real... Why is that?' A simple question."

He separated himself, and sat up next to Nodiah. As he did, he looked around the room noticing a few others make their way to the different balconies, listening in on the story. He wondered if any of them had heard it before. "I told her, 'because you can't possibly be real. Things that often seem perfect seldom are.' She laughed.

We spent the rest of the summer discovering one another's flaws. It was perfect. We decided in the winter we would get married. On a particular evening..." Keelin noticeably paused, making his way to his feet. His intensity grew, drawing in a few more onlookers. He began pacing the room, composing himself to tell the rest.

"...we were out wandering the trails together, just outside of town. We loved just going on walks and discovering things together. Had a great time. As we returned, we could first smell the burning. Black smoke filled the air... screams... chaos..." His words continued to be icy, jagged, but controlled. "The attackers came without warning, without cause, and our great leader, the illuminated Marcus had failed us. All of his claims of a connection... to the Creators... to the future... were lies."

We ran back to town only to see our friends, our families, our loved ones... slaughtered. Everything was burning. A large bald man, with tattoos covering his skull and black smeers of soot around his eyes stood in our path. He seemed to be giving out the orders. I drew my sword, putting Geniveve behind me."

Keelin began to act out the scene, crouching a bit and extending his hand as if he was armed. Another deep breath. He turned his back to Nodiah at this moment so that her eyes couldn't read him. She seemed to be a little too good at it. "He laughed. I thought he was laughing at me, but he wasn't. I heard it first. A *whoosh*.... and her scream... and I turned just as the flames reached her face. Another member of the attackers stood behind her, hidden behind the mask of a dragon. His laugh has haunted my dreams for a long time. I turned back..."

He instinctively turned back towards Nodiah in this moment. Now past the roughest part of the story, he found new confidence. His energy, strength, and volume grew as he continued. Word spread, and now there were quite a few people looking in. "...and I saw the back of that large man walking away. That same dragon symbol was on his back.

I charged, and he swung his arm around. I slid beneath. I thrust my sword up as I did, and caught him directly in the heart. He slumped, and fell to all fours. I made him look me in the eyes, and he spoke. 'You fool... chaos brings balance... Your heart... brings pain. We are not enemies. From the ashes of death, life springs.'

I placed the tip of my sword firmly against his throat. 'That doesn't mean we get to be the ones to create the ash.'

My eyes caught the faintest glimmer of something flying at me. Instinctively I reach out my hand, caught it, and threw it back in the direction it came. The vile exploded in a massive fireball as it struck that dragon mask. His screams... were satisfying... but I wanted more. The other took advantage, and ran."

He tried to gauge Nodiah's interest, allowing his eyes to find hers. They were glued to him. He looked up once more, chuckling a bit as a few of the men on the balcony retreated a bit uncomfortable at the intimacy of the moment.

She noted that this Dragon's description matched Rowan. Was he a Fire Breather? Did he have some connection to the story? Surely he wasn't the same. There had to be more to it. She watched as Keelin came face to face with his past. She had no idea what real loss felt like. She never had anything of her own to lose.

Exhale...

"High and low, I wandered. I began searching for someone with knowledge about who these men were. Finally, in a great book in the West, a man showed me a story. A story about the Creators, and the four chosen. Could these Dragons really be Fire Breathers? Did that mean it was all real? I began asking more questions everywhere I went. No matter how far my travels took me, every culture, every town, had some story about the four, and some connection to them.

The details often changed. Different lands had different encounters with these Fire Breathers. Some good, some bad. They had spoken to Earth Sculptors. They had watched Water Walkers. No one… not one person… had ever seen a Sky Dancer. The favorites of the Creators must be able to explain the chosen. I had to find this temple, but no one knew where it was. As I continued to ask, I was directed to come speak to a wise old man who lived in the base of a mountain. Supposedly the Sky Dancers had written a prophecy on the ceiling."

As if on queue, Fulgrim entered the room with his usual warm smile on his face. He seemed intrigued to hear Keelin's account of how things happened. The two shared a nod as he continued. "This seemed like the biggest stretch so far, but I had nothing to lose, so I went. I came… here… and began asking questions. I was met by Lothal and Seth, who introduced themselves as two of the three Alphas, leaders of the Wolves. I was taken to this very building, to this very spot. My motives were questioned.

Lothal in particular seemed weary. 'You know so much about us friend, who sent you?'

'No one! I come on my own accord, seeking answers, truth. My village has been destroyed, my love burned to death. I want the strength to ensure I never have to feel this loss again.'

Lothal seemed to perk up at the mention of that one word. 'Strength? It's strength you seek? Are you willing to become one of us to find it?' Seth didn't like this.

'He has no right, no claim, nothing to offer! This is madness.'

My eyes locked with Lothal. My intensity swelled as I thought about all that I had lost. 'I bring an undying hunger, an unyielding motivation, and an unbreakable spirit.' Lothal smiled, and then he appeared. Fulgrim. He looked much the same as you see him today. Maybe a little younger.

'Careful Lothal... There is power in this one. His words ring true.' It was quite the ominous introduction. Little did I know I had just met a man whose fate was completely intertwined with my own.

Finally pissed off enough to speak out, Seth addressed me. 'You are a Grey, seek knowledge from the mystics, the naturals, the warriors, and in one year you will face the trials. Based on what you learn, you will be assigned. But I doubt you last that long.' The animosity in Seth's voice must have bothered Fulgrim.

'That's quite enough Seth.' Fulgrim chirped in. 'We are the Alphas, and there are two ways to reach this level. You can challenge and defeat a current Alpha in combat, or... journey to The Fangs and retrieve one of the teeth of the Great Wolf. It is a nearly impossible journey. Only one has achieved this feat thus far. Regardless of the outcome of a challenge, the winner decides the fate of the loser. Death, banishment, demotion, promotion, slavery, whatever the winner decides is final.

No matter what happens there always must be at least three Alphas. If one dies, at least one new Alpha is to be named, though multiple may be promoted.'" Keelin paused, wondering if he was sharing a bit too much.

Nodiah's eyes and ears still were fixated on every word however. Everyone left seemed intrigued by this origin story. He couldn't deny it was captivating, which only added to his bravado in his performance. "He continued to tell me about the colors, each word fueled my soul. I had no intention of waiting a year. All of the Alphas began leading, and I followed.

They told me their version of the story of the Creators, and then showed me that ceiling. They told me of the White and the Black. How the Black would give his life if he had to. True guardians, and how the White would come in a time of great need. They will become a symbol of hope, of strength, but it will be impossible for them until they have come to an enlightenment of self. In order to achieve this, the White and the Black must journey together, in balance. For one can only appreciate happiness if they know suffering. There is no healing without first pain. There is no light without first dark.

My mind traced back to the Dragon, but this is when Lothal took over the story. 'And so the Black journeys to remind the White. To keep them grounded. To teach them what it is to be broken. If either gives in, the Creators will not speak.' It was at this moment, I had grown tired of listening. The story was no longer realistic. 'Anyone can challenge an Alpha?' I asked.

'Well yes technically, but…' Lothal tried to stop me.

'Then I challenge Seth, right here and right now.' Seth smiled, a devious confident smile. Fulgrim insisted we stopped. He accepted. I charged." Keelin put his hands on his hips, reflecting on how foolish he was. It took him a moment to swallow his pride and continue.

"In seconds, I had lost. Flat on my back as he choked the air out of me. Seth was amused by my effort and granted me the ability to stay. In fact, he insisted I face trial… immediately. His expectation was that I would be broken. I would surprise him.

Saoirse came, and while my body gave in, my mind stayed sharp. What did my mind want? Peace. What did my heart want? Forgiveness. I saw her eyes change as soon as that word was spoken. What did my spirit want? … Strength… Her act dropped. A small smile crossed her face. 'You passed', was all she said. Then I came face to face with the Alphas.

Seeing how our earlier encounter worked out, Seth insisted it was a waste of time, and that I should move on to the final trial. Since he technically brought me to trial, he was allowed to choose my final test." Wait… Keelin chose for Nodiah to kill the King. She would remember this.

"He chose The Fangs, and I accepted but on one condition. If I succeeded, not only did I become an Alpha, I got to challenge him again. Fulgrim resisted. Alphas fighting Alphas did no one any good. Seth gladly accepted. 'It takes more than brash arrogance, boy' he responded.

I was led deeper into the mountains. We journeyed for the better part of a day until we came to the edge of a great chasm. The sides were steep, and the drop was nearly straight down. It was a round chasm, and sticking out from the middle was a huge pyre extending up to the clouds. Jagged rocks covered its face, and I knew other unspeakable challenges lay in the way. Near the top of that pyre, a small cave. That was where I was headed.

'Good luck' Seth smiled, before giving me a firm push off the edge. I was falling before I knew what happened. My hand grasped for the cliff wall, but I was falling too fast. My body smashed into the wall, knocking the air from me. I was able to slow myself down, sliding down the side as best I could. A few seconds passed and then splash. Overwhelmed as I fell into the icy cold water, which I didn't even know was there, I fought my way to the surface, and then looked up at the challenge before me."

Keelin made his way over to a small display case. A glass dome covered two small items. He motioned for Nodiah to come look for herself. Inscribed beneath were the words. Fulgrim's fang... Keelin's fang... "I passed." The duo shared a smile, and Keelin glanced back at Fulgrim, as did Nodiah, in awe of what this man accomplished. He was the first.

"I made my way back, but Seth was waiting. 'Your challenge begins now, and you face us both!' I was hurt. I was exhausted. This was their plan all along.

Inhale...

Lothal charged, and I dropped to my knees. I tripped him, his body skidding right to the edge. As I turned around, Seth was running at me full speed, just as I had charged him before. As he swung, I ducked, caught his arm, and swung him towards the edge. Normally, he would've been able to stop himself, but he tripped over Lothal, and fell over the side. There was no grace in his fall. He hit every rock on the way down, and bounced off the wall several times.

Lothal tried to get back to his feet, but I advanced as he got on all fours. My foot connected with his ribs, and sent him over the edge. He rolled, and slammed into the wall. As Fulgrim and I looked over the edge, both were motionless on top of the water, face down.

Fulgrim of course smiled. 'I warned them.' A momentary look of concern crossed his face. 'Of course, now we only have two Alphas. We need a third.' I didn't know any of the Wolves, and I didn't particularly care. The first I saw that looked the part, I named. It was Rowan. He has proven himself worthy of the position, but his rise was luck.

Since that moment, I have used my time, and all of our resources to find a Sky Dancer... To find the White Wolf... Never thinking I'd find both in the same person. My battles have made me strong. My purpose has grown. My hunger for answers has become a force. I have led the Wolves to prosperity, and to a reputation as something to be feared! And yet... I never actually attach myself to anyone, or anything... because if I do, I might fail her... them... I might fail again. I need to know why these things happened to me, and make things right, so I can stop them from happening to anyone else."

The mood shifted. As if coming back from a trance, Keelin's body relaxed. He returned to the present, and refocused his energy. Most of the people who were watching now moved on. They felt it too. "The artifact I was sent to Malachi to get, it may be a clue. A piece of this puzzle. I don't know for sure, but there's a lot I don't know." Now tired of hearing himself talk, Keelin stopped, and sat, getting lost in the ceiling above.

Exhale...

Matthew Oakley

Chapter 9

Nodiah struggled to find words. She sat stunned. She never expected him to bear his soul. She never imagined his story was so conflicted, but it made sense considering his anger. He actually loved a woman, not because she was subservient, or because of the glory, or prestige. He loved her in spite of her flaws, and perhaps because of them. He was so strong, and yet in this moment he looked so defeated.

She closed the gap between them, sinking to her knees. She then placed two fingertips beneath his shoulder blades, and began expertly applying pressure, trying to release some of his unease. "Keelin, if the White Wolf is supposed to show itself... Well you came to me. If it weren't for your business with the King I wouldn't have been sold. How could I ever have come to you?"

She moved to his spine as her questions continued. "And after all of your sacrifice that led you here, are you really ready to leave again? To choose a replacement and go chasing after Creators that may or may not exist, not knowing where to even start? Are you sure any of this will even be waiting for you when you return?" She moved around to face him, and could read the answer in his eyes. She understood. Slowly she climbed into his lap, letting out a long breath.

"That's enough for me. I am with you Keelin, my Black Wolf." She smiled, running her fingers through her hair. "Oh! I know where to start!" As if a sudden revelation struck, Nodiah had done her best to block out anything to do with it, but it seemed unavoidable in this moment. "Beneath Torek, there's a temple, and in that temple there's an Oracle! She's been sleeping for centuries, but the King's advisors say she's been stirring lately. Something's off." Her expression became determined. "Lets go wake her up!" Her excitement was so pure, it caught Keelin off guard. It's the only thing that stopped her from thinking too deeply about her past.

The stories of Oracles were as old as the stories of Sky Dancers. Could it be true? Was Keelin so close to his answers this whole time? He almost hoped it wasn't. "Fate brought you here, not me. As for any of this waiting for me? No... I imagine not. Life will go on. New Alphas will rise. Our quest is much bigger than the Wolves. This is merely the starting line." He paused for a moment...

Inhale...

"To Torek then... again... Though I doubt they'll just let us in the front gate this time," he smirked. He tried his best to hide away his apprehension. This time there would be no backup, no guarantees, and no real plan.

Nodiah did the same, bundling up her nerves and filing them away. Returning to the castle once had been a daunting prospect. She'd completely lost it when he first brought up the idea to her. Now they were going back as enemy number one. She had forfeited the right to ever go back. She knew most of the people who would be waiting for them. For the first time, she thought of the other girls who belonged to Malachi. The so-called Sisters of Sabal. They were hardly sisters, but she still felt bad for them. She wondered how much they really knew.

She looked upwards, towards the various balconies and rooms, and frowned slightly as inspiration struck. "I can get us in," she said simply. She climbed out of his lap, and gracefully spun to her feet. Her mind wondered about some of the other members of the Wolves. There were many, she was sure, who would be thrilled if Keelin never came back.

It seemed a moment that required some privacy. She was about to suggest they move to somewhere that prying ears and curious minds wouldn't be a bother, but as she opened her mouth to speak, her stomach growled to life with a monstrous gurgling noise. She couldn't help but laugh, but only to hide the mortified feeling in her mind. Never, ever, had her body displayed such a basic need so blatantly. Yesterday's adventure, and the nights... exertion... had left her feeling even hungrier than before. She ducked her face, and let out another small giggle.

It was a tension breaker. One that Keelin was thankful for. He couldn't help but laugh a bit himself. Neither of them were very good at showcasing their wants, and this was a rare moment of need. "Breeding a monster in there?" He said with a soft chuckle. "Well you're in luck. The send off for the White Wolf happens to include a feast the night before. It should be ready anytime." He led the way back towards the dining hall.

Before they ever reached the doors, the smells caused Nodiah's stomach to growl once more. As they flung open, she was surprised to see just how much of an occasion this was. Every table was decorated, and streamers and ribbons were strung from the ceiling above. Long banners representing the colors of Wolves hung along the walls. The massive food table was covered with dishes that looked even more amazing than the first meal she experienced in the Den.

In the middle of it all, a small round table with four chairs. One for each Alpha, and as Keelin led her towards it, she realized the last was for her. She was truly speechless. All eyes were on them as they entered. Rowan shouted out something Nodi couldn't quite recognize, but in unison every-one stood and turned to the pair in silence. Keelin softly let Nodiah know what came next. "We will share our plans with the Alphas and they will each present you with something for the journey. Eat anything you'd like. You eat first, and the rest will file in behind."

It felt good for Keelin to give Nodiah a choice once more. Her only hes-itation was the idea of sharing plans with Rowan. He was an Alpha, and she would have to submit to his authority… for now… but her hunger overrode any animosity for the most part.

As she inspected the spread, she picked from an assortment of fresh fruits that were laid out in the shapes of bouquets of flowers. Nodiah won-dered how they pulled all of it off so fast, but there were more important decisions to make, like should she just get one chocolate or two? Being the White Wolf, she took three.

Eventually she returned to her seat, approaching the table reverently and wondering what the proper procedure would be. When no one appeared to guide her, she spotted a white scarf draped around one of the chairs, and gracefully took her seat. As soon as she did, the rest of the Wolves began to file to the table and fill their plates.

The tone was different on this night. There were a few hushed conversations, but not the typical roar of arguments and debates. It was almost peaceful. Everyone seemed to be deep in thought at what had happened. Everyone was contemplating the meaning of what was to come, and each dealt with a bit of uncertainty over exactly what the future held. Even Rowan and Fulgrim seemed oddly quiet. They were focused. Everyone was, except Nodiah.

She was thoroughly picking through the items on her plate, and taking the smallest bites, savoring the flavor of each and every piece. Every once in a while, she would perk up and ask one of the Alphas "What's this!?" To which, Keelin would usually answer, and then Fulgrim would provide some deeper insight to its origin or flavor profile. Keelin couldn't help but smile at her as she watched... It was cute.

In her mind, she had completely invested herself to the food. Each discovery of flavor was a moment of happiness. She popped a large strawberry in her mouth, and bit off the stem before locking eyes with Keelin, and smiling back awkwardly.

This is when the realization really hit. Part of her thought this was a horrid excuse of a celebration for her! Even Malachi knew how to throw a feast! The truth was these men weren't reverent, or in awe, or simply lost in thoughts. They were worried. The silence continued until most had finished their meal.

Keelin suddenly and without warning stood, and let out a truly guttural howl. All eyes quickly turned to him as his voice snapped through the hall. "My Brothers and Sisters! Tomorrow I leave. One must rise to take my place! Our code dictates we must have three Alphas. WHO AMONG YOU IS WORTHY TO TEMPORARILY FILL THE ROLE OF ALPHA!? Or maybe..." his eyes scanned the room. "Permanently. I secured my place through a challenge and so I offer you the same opportunity. Are there any among you who wish to challenge me?" He waited. Part of him didn't expect a response, but part of him hoped for one. Then it happened...

"I will..." A large round man's voice rose among the crowd. Keelin and Nodiah's eyes immediately locked on him, as did many others. His hair was brown and shaggy, a bit curly. His green robes seemed small for a man his size. In honesty, he didn't look like any of the other Greens really. He stood, confirming it was him that spoke.

Exhale… Nahko… don't do this…

Keelin began to reflect on the man who issued the challenge. His name was Nahko. He had been with the Wolves for five long years, since his village on Tsala, a small island west of Sabal, had been overrun by a rival tribe. He had been around long enough to watch challenger after challenger try, and fail in that time. Always, because of their pride. They had always been seeking power. Never for the good of the pack, never because they wanted something more for the Wolves, or the world.

He had never mentioned challenging the Alphas. Usually, he was a trusted supporter, and enjoyed his position as Green. The spindle that held the threads of fate was weaving a new story. The winds were changing. Keelin was truly surprised. He thought back to Nahko's trials fondly as hr reflected on the unlikely story that brought Nahko this far.

When he faced Saoirse's interrogation, he had given her the three most honest answers that he could. His mind wanted clarity, his heart wanted love, and his spirit wanted peace. In the moment, Saoirse thought he was crazy, but he explained more as they just sat and talked. Eventually, she passed him.

When he faced the Alphas, there was a huge dispute. Nahko had been a warrior all his life. His tribe had been feared all the way from the mainland, but his warrior spirit had been broken by the war that wiped out his people. He refused to fight anymore. As a result, Rowan had argued to the Alphas that he had nothing to offer. A Wolf must be willing to answer the call of battle whenever it was sounded. Fulgrim saw his quest for peace and realized that his selflessness was exactly what the Wolves needed. It was up to Keelin to give him his third trial.

This man wasn't an assassin, or a fighter, so the mission had to be fair. Keelin chose to send him on a rescue mission. He returned successfully, bringing back several pack members to the Den, as well as a number of artifacts and trinkets that had been taken from them at various times for various reasons. All of them were impressed he did so without a single moment of violence.

He was awarded the color Green, and had been living a mostly peaceful and productive life in Dachaigh, and occasionally wandering out to the surrounding areas. In his free time, he often debated the Blues, arguing about nature's extreme impact on the arcane and magic in general, or with the Reds about how nature's fury was stronger than any weapon they could wield.

Finally, Nahko bowed, and continued. "I would be honored to serve as Alpha in your absence." Rowan stood, of course he had an issue.

"Him?" Rowan asked with a shocked tone, while putting his hand to his forehead.

"Are you sure Nahko? You know what losing would mean." Fulgrim asked with a bit of confusion himself. Even he hadn't seen this coming.

Keelin stood tall, and approached Nahko, placing a hand on each shoulder. "You have always acted in a way that promotes the best interest of the Wolves. I don't need to fight you to know you'd be a great Alpha. As long as the other Alphas agree, you have my blessing." Nodiah smiled at this soft approach from Keelin. This Nahko must have been a pretty unique guy to get his blessing so openly.

"NO!! Unacceptable!" Strom charged towards the group. "Keelin, before he accepts this temporary position that you're handing to him, I challenge you for the permanent position of Alpha!" A collective gasp rose as the large beast of a man towered over Keelin, clearly seething at the idea a challenge wasn't going to take place. Nodiah felt her body tighten. She wanted to interject, but Keelin seemed to have things under control. He looked ready. Then Nahko shocked everyone once more.

"Wait…" He slid between the two, looking up at Strom, but only just. "How about you and I fight instead. You win, you become Alpha. If I win, I fill in until Keelin returns." The room went silent as all eyes turned to the Alphas for approval.

Rowan sat back in his chair, with an expectant smile on his face. Almost too expectant. "I consider this a win win for the Wolves. This is a great test, which will provide a worthy replacement." Fulgrim seemed equally bothered by just how happy this all made Rowan, but he nodded, and all eyes fell to Keelin.

"Very well, Nahko will represent me… here and now… to determine the new Alpha." Tables immediately began to clear out, giving them a ring to compete in. Keelin took Nodiah's hand, and led her to a safe distance. He looked to Strom, who was cracking his knuckles, and a few other choice joints, with a smile on his face. His eyes then turned to Nahko, and doubt crept in.

The Green Wolf surprised everyone as he closed his eyes. His nostrils flared as he seemed to take in the scent of the room. His entire aura became surprisingly calm. His hands pressed together, palms meeting. The Wolves collectively grew nervous. Was this Nahko refusing to fight? He let out a slow, measured breath and waited for Strom to make his move.

The large Red seemed more confused and frustrated than anything. "Are you? Are you meditating? Praying? It matters not. All this talk of prophecy." He waved his hands dismissively. "Of destiny... It's time the Wolves sharpened their fangs! Men not of words, but of actions! We return to chasing treasures, not fairy tales!" A few among the crowd seemed to agree with Strom's sentiment, though not many. Keelin was visibly angered. His grip on Nodiah's hand tightened to the extent that she winced just a bit.

"I shouldn't have let him do this. He's going to get killed." Nodiah moved to comfort him, placing a hand on his chest, and leaning in to him. "This is wrong." It took every ounce of restraint Keelin had not to take his place back. He couldn't. He knew that. Nahko's blood would be on his hands.

"He speaks for the skeptics. It needed to be addressed," Nodiah murmured back. She was completely entranced by the moment at hand. It was charged in a way that was truly hard to describe. Strom roared loudly, though it missed something it seemed. It wasn't as impressive as some other noises she'd heard, Nodiah thought. Then he advanced. He ran full tilt, head lowered, directly at Nahko, but he didn't move. He didn't flinch. What was he waiting for? Nahko didn't even bother opening his eyes.

The room grew tense in anticipation as the gap closed. Finally, the moment came. Strom cocked back his fist... and then collapsed to the ground. He was paralyzed, eyes open, conscious, but completely still. All eyes turned to Nahko who seemingly hadn't moved at all.

Keelin approached Strom, and began speaking at a volume that was meant for all to hear. "Have you learned nothing Strom? Power doesn't come from muscles. It comes from the mind. You have lost." Keelin turned back to Nahko, trying to reconcile exactly what just happened.

He remembered back to when the pair had shared a conversation about being able to strike a man's spirit from his body, but Keelin didn't think it was actually possible. He didn't have any other explanation though. He looked to Nahko for an answer, but he still hadn't moved. This technique was one Keelin would insist on learning if he made it back... If...

Keelin stood on one of the nearby tables, and addressed the crowd once more. "I believe we've had enough excitement for one night, but before we leave, there are two Wolves who's fate must be decided. Strom's... and Saoirse's..." The energy turned once more, back to anticipation. He motioned for Nodiah to join him. A bit of relief took over his mind. His work was done. There were now a couple of decisions, and a nights rest between him and leaving the Den.

Nahko finally opened his eyes as Keelin spoke. He looked down over his shoulder at his opponent, and with a surprisingly kind and sympathetic tone, he spoke. "You still have so much to learn. I truly believe you could have benefited from the changes that are upon us. You still cling to pride... foolish pride... Your mind is blocked from anything other than power. Your heart is filled with greed, and your spirit has withered. For this reason, my judgement is this. You are banished from Dachaigh in the hopes that out in nature, you find a new appreciation for the world as it really is."

A collective noise of surprise rose from the crowd, particularly the other Reds. It seemed an unlikely choice from their new Alpha, but it was one that was incontestable. His word was final. Nodiah's word would be as well.

She considered Saoirse carefully, remembering the bitter jealousy that she displayed. She thought of the obsessive longing that filled her heart. This wasn't as easy as she expected it to be. "Saoirse, so long you have lived without satisfaction of your own. You allowed your whims to defeat you. You completely abandoned your duty to the Wolves for selfish pleasure." Saoirse's head ducked in defeat.

"But I have heard of your service in the trials, and how even the strongest among us have not been able to help but surrender to you." She paused, letting the words build in her mind. "My decision is this. You will stay in the Wolves, but in a position that brings you some peace. You are relieved of your role as Temptress, and will become a Black, sworn to do whatever it takes to protect and..." Nodiah's eyebrows lifted... " serve the Wolves...

and the Alphas. After all of your service as a part of the trials, you deserve this position."

The reactions of the two Wolves couldn't be more different. Strom staggered to his feet, and made his way to the main room, looking up towards the balconies above. Keelin followed, and tried to see what caught Strom's gaze, but no one seemed to be there. On the faintest hint of a whisper, Keelin thought he heard "I'm sorry" escape Strom's lips. Maybe there was more to this mountain of a man than he ever let on. With that, he was gone. Strom didn't bother grabbing anything. He simply walked out the front.

Keelin walked back into the room just in time to see Saoirse wrap her arms around Nodiah with a huge smile. Tears streamed down her face as she hugged the White Wolf tight. It was a bit out of etiquette, but one could hardly blame her. As she separated, a hand slid down across Nodiah's backside with a playful grab. "I still want some of that, so come home safe ok?" She said with a smile and a chuckle. Keelin's eyes flicked to Nodiah. That word again… home… how would she respond?

She smiled as a warm chill slowly built up in the back of her spine. She was home… and now they were leaving. She took in the room, eyes circling to all of these people. She thought about the stories she knew, and all of the ones she didn't. These people were only Wolves, because they believed they were. Her eyes found Rowan's, and much to her amazement he seemed to be happy. He smiled, and nodded gently in her direction with approval.

Fulgrim took over the scene, approaching Keelin. There was a true sadness in his eyes Keelin thought, but behind it… hope. "My friend, you know what must be done." He held out his hand. From Keelin's pocket, a small amulet on a chain came forth. In the middle, four wolves chasing each other in a never ending circle. Keelin looked down at it fondly, and then with a bit of a stutter in his own breath, handed it to Fulgrim.

Fulgrim approached Nahko, but Rowan interjected. The room again felt silent as everyone wondered what he was up to. This wasn't the time for another debate. He took the pendant from Fulgrims hands, opened the chain, and slid it around Nahko's neck. "There's no need for formalities tonight. He's earned his place." Keelin wasn't sure of Rowan's motives, but maybe the Wolves were in safe hands after all. "LETS BREAK OUT THE GROG!" Rowan roared, and the crowd cheered back to life.

Matthew Oakley

Chapter 10

Finally, a true celebration began. Large barrels were rolled into the room from the kitchen area, and immediately tapped. Clay mugs and glasses were passed out to the crowd quickly as cheers erupted. The mood was jovial, and electric. The tables were returned and the Alphas made their way back to the center.

A large black bottle was brought forth and placed on their table. It was curved towards the bottom, and narrowed at the top. Rowan and Fulgrim's eyes grew wide as they looked on excitedly. Keelin however couldn't shake the somber reality of what had just happened. Keelin grabbed the bottle, and five more ornate looking glasses, and began pouring. The vibrant purple liquid flowed out smoothly into each glass. He started with Nahko, and made his way around to Nodiah, who seemed hesitant, and then poured his own glass last. "This we call twilight. The Sky Dancers who painted the ceiling brought it to us. They told us to only use it when we believed a Sky Dancer was in our presence."

Alcohol of any kind was forbidden for the Sisters. She wasn't sure she wanted to lose her senses around the rest of the Wolves. Never mind the fact she wasn't sure she was a Sky Dancer either. Her eyes looked up to Keelin, and the words came flooding back. *I will protect you.* She was safe... She raised her glass, and leaned forward to kiss his cheek, but he had backed away. He sat at the closest table, but immediately she followed. "What are you doing?"

"I am no longer an Alpha." He said reluctantly. His head sunk in defeat.

"Neither am I." She stated with a firm resolve. "You are my Black Wolf however, and you can't protect me from all the way back here." Without hesitation, she grabbed his chair, and dumped him on the floor with a swift shift. She then dragged the seat over to the center table, and placed it next to hers.

He gracefully managed not to spill a drop of his drink, but did tumble to the ground. He popped up a bit embarrassed, but more at his thoughts than his actions. He took his seat next to her with a grin of humility on his face.

Finally she raised the glass to her lips. It was a bit... underwhelming. For something that was supposedly brought to them by the Sky Dancers, it didn't taste like much. She looked to Keelin, who didn't seem to react to it one way or the other. The other Alphas however seemed completely entranced. Rowan was just staring at his cup in silence, while Fulgrim had closed his eyes. Each seemed to be searching for deeper meaning in this fluid, which felt silly to her.

As time passed, most of the Wolves came up to them, paying their respects and wishing them good fortune. As some began to turn in for the evening, and both Keelin and Nodiah had their share of drink, Fulgrim took center stage once more.

He slammed his staff down on the table, refocusing everyone's attention. Nodiah jumped, a reaction enhanced by her current inebriation. "As is customary when any of our own venture out on a quest of this magnitude, especially in the case of the Black and White Wolves, we as Alphas will present you a gift. Something we believe you will find useful for the journey ahead." He smiled, and took a step back allowing Rowan to approach.

He pulled out a large silk bag that was beautiful in its own right. Swirls of black and purple covered the soft fabric reminiscent of the night sky. He reached in, and pulled out an arrow, handing it to Nodiah with an intriguing amount of care. "Let me explain, this arrow is made from the King's throne in Torek. Yes that King. I nabbed the wood when we were in the castle. May it remind you there is more than the now. Remember your past, and aim towards your future." He bowed, and backed away, leaving the duo to try to comprehend his surprising thoughtfulness.

Nodiah was completely speechless, but she only had a moment before Fulgrim approached. He produced a black cloth, with something wrapped inside, and motioned for Nodiah to lower her head. As she did, he opened the cloth and pulled out a thin necklace, placing it around her neck. Something heavy pressed against her chest, and as she looked down to see what it was, she again was stunned. "Fulgrim I can't… It means…" she tried to refuse, but was met with his usual smile.

"You can and you must. This fang has long served as belief in the impossible… strength… and hope… We don't need this now. We have you. It will serve you well Nodiah." He firmly grasped her shoulders, and stared deep into her eyes once more. She could feel his vision penetrate her very soul. "Even if you don't find where you're going, even when all your strength is gone, when you face the impossible, remember what you've already done. You are so much more than a slave, and you always have been." Nodiah couldn't hold back.

Tears streamed down her face, overcome with emotion she hadn't felt since the cliff top. This was a decisively happier moment. There was joy, humility, and love, and so many more things to feel. She had eyes on her most of her life, and yet this was the second time she felt like anyone had actually seen her. Keelin was the first, but they had shared so many experiences. Fulgrim seeing her was genuine.

Her mind moved forward to what Keelin would give her. What else could he possibly give her that he hadn't already? All of this was because he saw something in her that she didn't even know was there. Maybe he wouldn't give her anything since he was coming with. He could see the anticipation in her eyes, her heart happy, and that made him smile. "I'm not an Alpha anymore…" he spoke softly.

Nahko must have heard the words carried on the wind. Suddenly he popped up from the back of the room, and approached. Keelin wondered when he even left. The large man was surprisingly stealthy. He caught his breath a bit, and then moved towards Nodiah.

"A warrior with an arrow… needs a bow…" He presented the weapon, which had an immaculate amount of detail carved into the wooden structure. Wolves were running through a forest of trees, complete with a moon shining down, and a creek twisting around to the side. "May it serve you both, and show you that when you are stretched to your very limit, that is when you are in fact your most dangerous."

Keelin's jaw dropped. It was the first time he was mentioned, and the gift was so amazingly on point. How in the hell did he come up with this so quickly? The bow must have been something he had. Something he was working on for a while at the least.

Keelin rose, and grasped Nahko's forearms. "Thank you brother, you will be a great Alpha. Excuse me..." The emotion of it all had gotten the better of him. He was exhausted in every way. He made sure to grab Nodiah's hand, and give it a heartfelt squeeze before retreating once more.

Nodiah was still looking over the bow. A real weapon! The beauty... the power... It was a message. "Thank you so much." she said reflectively. "I'm not sure I know how to use it, but I'll learn! Excuse me..." She felt her cheeks flushing as Keelin squeezed her hand, but he wasn't allowed to just walk away from her again. Not now.

She grabbed the bottle from the table, and chased after. Her steps were a bit staggered, her head buzzing pleasantly as she walked after him. "Keelin..." she giggled girlishly. "That was rude, I was enjoying my party!" she said stupidly, not even really considering the words. She lifted the bottle back to her lips, and took another drink, the liquid dripping from the corner of her mouth. She chased after, but he didn't give a reaction.

Finally, Keelin led the way back into his room. They thankfully had a few moments alone. The air that filled the space felt thick. She could barely take in a full breath. Their chemistry was explosive....dangerous... Her teeth grazed her bottom lip as she said his name once more, this time in a low growl. "....Keelin..."

The tension was electric, and yet Keelin felt like everything was slipping away from him. His life, his position, his home. He couldn't shake it. "Ten years... Ten years ago I walked into this place thinking I could take it over." He sat on the edge of the bed, leaving her standing with the bottle. His gaze was distant as he continued. "Ten years later, I accomplished what I set out to do. Well, I had. I'm not even an Alpha anymore. I'm nothing. I'm a sheep in Wolves clothing, consumed by you, by stories..."

He could feel Nodiah was going to try and calm him, but he cut her off. "I....I don't know if any of this will be waiting. I don't know how, or if, what we're chasing is even real." He shook his head at the thought, maybe this was all crazy. "But if there's one thing I'm not, it's a liar. So I will protect you, and I will take you as far as I can, but I don't know how far that is." He stood, facing her and trying not to lock eyes.

Her head was buzzing harder than ever, but rather than blurring her world around her, she felt hyper focused. She saw his glow, radiating doubt and worry, and conviction. It was stunning. Halfway through his speech she realized she was holding her breath. She let it out slowly.

His faith seemed so unshakable. She had killed the King because of him. It was still too incredible to consider real. She remembered the moment as if she were removed from her body, watching flashes of it go by. That had been someone else in the throne room, and she wasn't sure where that girl was now. She would not allow herself to be pulled into this frenzy of doubt with him as he continued.

"I need you to be ready. Unwavering, unshakable, enduring... because I don't know if I am." His eyes watered as he fought back those feelings of doubt. "But I don't have a choice." The moment was as raw as Keelin got. He had become comfortable enough to express his true feelings in this moment, perhaps at the cost of hurting hers. He kissed her passionately before she could respond, trying to transfer all of the feelings of his heart straight through their lips.

She fumbled back, and then pressed closer, her heart beating against his. "Do you feel this?" She asked clearly. "Do you really believe that this... this moment... this past week... means nothing?" Her words were precise daggers stabbing out at his darkness and doubt... but they missed. His only thought was how much had she drank? Of course he felt it, and he was glad she felt good. Of course it all meant something, but she was yet again unable to see past the now. It was what was in front of them that scared him.

"No... of course not. It means the world. To the Wolves, to you, and to me. No one can take away what has happened." That much was right, though there was clearly a bit of frustration in his voice. He tried to cough it out, and then change his tone. He took a swig from the bottle and then continued. "You're right, it's just... a lot. If this is my last night here, then I can't imagine spending it with anyone but you."

He took her hair in his hands, and pulled her down on top of him as he collapsed onto the bed. He looked up into those amazing blue eyes that were now looking down at him, and in a moment, all that doubt faded. Maybe she was right after all. Maybe there was something to the "now."

She felt him relax beneath her. She ran her fingers along his sides, creeping under the hem of his shirt. His skin was hot, almost burning to the touch. She playfully bit his bottom lip, and continued. "So how..." she breathed into his ear, tracing the lobe with the tip of her tongue before biting again. "Are we..." She continued down his neck, kissing and biting playfully on his shoulder. "Going to spend it?" She withdrew from him slowly to the end of the bed, then moved back from the bed a few paces, and knelt down. He seemed to have lost control... she wanted him to take it back.

What followed was a few hours of thoughtless, passionate, fun. Her plan worked, and he established control throughout. It was important to him that he was able to let her feel good for a while. This wasn't about the emotion, or the thoughts, or the power however. This was just instincts and desires, and both enjoyed every last moment.

As things settled down, she moved back on top of him and just stared down with a playful smile on her face. His eyes were lost in hers once again... "Nodi you are quite possibly the most fascinating creature I've ever met in my life. That's saying something. I've been a lot of places. Strong... beautiful... graceful... A wild lioness set free amongst a pack of dogs. I cannot wait to see what else you have locked in there." He pressed his hand against her heart gently and smiled.

As he placed his hand on her, she could feel it all. It seemed this transference was working better than ever. She could feel every ounce of want, need, fear, satisfaction... He didn't fully trust her. She truly was a lioness to him. There was still a level of fear that if he let his guard down, or somehow failed her, she'd pounce. Maybe he was right. He had shown her what she was capable of. The blood-lust that destroyed the King was something she had never imagined.

She let out a pent-up breath and responded, "And you are like no man I have ever met in my life. You..." she smoothed her palm over his hand, interlocking her fingers with his. "You see me." She wrapped her arms around his neck, and embraced him tightly. This time, it was an embrace of safety, comfort, and belonging.

Maybe it was the booze, or the exhaustion, or just her presence, but finally Keelin's emotions got the better of him. As she embraced him his tears began to fall. Each tear felt like pounds lifting off his very soul. He had as many questions as he had answers, but he no longer doubted. This was meant to happen. He was close. He had to push through. For Gen...

Inhale…

His eyes closed.

When they opened, he was somewhere new. A small hut with a thatched together roof. A fantastic smell overtook his senses from nearby. He walked out, only to be surprised by the bright sunshine that blocked his vision. "Well good morning love!" That voice... What?... How!? It couldn't... "Genevieve?! You… You're here!?"

"Well of course silly. Where else would I be?" Her smile… it was perfect. Keelin ran and threw his arms around her with force. The tears returned to his eyes. "I won't let you go. Not again…" He hardly noticed her awkward body language. She seemed to be confused.

"Keelin? You're worrying me? What are you talking about? Did you get into the wine again?" She was so sweet, always smiling, always happy. It was one of the only things that frustrated him about her. He never understood how she was always just so positive. She saw the good in everything.

"No... I just missed you, that's all." He chuckled a bit to himself.

"You've only been sleeping for li… Keelin… who's that?" He turned just in time to see him approach. The man in the mask. His heart sank. "RUN!!!" Keelin yelled out. He turned back to Genevieve but it was too late. Fire climbed up her body, but it didn't even seem to hurt her. The flames danced and swirled on her body, reflecting in her eyes as she stood there, staring him down.

"Why didn't you save me Keelin? Why didn't you stop him? He's one man. You failed." She smiled… a sick, deranged, twisted smile. "You're going to fail again. You are no wolf. You are nothing. She will devour you." Her hand lifted and pointed behind Keelin. He turned to see who she was motioning towards. It was Nodiah, covered in blood, howling at the sky above with an equally twisted smile on her face.

"NODIAH!" He sat up with a jerk, his eyes popping open as he gasped to catch his breath. A dream… It was a dream… it felt so real.... Something… wasn't right.

Her eyes closed...

The only sound Nodiah could hear was that of dripping water. The darkness was impenetrable. The whole room smelled of decay, the stench of death, and worse... so much worse. She could feel was the pain particularly in her lower back, along with fatigue, hunger, fear, and cold. The cold of the steel manacles around her wrists, neck, and ankles. The pain was all she could focus on. She tugged against the chains, feeling the all too familiar metal bite into her flesh. It let her know she was alive. It was the only way to cope with the thoughts and panic and despair that her life had become. The taste of blood on her tongue was back as well.

He was there somewhere. Watching, planning and breathing in her suffering; drinking it down in gulps. He was living off of her pain and desperation, but she refused to talk to him. Not a word. Not a sound. Not after what he just did to her. She turned 18 on this day...

"NODIAH!" The sound of her name tore her from her sleep, from hell. Her chest was heaving as the darkness closed in. She had to escape. She panicked. Blinking her eyes a few times, the darkness gave way. There was moonlight, she wasn't where she thought.

Finally her breathing slowed. It wasn't until she noticed Keelin sitting up that she was able to truly come back to the present. One look at him was all it took to realize something was wrong. She raised her hand and gently ran it up his spine. He jumped at the touch. He was truly terrified. "Keelin... slow down... It's me..."

He took a few deep breaths, allowing his body to press into the touch of her hands as they raised up to his hair. "I... I'm sorry. Just a dream." He wanted to tell her more, but he couldn't. They didn't need more to deal with. Genevieve was gone, and that was the end of it. "We should get ready..." Keelin left the bed, still numb. He didn't really have a sense of what time it was, but he knew it was time to leave. It was time to find answers. He approached her, giving her a firm kiss as if to make sure he wasn't still dreaming, and then began gathering his things.

Chapter 11

Nodiahs list of possessions could be counted on one hand. White robes. Fang necklace. Arrow. Bow. There wasn't much to gather. She sat and watched Keelin move around for a moment, but she still felt the cold metal clinging to her body.

In an attempt to warm up, she slipped from the bed and headed back to the shower. She wasn't sure the next chance she'd have to take one, might as well make the most of it. After turning on the water, she stepped back and looked at herself in the mirror. The bruises Keelin left were nearly gone. Her fingers grazed her neck, half expecting her collar to still be there.

She stepped into the warm water, thinking it would do the trick. She tried to convince herself she was ok. She wasn't alone anymore. She was safe… She was a Wolf. She had Keelin. It didn't work. She let the tears fall down her cheeks. The shower walls moved in towards her. Chains wrapped around her lungs, squeezing. He was still down there, in the temple, and she was going back.

Her eyes closed...

She felt the cold steel tighten around her neck once more. She collapsed to her knees, unable to support her own weight anymore. He was there. He paced. He circled her. This man who claimed she was nothing. She was a tool for the greater good. The key to a door. A Vessel.

She listened as he made his circle, not bothering to stare into the darkness that surrounded her. She waited for him to get in front of her, and then with all of her might, she lunged. The chains around her wrists went tight, pulling at the bolts that fastened them to the floor. She gritted her teeth, and screamed as she pulled with everything she had left. He just smiled.

He continued walking his circle. "This is for your own good!"
THWACK!
The whip lashing down across her spine took away all the fight she had left. Her head fell to the ground as her body folded, exposing her back even more.
THWACK!
She tried to scream, but was unable. Her back arched and tightened in an attempt to escape the hurt. The pain radiated up through her spine, leaving the rest of her body numb. There was just the pain. If this was preparation for what was to come, then she wanted no part of it. Panic took over.

Without a voice, she was nothing... just a Vessel. She began to hyperventilate. He was winning. Her hands were suddenly freed, but she had no strength left. Her entire body collapsed forward once more, sprawling out on the cold ground, still struggling to find a breath as the tears rolled down her face. Finally, he left, but he'd be back.

Keelin gathered a few sets of clothes. Some of which he hadn't even seen for quite some time. He usually stuck to his Wolf robes. While rummaging through the fabrics, his hands stopped on a long thin red scarf... her scarf... damn. Even in a nightmare, seeing her brought some comfort and motivation. He couldn't fail.

A sudden thud in the bathroom shook his focus. He ran in, nearly falling himself as he discovered Nodiah laying on the shower floor motionless. "Nodiah! Are you ok?" She looked... cold... Long gone were the mesmerizing eyes of a White Wolf. This wasn't the numb face of a slave, nor was it the focus and poise of a Sky Dancer. It was vulnerable... scared.

Her body convulsed in his arms as he lifted her up and moved her back to a chair in the corner of the bedroom. He ran back to get a cold rag, but it was clear Nodiah's head was somewhere else.

"There's a priest coming today..." A girl sat in front of a large mirror brushing through her dark locks. "The King is giving him run of the Sisters. He needs a new girl to serve the Oracle. It's a great honor, but a huge responsibility of course."

Nodiah scoffed, shaking out her hair and combing through it with her fingers. "How hard can it be? She's been asleep for centuries. Are you sure she's even real? How gloomy, serving a living statue all day down there in the temple. Who would ever want to do that?"

The other girl smirked, rolling her shoulders with a shrug. "I wouldn't worry about it. With your attitude, why in the world would anyone ever pick you?"

Keelin placed the rag against her head, but she still appeared to be gone. He reached for a bottle nearby, and poured some on the cloth. "Gonna sting a bit." He pressed on the rag, noting that the cut wasn't that big, but her blood pressure must have been high because it just wouldn't stop. He shifted her hand to the rag, and wrapped his arms around her.

As if the hug flipped a switch, Nodiah came back. She cocked her head to the side and tried to process what was happening. "Keelin? Are you ok?" She remembered his panicked retreat from the bed, and his nightmares. "It was just a dream right? Do you want to tell me about it?" It was as if her fall in the shower had never happened, except for the headache and her blood saturating the rag in her hand. Anything to get the attention off herself though.

Keelin wondered if she was hiding something, but there was too much going on in his own mind to figure out what. Maybe she just hit her head harder than he thought. "I'm fine. You on the other hand. You're lucky you didn't knock yourself out." He wasn't fine, but this was not the start to their journey he was expecting. With his usual immaculate timing, Fulgrim made his way into the room.

"The time has come." A momentary glance of worry came over his face as he saw the bloody rag pressed against Nodiah's head, but he let it pass as he left the room.

"I'm going to grab my last couple things and then we'll be done alright? I'll meet you at the stables." Keelin needed separation. He needed to clear his head and forget the Nodiah from the dream.

With a deep sigh, he walked out of the room and proceeded to the main hall. There he went to the case and grabbed his own fang. From the shelves, he grabbed a couple books. They were epic stories of heroes long gone, if they ever existed at all. He then moved to the food storage and grabbed a few rations and a canteen, normal survival gear, and then to the armory to pick out some weapons. He settled on a small dagger and a fairly large broadsword.

All of this was an attempt to keep his head clear, but the images kept coming. The image of Genevieve pointing, and Nodiah approaching was becoming more clear. The blood running from Nodiah's mouth, covering her hands was unsettling, but it was the wicked, dark smile on her face that he just couldn't shake.

"You know sometimes the future we are afraid of." Keelin nearly jumped out of his skin as he heard Nahko's soft voice behind him. Nahko chuckled a bit as he continued. "Is the exact thing that will lead to our destiny." Timely words from an unexpected voice.

"Nahko, friend... I needed that." It was truly what Keelin needed to hear. He was afraid. Afraid of what could be. Afraid of losing everything again. Afraid of the power Nodiah seemed to possess, but that power is the reason why they were here. He couldn't be afraid of it, and yet expect to show her how to use it. It would only hold her back.

Keelin gathered himself as Nahko approached, and extended his hand to him. "Don't be surprised if your answers come from somewhere you never expected." Again Nahko's words resonated with Keelin's soul. He was ready. He had to be. Instead of shaking Nahko's hands, he wrapped his arms around him with a firm embrace, and then headed for the stables.

Nodiah watched Keelin leave the room. He didn't even look at her. It was a retreat. He wanted to get away from her. Again the panic swelled into her throat as she wondered if he would leave her behind. Maybe this was all a joke. She was nothing more than a damaged slave girl. She grasped Fulgrim's fang which hung around her neck, squeezing hard until the point dug into her hand. The pain took her back.

She closed her eyes

The High Priest was a small man, with a weak chin and what appeared to be a kind, but fake smile. His dark eyes he couldn't hide. They burned with an anger that could not be controlled. He strode across the span of the harem, considering the girls carefully. There were 12, standing in line ready to be inspected. "This will be a position of great honor! No longer will you be a servant to man, but to the Oracle, and the Creators themselves! You must be pure of heart and strong in your faith, less you anger the Oracle. If that happens, we may have to live without her wisdom forever. This, in her temple, is blasphemy, and will be met with punishment accordingly."

Reality faded back in, her skin covered in goosebumps. She looked around the room once more, forgetting that Keelin had left. She tied her hair back away from her face, and then searched around the room for something to dress her wound. She found several strips of fabric, and tied them back into a headband that was also effective in covering her cut.

As she checked the room, she put her white wolf outfit back on, and then took her Grey robe, and tied it around her waist letting it hang down behind her. She found a leather belt with some gold studs, and fastened that around her as well. If she needed to hide her self, the extra items may come in handy. Finally she searched for something to cover her wound. She settled on a long strip of red fabric that she fashioned into a head covering of sorts. As she took one last look around, another flash of vibrant red caught her eyes. It was a thin red scarf, which she picked up and used to tie her arrow, and her bundle to her bow.

She made her way to the stables just as Keelin finished saddling up the two horses, a confident mask on her face. "I am so glad to leave this place, it's been so terribly dull here." She said with a smirk.

Keelin bit his lip and shook his head a bit. "Oh yes, so uneventful. I can't wait to get somewhere exciting!" He noticed the headband, a clever disguise and fitting for Nodiah. Typical Nodi, never willing to show weakness.

The horses were similar in appearance, both giants in Nodiah's eyes. They fittingly had a beautiful black and white pattern running down their bodies. Magnificent black manes ran down their spines. The duo quickly packed their things, Keelin slid on a piece of black leather armor that covered his chest and shoulders, and with one final look back, they were gone. No fanfare, no crowds, no ceremony. They left Dachaigh, possibly for the last time.

Matthew Oakley

Chapter 12

Keelin pushed the pace from the beginning for a couple of reasons. He wanted to get far away from the mountains as quickly as he could. The sooner he could put it behind him, the sooner they could focus on what was ahead. The other reason was that it made for an exhilarating ride! The wind flowing, the sun just barely creeping up on the horizon, genuinely made for an enjoyable journey.

Nodiah had rarely ridden on her own before, but she had the control over her body she needed to keep pace. She couldn't help but smile as they raced through the Outlands. All the darkness in her body vanished as they flew towards the horizon. She felt free, and a part of her just wanted to ride off forever. It was much less painful this time, which helped. Unexpectedly, Keelin slowed down. Her eyes pulled to the horizon, wondering what he saw, but he just looked back at her.

As she pulled alongside, Keelin caught his breath and smiled at Nodiah, locking eyes. "Having fun yet?"

"We… HEY!" Before she could answer he raced off, kicking up a cloud of dust that enveloped Nodiah and her horse. "You little…" The chase was on. She managed to close the gap quickly, minus a few stumbles and near falls that left her white knuckled. She knew she was pushing her animal a little more than she should, but he didn't deserve the satisfaction of that stunt. She was nearly on top of him before he realized what was happening.

Keelin knew not to push, instead pulling back slightly and letting Nodiah run ahead. She deserved this moment. The smile on her face was worth it as she blew past, and returned the favor, leaving him in her dust. They continued for hours, alternating between these full tilt desert races, and slowing to let their horses, and their own bodies, catch a breath. As the sun began to reach its peak, the pace slowed. "We should look for somewhere to set up camp. It's too risky to travel at night with just the two of us."

"Torek will probably be busier at night anyways. Makes sense. What about up there?" Nodiah pointed to a flat plateau in the distance. It was in the open, but gave them a view in every direction. It was only eight to ten barrels tall, but it still would be safe, which in the Outlands was something they needed. Between scavengers, wildlife, and the weather, it had its own special breed of danger.

They led the horses up to the plateau, both still smiling from their day of travel, but exhausted. It was sunset before they reached the top. As Keelin attempted to dismount his legs weren't ready for it. They had ridden a bit longer, and harder than he thought. He ungracefully fell to the ground below, and just laid there. Nodiah eased off her horse, touching down carefully on the balls of her feet. Her legs were shaky, but she had no issues standing much to her delight, and his dismay.

She sauntered over to him, her feet on either side of his face with a huge grin stretched from ear to ear. "Very graceful, can you show me that one? It seems important to know. In case I ever want to look like an absolute fool!" She laughed, looking down at him and for the first time in a while she was able to just be in the present.

Keelin was left with a choice. Frustration would do him no favors here though. He chose a lighter response. "It's taken years of practice, but I've come to be quite the master of looking like a fool. I'm sure I could show you a thing or two. Though with your skill of making people look like a fool, it seems we're two sides of the same coin."

Perhaps distance from Dachaigh really was all they needed. Things felt relaxed. There was a quietness, a stillness to it all. Keelin wondered if it bothered her at all. Being still didn't seem to be her strong point. Maybe there was an opportunity there.

She backed off as he rose, turning away from him and looking out into the vast expanse. It left her feeling exposed, open, small. Nodiah had always been enclosed in walls. The wind picked up some, and as the sun set in the distance, she couldn't help but stare at the streaks of dusty gold, pink, and purple as they shot through the open sky, but that didn't help her small feeling in the least.

He dusted himself off, and began unpacking. "Different out here. Calm before the storm as they say." His eyes found her again, as they often did. She was still distracted. Something else had her mind.

"It's beautiful." She meant it, even if she was uncomfortable. She shifted from one foot to the other, stretching her legs, still looking out to the horizon. She wondered about his nightmare, his fear. She could taste it, and here he was, seeming to still carry it with him. Both of their dreams stretched between them like a wall of bricks. Finally she turned to him, and after a moment she asked… "Do I scare you Keelin?" It seemed absurd, but she couldn't shake the feeling.

Exhale...

How did she know? Could she read him that well? There were so many ways to answer the question, but there was no way of avoiding it. *I own you, why would I ever be scared of you?* He thought it. He almost said it. What he did finally say didn't feel much better. "You cut off a King's...... jewels.... that would scare any man!" He tried to laugh it off, but her glance let him know he wasn't getting away that easily.

"You… You captivate me. You excite me. You inspire me. You surprise me, and yes… you scare me. Not because I think you're going to kill me in the middle of the night or something. If you wanted to do that, you would have. You scare me, because in spite of being a slave your entire life, all you know is control. There isn't one situation, one moment, where you haven't been the one pulling the strings. You scare me, because you will do anything in this world for what you think freedom is… and yet you have no idea." He could feel the intensity and sincerity in his words swell, but it was too late to go back. "You scare me because without you, I can't get where I'm going. I can't get the answers I need. You scare me, because I need you."

It was as honest as he could be. He did. She was his connection to the Creators. It was a valid answer, but he couldn't stop himself. "But not this. Not this shielded up, walled off, armored up soldier. I need the one that's willing to believe in something bigger than herself. The one that isn't just along for the ride. The one the isn't afraid to feel, and getting to that one…

that scares the hell out of me." He looked off to the horizon once more, not sure how she'd take any of it.

She could feel her muscles tighten. Her back stiffened with anger. After everything that happened he still could not see her for who she was. It was always about what she was, and what she could be, and what she could do for him. *I need you. Ha...* "And what if you are all wrong. If I'm not a link to anything. What if I am the last of nothing? When I am once again a slave... Your... slave. Will you still need me then? Or will you just keep me around to use for your pleasure?" She snarled, unable to hide her anger any longer.

The truth was she was angry because she needed him too. Master, lover, protector, abuser... She could not compartmentalize these aspects of who he was anymore. It had been her main defense. Her emotions towards him swirled in her like one of Saoirse's spells, and it left her feeling stripped bare. She hurt.

His intensity rose to match. "What in the hell do you want me to say?" His heartfelt plea had been swallowed up by her ego. He didn't deserve this, and yet she was proving his point. As if the Creators themselves felt the intensity of the moment, lightning crackled in the distance. It was still quite a ways off, but where the beautiful sunset had been just before, darkness and clouds crept in.

"This is exactly what I'm talking about! Go ahead, put up your walls, stay in your fortress. Protect yourself. Go numb. What if I'm wrong? Well then this has been a big waste of time hasn't it?" He paced, trying to think through his words, but all he saw now was his nightmare. He saw her covered in blood, smiling, laughing. "What if I'm right? Ever think of that? I've been scared of failing this entire time, and you keep trying to pump me full of this belief that I actually deserve any of this! That I deserve you, but it's you! It's you that's scared." He closed the gap between them a step or two, and they began circling one another.

"It's you that's afraid because for the first time in your life, you may actually be something, and I've led you to believe that you are something. So now, what if you're not? You can't go back to nothing. It would kill you. I get that, but damnit Nodi you were never a slave. You have owned your destiny from the moment your feet touched the ground. The only one holding you in chains... is you."

He looked off towards the coming storm, and then inspiration struck. "Remember our game? I won. I want my prize right now." He aggressively, violently approached her, thrusting his pointer finger into his cheek. "Hit me. Not a slap, no holding back… Hit… me. With all of the force, and heart, and emotion you can find. Put it all into your fist, and knock my ass out. Do it. COME ON!"

His prize. Of course he wanted his prize. She lost it. "Your one thing… Your prize. Our game…" she managed to start calm, but her next words exploded from within. "This is not a game, Keelin. I AM NOT A GAME OR A PRIZE!" Hot tears spilled down her cheeks and before she realized what was happening, she pushed him hard. It wasn't a hit, and she could never match his strength, but she knew he wasn't ready for it. Her eyes widened as he sprawled backwards. She was shaking… she turned… and ran.

Inhale…

Keelin clumsily fell to the ground, but now was angrier than ever. "That's not what I said! I said…" she was already creating a gap between them. "GO ON THEN! DO WHAT YOU ALWAYS DO WHEN THINGS GET OUT OF CONTROL! RUN… HIDE… YOU CAN'T RUN FROM WHO YOU ARE. FROM WHO I AM…" His voice lowered, figuring she wasn't listening much anyways. "I'm your Black. I will protect you." He paused for a moment, hoping she'd stop or turn or something, but she just kept running. He took a long swig from his canteen, got on his horse, and began to chase her down.

She ran, and ran, and ran. Her feet slapped the ground, kicking up dust as her lungs started to burn. Soon she was enveloped in darkness as the sun finally gave way to the darkness. As long as she kept moving, her thoughts could not catch up with her, but Keelin was right. She was running from her fears, and they were following right behind her.

He was caught off guard by her speed. Maybe he gave her too much of a head start. She descended straight off the front part of the plateau, sliding down with ease. It was too steep for the horse, so he turned back to the path, and then began to close the gap.

Sound was his guide more than anything else as the darkness took over. He wouldn't have that for long once the rain reached them. He had to get to her. Occasionally lightning lit up enough of the sky that he could find her outline, but it only lasted a moment.

The first noise he heard was the heavy thundering of hooves. Running horses… Wait what? Panic set in as Keelin pushed his horse as hard as it would go, but he lost her. Another crack of lightning lit up the landscape. He thought he saw a group ahead, but he wasn't sure. He pointed his horse in that direction and pushed the pace to the brink, but it was impossible to see. "NODIAH!" He screamed out in vain. Had he failed? Was it over? Just hours after leaving… it couldn't be. He couldn't stop.

Nodiah could hear the hooves gaining on her. She pushed forward with all she had left. She turned to scream at Keelin, "Just let me… Who?" It wasn't him. A rope tightened around her waist, and she felt her feet get yanked out from below her. "KEELIN!" It ripped from her throat as she was dragged onto a horse. There was no light left. All was dark. The rain started to fall.

He sat, waiting for some kind of sign. He hoped for the faintest amount of light, anything that would help. The only place near was Torek, that had to be where they took her. He thought he heard his name, but couldn't be sure. Going in the wrong direction wasn't a risk he could take. He sat in the dark as the rain trickled down, and began to think about how he'd get inside the castle alone.

The thoughts didn't last long. A lantern sparked in the darkness to reveal a figure about twenty yards from Keelin. "Lose something?" a voice called through the rain. It had a strange accent, and a distinctive high-born tilt to it. The lantern bobbed closer to show a short man, more of a boy really. It was a strange site. He sounded noble, but his attire was that of an old salt. A curved sword hung at his side.

He held up a hand. "Peace friend. We mean you know harm, but if you want to see that little fox of yours again, you will lose your weapons and come quietly." Keelin did his best to control himself. He couldn't remember the last time he was caught so unaware. This man seemed to be a part of the darkness itself. How long had they been watching? Where had they come from? He drew his sword.

More noises from the darkness and another lantern let Keelin know he was outnumbered. With a disgruntled sigh, he stabbed his sword into the ground. "You hurt her, you will suffer a fate worse than death." He shot out coldly towards the small man.

The man smirked back, "I'll hold you to that. The name's Liam. And my Captain just wants to have a word with you. It's just business Keelin." Liam snapped and a few more figures became visible in the dim light. "I believe I have an old friend of yours here. What was it? Storm? Stan?" The mountainous figure loomed closer, refusing to look at Keelin.

"It's Strom."

"Ah yes, Strom. Do us a favor eh? Get his weapons."

"Strom you son of a bitch. Why am I not surprised?" Trying to cope with the sudden appearance of the former Wolf, and wondering who else may be involved, took all of the fight from Keelin. This alliance felt new, but it was hard to say.

Keelin raised his arms, allowing Strom to search him as his eyes found Liam. "Business? You steal a human life. My property. And you call it business? Alright then, let's go meet your Captain so I know whose neck to snap after I take out ole Strom here. You have no idea who I am." This was as close to Nodiah's primal state as he could imagine. This was the same kind of rage as when the Dragons showed up. There was a quietness to it. A storm brewing… a confidence building. He'd pick his moment… "Lead on…"

"Careful Keelin. There aren't the same rules out here." Strom remarked as he inspected Keelin's sword.

Nearby, Nodiah was unceremoniously dumped on the deck of a large ship. Lanterns hung illuminating the deck every few feet. She looked up at a woman she presumed to be in charge. Her long tight braids ran down to the middle of her back, entwined with beads and feathers. Her rounded out shoulders and long muscular frame told Nodiah this was a fighter. She was heavily covered with tattoos from what Nodiah could see. They ran up and down her arms, and along her neck. Her deep bronze colored skin glistened in the flame light.

"Captain Jashilyn Majila of the Vendetta welcomes you aboard pretty thing." Nodiah watched as the Captain looked to the crew. "Are you sure this is her? I had expected her to put up more of a fight." The Captain approached, crouching down to get a better look at Nodiah. "I hear a Sky Dancer was spotted a week ago, leaving the Sabal capitol and heading South. I rush all this way, and this is it? I hear you've been running around with Wolves? Ah yes... here it is." She spotted the wolf emblem on Nodiah's shirt. "It appears our new crew mate spoke true." *New crew mate? Who?* Another stepped towards the Captain.

"Cap, Liam and the others approach. They have the Alpha." A sinister smile crossed the Captain's face.

"Very well. I think we should... oh look, she's coming around now."

Nodiah stirred, as she murmured to herself. "Keelin..."

"So it is her. Put this on her. We can't underestimate our new friend." Nodiah's eyes moved up to see what was coming. Much to her horror, a metallic collar approached her neck. She tried to resist, but she had nothing left. It locked around her throat, and a chain was threaded through a loop securing her to the deck. She wanted to scream, but there was no point. "Now, let us greet our guests properly."

After a while, Keelin and his captors approached the Vendetta. So they were corsairs. It was a little surprising to Keelin, because he hadn't realized they had gotten so close to the coast. Corsairs were fewer in number than they once were, but it also meant the ones that were left were good at what they did.

Strom followed Keelin, forcing him up to the top deck as the Captain awaited them. As soon as he was onboard, crew members began running around preparing to cast off. That would complicate things. He didn't dare look for Nodiah. Seeing her would jeopardize his emotion, and could cause them both trouble.

"Keelin my friend, as Captain of the Sea Hawks, I welcome you aboard the Vendetta!" Keelin took in her appearance. She had an intimidating look, from her weathered bronze skin to her fierce dark eyes. She looked every bit the part of a female corsair captain, but he wasn't sure he had ever heard of one before. Her tattoos were common, but familiar. Her arms. They were the same as Nahko!

Keelin settled back into a chair as she continued. The rain picked up, but they both did their best to ignore it. "Please make yourself comfortable. Can I offer you a drink?" She smiled politely. He tried not to show his concern, centering himself in the moment and preparing to engage in conversation. The ship lurched to life, and began to make its way out into the waters.

"Something strong preferably… Captain is it? Your mate Liam tells me you have business to discuss? All I know is you have something that is mine." Keelin held firm, his confidence oozing through his posture. "Why don't you start by telling me about your tattoos there? Quite lovely." A bit of a crazed smile took over. He was selling every word, coated in charm and charisma.

Keelin watched as the Captain leaned back in her chair, studying him. She stood, then approached him, circling him like a shark. A crew member produced a couple glasses of some kind of drink. Keelin could smell its strength before it ever got close.

"Please, call me Jaz... And these?" she asked innocently. Her fingertips traced the exact markings in question. "Call it a… family tradition." Keelin's heart sank. The Wolves were in danger.

Her hand moved up to his jawline, pulling his gaze to meet hers. "I suppose I do have something of yours. Or rather, you want something that is now mine!" Again she smiled. "My men told me she was running from you, trying to escape." She cocked her head, looking at Keelin quizzically. "She must have been rather poorly treated to run off into the desert with no food, nor drink, nor a horse to ride. I don't imagine she would have lasted more than a day or so. Truly, you think you'd take better care of your things. You're lucky my Hawks found her first."

Keelin stood and began circling as well, the two engaging in a duel of wits. The rain increased to a downpour. The Captain made a slight nod, and from somewhere up the deck Keelin could hear metal jangling along the wood. Moments later, Nodiah was led on chain and collar, and then reattached to a bolt closer to the two of them. There she was, cold, blank, and bruised. She was just an empty shell. This wasn't her at all.

He immediately approached Nodiah, and tensions on the ship rose. He picked up her chin forcefully with one hand, and began inspecting her. As his eyes crossed her sight line, he winked, hoping she saw it. Then he turned once more, and returned to circling with Jaz. "You damaged her pretty good."

The Captain was taken back. "You can't blame me for all of that. She doesn't seem too happy to see you. Why don't you tell me, Keelin, Alpha of the Wolves, what is she worth to you?"

She knew his name. She knew his reputation. She knew too much. Strom had something to do with this, and possibly Nahko. He had to play his cards carefully. "A disobedient, clumsy slave, willing to run off into the wild." The words stung Keelin to even say. "She'll likely off herself one of these days. The only reason I went after her is because of how much I paid for her to begin with. I'd at least like to get my money back." The words hurt to say, but this Captain was no fool.

"I tell you what Jaz. You give her back, we all have a drink, and we all go our separate ways." His pacing stopped. He took a sip of the drink and raised his eyes to meet hers. "Or… you cut the theatrics and tell me what you're really after? You know me, you know my name, you know the Wolves. You must be wanting something specific. Maybe we can talk business after all?" He took a bigger swig of the drink, strong, yet disgusting, with a bitter aftertaste. As he tried to swallow down the harsh liquid, the burn got to his throat, and he let out a rough cough. "Like, I can show you where to get some better booze." *Breathe… Wait for your moment…*

The entire crew let out a good laugh at his coughing before the Captain responded. "Not to your liking eh? Well I suppose that will be your first lesson aboard my ship. Beggars cannot be choosers. I suggest you apply this across the board and watch your tongue. The leader of the Wolves is quite a valuable hostage to have, but nothing compared to the King's assassin. And you're not even an Alpha anymore are you? Strom here has informed me of a new Alpha. Someone I happen to know quite well." She gave a quiet laugh, her fingers tracing along the tattoos once more.

She crossed the deck, and approached Nodiah, stroking her cheek in the same fashion Keelin had before. A crack of lightning flashed across the dark sky. She firmly grasped her hair, snapping her neck back and looking down at her eyes. "She is sweet, tempting to keep her to myself. My Hawks could use some entertaining!" She let out a mock sigh of debate. "Hmm... The question really is, who should I ransom her to? The royal family of Sabal? I am sure they would pay handsomely for her. And of course the Queen of Ogla has issued a proclamation saying she will pay any price for any information of the Sky Dancers. And then there is you."

Jaz dropped Nodiah, and approached Keelin once more. "Who just wants your monies worth. Or so you claim." She looked over her shoulder to Liam.

"Have a go at her yourself. If she's just a slave, I'm sure Keelin here won't mind much." Her eyes locked onto Keelin as Liam approached Nodiah. He pulled her roughly to her feet by the collar, pressing his face deep into her hair and inhaling deeply. His hands began wandering her body, freely groping and squeezing as they went.

As much as Keelin wanted to end Liam, something wasn't adding up. If the Captain had all of these connections, she wouldn't be facilitating this meeting. She was trying to get something out of him. He couldn't give in yet.

The Queen of Ogla and Keelin had crossed paths before, and honestly that wouldn't be the worst of circumstances. As Liam continued, all of Keelin's thinking stopped. His anger began to swell. "Would you stop your talk of Sky Dancers! She's nothing more than a dead King's trophy. Not even worth your time. I'm going to give you one last chance. Leave her be, and let's talk business before things get messy." Keelin had a sudden stroke of inspiration. The Captain was all ego. Maybe he could use that against her.

"There is another option." Keelin watched as the Captain's head cocked once more.

"Oh, please enlighten me." She said playfully curious.

He placed his arms casually on Jaz's shoulders. "We could forget about her. Do you know how many people out there want me dead? You deliver me, get your payment, and then we spring our trap. I escape, we move on to the next town and pull the same thing. Think of all the money you could earn!" Keelin played up the performance to a maximum. Every word was over dramatic, and emphasized by broad strokes of volume and gestures. "All the while pissing off Queens and Kings on all four corners of the map. Plus, there's something about you, about your style. I don't think we're all that different."

Now desperate to sell his point, he leaned in moving his hands to the back of her neck. He pulled her to him, and kissed her lightly. The entire crew fell silent as Keelin dared to touch their Captain. Hands moved to weapons all the way around.

The Captain allowed herself to indulge in the kiss, letting out a small smile as her fingers found their way up into his hair. Then as they broke, he felt her fingers tighten, and she yanked his head towards hers, connecting her forehead to his nose with a vicious smash. "Nice try, but I have my eyes on bigger things than a mercenaries bounty." She snapped her fingers and the crew advanced towards him. Liam stepped away from Nodiah, but still hung towards the back as Nodiah seemed to become present for the first time.

"Keelin…" She whimpered out, half in desperation, half in sadness.

His eyes watered, but he did his best to focus. He was running out of options as he watched the Hawks close in. "You need your Hawks to fight your battles I see. I get it. I'm not in the mood to hit a woman anyways." He backed up, but realized he was surrounded in short order. He had one move, one chance.

He ran full sprint at Nodiah. From his pocket he pulled out his fang, grabbed a fistful of her red hair and yanked her back. He raised the fang to her throat and yelled out, "She's no good to you dead. Call them off. We can take you to a treasure far more valuable than either of us." He wasn't sure how true that would be, but he had nothing left to lose.

The Captain let out a low growl of a laugh. "Not in the mood to hit a woman, but you won't hesitate to use one as a shield. What kind of a man are you Keelin?" She approached the pair slowly. "You're bluffing. Do it."

Nodiah gasped, he wouldn't do it. He couldn't. The world around her disappeared once more… The Priest's voice became clear.

She closed her eyes…

"This is your doing. Lust and envy are the most contemptible of sins, and you tempt all of those around you in one way or another. Filling heads with fantasy. I am tired of all of the talk about you. Your destiny is here. You must be punished. I have no other choice." The Priest's voice echoed in her ears, along with the clanking sounds of the shackles.

"The Oracle!" She snapped back to the Vendetta. "Wait… I can take you to the Oracle…" Keelin hesitantly moved away from the Captain. None of this sat right with him. What would Jaz do once they got there? Just let them wander off? They gained nothing.

He whispered in her ear "You are a terrible negotiator, don't do this." He then turned his attention back to the Captain. "No she can't. Look at her! She just is trying to give herself a way out. Now… if you keep walking, the only thing she'll be able to show anyone is the after life, so back the hell up." It was his last chance. She had the Oracle, he had nothing. No matter what happened this didn't fare well for him.

The Captain ignored him as if he wasn't even there, instead focusing on Nodiah. "The Oracle? You can really deliver her to me?"

Nodiah hissed as the fang bit into her skin a bit. "Yes! I was chosen to be a Vessel in the temple under Torek. I know the way. Just don't let him… kill me!" As she talked, her hands gripped the chain attaching her collar to the ship. She tugged it, feeling it loosen from the water soaked wood.

Her eyes closed…

The burn returned to her body, pulsing through her veins as her chest heaved, trying to catch her breath. "I'm sorry it came to this. If you just stop attempting to escape, we can make this so much easier. Accept your fate."

"I'll never stop. I will escape. She isn't going to wake up. You're just doing this for yourself." His laughter filled the room, letting doubt creep in once more.

THWACK!

That same spot. Three years later, he always found that same spot. It never had a chance to heal. She felt the familiar pull of the chains as they tightened. She gave everything she had to break free. Something moved. The bolt gave a little. This was it.

Her eyes opened, and she was back. "Please, I promise I can…" Suddenly the bolt popped from the wood and Nodiah had a weapon of her own. She snapped the chain like a whip and with a quick fluid motion, it wrapped around the Captain's neck.

With another flick of the wrist, she had Jaz pinned against her, Nodiah's chest pressed against the Captain's back. Keelin managed to hang on, still holding the fang up to her neck. "Bad at negotiating huh?" Nodiah spat with disdain as she carefully shuffled her weight.

"YES!" Keelin replied emphatically. This wasn't negotiating, this was a hostage situation. Even though the Captain seemed at a disadvantage, neither of them were taking her positioning lightly. Lightning cracked once more, and the Hawks circled the trio, closing in as Liam took the lead.

"Now now, let's not be hasty." They were still outnumbered, and the crew knew it. "You give us back Captain Jaz, and we all go see the Oracle. We've already shown we can track you down, so even if you do escape, we'll follow you, we'll find you, and we won't be so generous." His threat was empty, and they both could sense it.

Someone had to do something As usual Keelin took the lead. He raised his voice and made his move. "Alright slave, I'm going to let you go. Think about what you're doing." Keelin removed the fang, and positioned himself in front of Nodiah and Jaz, giving them at least a little bit of a buffer. "Now when we started this negotiation, I gave your Captain a choice, the easy way, or the messy way. Looks like you chose..."

Running on pure adrenaline, Keelin charged the crew. Liam lashed out with sword in hand, but Keelin easily vaulted him, now putting himself in the center of the Hawks. He threw an elbow at the youngest face he could see, catching him off guard and knocking his sword in the air. He grabbed it while dodging the attempted tackle of another. He then took his fang, and grabbed it between his pointer and middle finger, sticking out like a spike. He was ready.

"ENOUGH!" The circle cleared, and Strom stepped in. "I'm sure you've figured it all out by now. All of the lies. All meant to get you out of the way. You never deserved to be an Alpha. My little fight with Nahko was all for show. It let me leave, so I could let our Captain know what you were up to. You walked right into this, and now... now Keelin. I end this." He cracked his knuckles with bravado as the two began to circle.

He was lying. He had to be. All of it? How long had he been working with Jaz? How long had Nahko? This plan was years in the making. It couldn't be. He would pay! Keelin had no intention of dropping his weapons. This wasn't a challenge for Alpha, and Strom was up to something.

As the pair continued measuring each other up, Keelin suddenly lost his balance and stumbled forward. The crew's laughter roared on-deck as, he turned back to see the grinning Liam standing nearby. Keelin returned the smirk and let Liam know, "You're next."

He felt the vibrations of the wood as Strom started his charge. He managed to narrowly avoid him, but Strom couldn't stop his momentum. He smashed head first into Liam, and both hit the deck with a loud crack as the boards beneath them gave some.

Now that Strom had his back to him, Keelin could see the massive sword sheathed along his spine. As the giant stood, he pulled out the sword, and continued the offensive. Keelin blocked, but every blow felt like he would be sent crashing through the floorboards, and into whatever lay below. His smaller sword began to bend and crack under the weight of Strom's heavy smashes, until finally it gave, snapping in pieces.

Sensing the opportunity, Strom boldly raised his sword overhead, preparing to bring it down with his full weight. Keelin saw an opening. He quickly shifted to his feet and swung an uppercut straight into Strom's neck, but much to his surprise it didn't stop him. Strom continued the swing, clipping the fabric of Keelin's pants and pinning them to the deck. He struggled to rip free, but Strom was on him in no time. A right hand smashed into Keelin's jaw, knocking him back and ripping the fabric. Keelin had to take the offensive.

He charged, wrapping his arms around Strom's waist and pushing him back, but Strom hammered down on Keelin's spine, flattening him once more. He lay at Strom's feet, trying to gather himself when he heard the sword pry free.

He jabbed the fang forward, slashing at Strom's ankles. The sword dropped, missing Keelin's head by inches as Strom roared with pain. The fang then found its way into his calf, sending Strom down to one knee.

As Keelin rose, his fists picked up the pace. The combination of jabs and stabs continued up until he felt the fang sink deep into Strom's chest between two ribs. He heard the air leave the big man's lungs. Each punch just further fueled Keelin's rage. A swift punch to the neck left Strom on all fours.

As Keelin eyed the sword, the crew went silent. They knew what was coming. At least they thought they did. Keelin lifted the sword. "This is for the Wolves…" A piercing howl followed as Keelin raised the sword high. True fear finally set into Strom's eyes. That was what Keelin wanted. He swung down with all his might, driving the hilt of the sword straight into Strom's skull, knocking him unconscious. He turned to the rest of the crew, pants torn, blood spattered everywhere, breathing heavily with a glint of madness in his eyes… and waited.

Nodiah clenched the chain tight around Jaz's neck, as she struggled. "You little… I'll kill you. Just you wait." The Captain tried her best to intimidate Nodiah, but she was having none of it.

"I wonder what your head is worth Captain," Nodiah sneered in her ear. She watched the scene play out in front of her. She wanted to help, to be by Keelin's side. She felt the same kind of ferocity running through her veins as before. It was a high that was addicting at best. She was in control however, and needed to stay that way.

Slowly she edged back towards the side of the boat. Jaz continued to struggle, but Nodiah was able to constantly shift her weight and keep the advantage. Her backside pressed against the railing. Nodiah knew what she had to do. She waited to lock eyes with Keelin, and then flung herself backwards, dragging the pair over the rail and into the water below.

Keelin couldn't stop her. He had no way to get to her in time. He was still trying to figure out the logic behind it all. First, he promised to take care of Liam, and he intended to do just that. He pointed the sword in Liam's direction, and took control. "Howl."

"What?" Liam looked perplexed at the request.

"Howl… now…" he repeated firmly.

"I ain't your dog," Liam shouted defiantly.

"No, but you're no man either. If you want to escape with your life, then you'll howl." Liam gauged the look. Keelin stepped forward, pressing the point of the sword against the soft part of Liam's neck. A pitiful attempt of a howl escaped between shallow nervous breaths. Keelin smiled, and pivoted.

The entire crew circled with him until finally his back was against the same railing. "Gentlemen, and dog, this is where I bid you good day, but you should leave this ship while you can. For even if your Captain does somehow manage to escape, the next time I see you there will be no hesitation, and no mercy. You will be attacked, pounced, mauled, disfigured, and dismembered by the Wolves." Keelin eyed each and every crew member as he made his promise. He lowered the sword, and then thrust the hilt straight into Liam's groin. He vaulted the railing, and leapt for the water.

Matthew Oakley

Chapter 13

As soon as he broke the surface, his eyes searched for Nodiah and the Captain. They weren't too far away, and neither was the shore. The Hawks weren't going to just sit there, they had to act.

He swam in Nodiah's direction and hoped he wasn't already too late. The battle between the two women was intense. Each seemed more content to drown the other than survive. Jaz had been struggling for air long before they went overboard however. Nodiah could feel her desperation, and in a way it gave her strength. Every time Jaz went under though, she pulled at Nodiah and brought her down with. Nodiah struggled and sputtered with gasping breaths as she looked up to see the crew watching, and orders began to ring out. "KEELIN!" She screamed, hoping he was somewhere nearby. She began moving towards the shore, but Jaz grasped her collar and pulled her under again. "Kee..."

Keelin watched the pair sink below the surface as he approached. He swam down, grabbing a hold of Nodiah's waist, but immediately felt the Captain wrap herself around his back, her arm gripping tightly against his throat. He swam with everything he had towards the surface. Somehow he managed to break through, and then immediately attempt to speak. "This is stupid! Let's settle this on land!" He clawed at the water trying to make any progress he could. The waves luckily were helping.

Finally he got to a point where he could stand, the women too exhausted to fight at the moment. As soon as his feet touched, he flung Jaz over his shoulder, and into the water in front of him. "We don't have to do this. This… thing… She isn't worth your time."

Every time Keelin had to speak of Nodiah as such, it hurt, but he had no choice. Rage filled Nodiah to the brim. She just risked her life for him. The

Captain was helpless, why was he keeping up the charade? They should be running for the shore. If they were caught, it would mean death for them both, and yet he continued.

"I jumped in to save you Captain. I can't do business with a dead woman. Let's figure out how to help each other." Keelin didn't know much at all about Jaz, but she had proven to be quite the foe. Where Nodiah was wild, uncontrolled, and unpredictable, Jaz was measured, precise, and thoughtful. Keelin could appreciate that.

Jaz pulled herself to her feet, bent over, and vomited up what seemed like a barrel of seawater. She wiped her mouth on the back of her glove, and drew out a solid black sword. "You jumped in to save me? You are both an idiot and a liar." Keelin put himself between Nodiah and the Captain. "If you wanted to do business with me, you would have killed her the moment she attempted to strangle me. You may be her Master, but she is certainly not your slave. You want to prove yourself? Kill her."

Tensions rose. Keelin did his best to hide his surprise, but he knew he failed. The Captain continued to challenge him. "I'll bring her head to Torek and collect the reward. They won't care if she's dead or alive, she is the most wanted woman in Sabal. She killed and dishonored the King. This… thing… is a monster, and I'm betting you're the one who created her."

Nodiah snuck to the side, wrapping the chain around her fist, no longer willing to stand behind Keelin. The pair seemed quite locked on each other anyways. "What is it? Did she save your life? You want to do business than hurry up and prove i..." A few small splashes and then a loud twang filled the air as the chain connected with Jaz's temple and the Captain collapsed on the ground. Nodiah inspected the fresh blood on the metal wrapped around her knuckles, and then eyed Keelin, debating whether or not to swing again.

She thought she could handle whatever he had for her, but not this. Not from someone who referred to her as a thing in front of this other worthless excuse of a woman. Nodiah bit her lip, feeling the animalistic rage building up. It was intoxicating in its own right, to feel powerful. She dropped her gaze to the limp body laying in the water in front of her. "Let's kill her."

"What is wrong with you Nodiah?" Frustration took over any thoughts of a happy reunion. "It was an act. If they believe you're nothing to me, they stop chasing you. I was trying to protect you!" His anger and confusion seethed through every word.

At this moment he wasn't sure what to do with her. He was concerned for Jaz, and was wondering if Nodiah would actually hit him. "No. You don't get to kill her." He charged Nodiah, catching her off guard. "You want to hurt someone, here I am!"

His words rang in her ears. One swing, and she would be free. Her fingers clenched tightly. She was ready. This was it. As he approached, she cocked her fist back, but he caught her wrist. His other hand found the back of her neck and pulled her mouth to his.

Instead of the usual passionate kiss however, he extended his tongue, licking across her lips and then up her cheek to her ear. The move was entirely intended to create shock. Her eyes widened. She pushed him off and moved to swing again, but he spoke. "White wolf or not, you will listen. I'm done with these games." He had positioned himself between Nodiah and Jaz as he continued. "This is your fault." Finally they locked eyes. He had to get through.

She couldn't begin to process. She looked down, then her eyes flicked back. The power faded as she softly responded. "I know." It didn't satisfy Keelin. That's not what he wanted. This wasn't the time for her to hide behind her submission. What did she know?

"No… you don't know. You don't have a clue." The Hawks were coming, they didn't have much time. "The Wolves are compromised. My life is on the line, and you won't get out of your own damn way." He wiped his face with the back of his hand, and then looked towards the ship. "We need to move. I'll deal with you when we're safe."

He moved to Jaz, slinging her over his shoulder. He knew she wouldn't like this, but he was done with her negotiating. Nodiah froze. He didn't even care enough to yell. He was uninterested in her. He was more concerned about his own life than hers. She coiled the rest of the chain up so it wouldn't drag on the ground, and followed after.

Once they were into the island a bit, she finally spoke. "I got scared. You… I ran… You just make me lose control, and if you hadn't come after me, who knows what they would have done." It was as if she was recapping the events to herself. "I nearly got you killed, and now we're stuck with this… this…" *thing*. She stopped herself.

They approached a small, dry cave set deep into the shadow of a grassy hill, disguised by brush. It was a good place to stop, if Keelin let them. If he even wanted her anymore. It was hard to say exactly where they were at this point.

She circled around in front of him, blocking his path. "But why? Why would you want me to hit you? Don't you know what I've been through? What I've..." She paused, gathering herself. The last words came out as a hollow whisper. "Don't you know what you are to me?" Her eyes pleaded for him to see truth.

Keelin moved towards the cave, feeling Jaz begin to move just a bit. He didn't say a word, instead starting to inspect Jaz's body closer, and searching her. Nothing in her pocket, but she did have something around her neck. He yanked off a thin strand of leather, and stared at the keys attached to it.

Still saying nothing, he moved towards Nodiah, and unlocked her from her collar. He grabbed the chain, and forcefully ripped it away from her. He then used the chain to wrap up Jaz in a way that made it difficult for her to stand on her own. Once she was secure, he finally turned back to Nodiah. "In order to pull this off, we have to be willing to do just about anything. We have to push ourselves. We have to be able to trust ourselves." His eyes shifted towards the cave entrance.

"You think Jaz is bad? There are things after us that are far worse than a smooth talking corsair and a boat full of scum. I need to know that when our backs are against the wall that you'll have mine. You don't have to like me. You don't even have to trust me. I'm not sure that you can, but I need you to obey..." As soon as the word escaped his mouth, he regretted it. "I need you to listen to me. What am I to you? I am your OWNER!" He paused as the words echoed through the cave.

He needed space. It was the closeness of their relationship that was causing so many issues in the first place, but he couldn't back away from the truth either. He continued in a softer tone. "I am... your protector. Your guardian. Your Black Wolf. I am the one who will break you. Strom may not believe, but my thoughts on you and the White Wolf existed long before he ever came to us." He couldn't look at Nodiah. He leaned against the cave wall and focused on Jaz. "I am the one who will set you free." It was gentle, but powerful. They hung in the air with all of the intent he could muster.

Nodiah moved farther back in the cave and shed her wet clothes, wringing them out and spreading them on the ground. She curled her knees up to her chest, wrapped her arms around then, and rested her chin on her arms. There she sat, and stared out the cave opening into the night. "You really think the Wolves are compromised?" Nodiah asked in a small voice. "Just because Strom, he's not a Wolf anymore anyways."

Keelin's frustration grew. The instability and inconsistency of Nodiah's temperament was hard to understand. He wanted to help her in so many ways, and yet every time the conversation came up, she shut down. He walked in farther, and sat behind her letting her lean back on his shoulder. "Nahko and Jaz are family. They have the same markings. Strom had been coming and going which no one knew. I… I don't know. That's the worst part, I don't know what to believe." It was a startling revelation even to himself. He was lost.

Nodiah shook her head for a moment. Strom And Nahko working together didn't make sense. They had traveled almost a full day before stopping to make camp. Jaz's men had gotten lucky. Just because they were family, didn't mean they were allies. They were such different people. Keelin was wrong, but she wasn't about to tell him that.

"But I believe in you. I believe you're worth fighting for. It doesn't matter who you turn out to be. I'll keep fighting for you." *In who you are, not what.* He thought it, but then decided saying it wouldn't help. He moved back to his feet and made his way towards the entrance. "I'm going to get a fire going just to be safe. No reason to leave anywhere just yet." Then he disappeared into the trees.

At about that moment, Jaz stirred, sitting up groggily against the cave wall. "You know, you two have the most messed up relationship I have ever seen. A slave in love with her master. A master who cares too much for his slave. Pah! You don't see what he sees. You are no slave. No matter how much he paid for you, he doesn't own you. You could kill him any time you chose, but you're weak." Nodiah felt what she was doing, but she couldn't help but listen. "Normally, I would appeal to your sense of freedom. I know we could work together. But you don't want to be free do you? You think if you do well enough, he will love you. You're wrong.

You are nothing more than another piece to his puzzle, and I'm going to prove it to you." Nodiah locked eyes with Jaz, anger swelling once more.

"Big words for someone bound in chains. I could kill you at any moment," Nodiah growled. Her words were empty. The more she thought about Jaz's statements, the more they lined up with what she was feeling in her core. It was as if she could see her soul, and all the dark stains that marred it. She couldn't risk defying Keelin again. Somehow Jaz was still in control.

Keelin returned with wood, breaking up the conversation, and Jaz began working on him as well. " So I take it this means we are done pretending to be friends ey Alpha? Odd way to do business..." she quipped with an insidious grin. Keelin approached, tempted to smack the smirk off her face.

"I was all for making a deal until you decided to try and kill me." He placed a finger under her chin, and lifted her eyes to his. "First, she could in fact kill you, at any moment, at any time. She didn't just assassinate the King, she disfigured him." Keelin shuttered a bit at the flash back. "Secondly, if I wasn't still willing to figure out something you'd already be dead. What we do with you now, that's up for debate." He dropped her chin, giving her a playful smack and then returned his focus to Nodiah.

"So, we rest for a few hours then we had for the Oracle!" He smiled lightly, waiting to see how either woman would react. Jaz spoke up first, clearly bothered by Keelin's touch "Actually, if I had been trying to kill you, you would be dead. I would have let the crew have a bit of fun with you, but I have big plans for you Keelin."

She shifted a bit against her restraints, tilting her head towards Nodiah. "Her as well, if she will stop whacking me in the head with these chains. Cheap shot by the way." Nodiah watched with a level of detachment. She wondered how long Keelin planned to keep up the slave charade, or if it even was a charade anymore. She said nothing as he mentioned the Oracle. It was crazy to take her. She would never be able to be trusted. What did he see in her that Nodiah couldn't accomplish? She didn't voice her objections, slaves don't do things like that.

"I do believe we can help each other," the Captain continued. "As you said, you can't do business with a dead woman. These chains are like ice, I'm soaked through, and I have an injury that needs attention. I am unarmed, let me out of these things." She flashed a predatory smile at

Keelin and lifted herself up a bit more. "You can search me yourself…"

Keelin wasn't particularly phased by anything Jaz had said until she made the comment about the search. Her eyes flickered with a hint of flirtation, and Keelin considered it. He had caused Nodiah enough damage. He did look to her, for approval. He was actually looking for Nodiah's permission, but he didn't need it, and instantly felt silly for even waiting. He turned back to Jaz, inspecting the wound on her head.

It truly was a nasty gash, so for her sake he undid the chain, and then casually searched her body for possessions again, not really thinking about what he was doing. He didn't give her any more attention after, instead moving to Nodiah's side. "You ok?" He asked softly. Nodiah tensed as Keelin slid up next to her.

This again. He was just as unstable as she was. Now it wasn't angry Keelin, or Master Keelin, or uninterested Keelin. This was the Keelin that cared about her, but for how long? She stayed quiet for a while, then tilted her chin towards Jaz. She gave Keelin a bit of a disapproving glance before rising to her feet. She struck like a snake, quickly and quietly pushing Jaz against the wall as she shook off her chains.

"Boots." Nodiah ordered roughly. Jaz grinned as she slid them off. A small revolver slid across the ground. Jaz shrugged. "Useless, powders wet." Nodiah continued her search, snatching off Jaz's belt and slinging it across the cave. Next she pulled away the rough leather Jaz had tied around herself as a skirt. A blow gun was strapped to her leg. Jaz raised her hands with a mock surprise on her face. "What? That's always there. I don't even notice it anymore!"

By now, Nodiah was enraged. She tore away Jaz's bodice, revealing a small leather pouch, and a bone dagger tucked below her chest. Nodiah grabbed them both, but as Nodiah ripped the weapon away, Jaz showed anger for the first time. There was no retort or explanation as Nodiah threw it away from her.

Keelin noticed, and wondered what was so special about this dagger to draw a reaction. He quickly grabbed it. He took a moment to take in the two standing before him, both ready to explode. The pair locked eyes, exposed, but willing and eager to kill if it came to it.

Nodiah turned away, flashing Keelin a scathing look for his pathetic search, and letting his guard down. She then gathered some of the wood, and moved farther in the cave to start the fire. She kept her back to Keelin in particular and set about rather skillfully building the fire. This left Keelin and Jaz to speak.

"You mentioned helping us. What in the world could you possibly be able to offer me?" Keelin asked rather intrigued. Jaz raised her brow at Keelin, stepping into him. Keelin couldn't help but think just how different her and Nodiah were, in every way. Both were exceptional, but different.

"I can offer you many things," she purred, trailing a finger along his collarbone. "But I need some information first. What exactly do you intend to do once you reach the Oracle? What is the point? I need to know what you hope to achieve before I can figure out how I can help." It was a fair question. Telling Jaz the truth would certainly give Jaz an advantage, but if he lied they may not get anywhere.

"I believe she is a Sky Dancer. She can take us to the temple. At the temple, we can talk to the Creators. In order to find the temple, we need the Oracle." It was a bit more truth than Keelin wanted to reveal, but it just spilled out.

Her presence left little room for comfort. Jaz's eyes flicked over to Nodiah as she processed. "A Sky Dancer? I had heard a rumor. You two have a lot more problems chasing you than me. The Queen has put out a bounty on her. If it's true, she believes she is the last of her kind." Jaz paused, considering her words once more. "What makes you think she is a Sky Dancer? She's got beauty, and skill, but who cares? How would we convince someone else she's a Sky Dancer hm? It takes more than red hair." Keelin didn't have an answer to that question. It was a belief. It was a presence… an aura. She pulled away, stepping towards the mouth of the cave. If Nodiah glided on the air, Jaz blazed through it.

Keelin could see that her tattoos wrapped around her shoulders and back, traveling all the way down her body to the back of her thighs. It seemed that this move to the mouth of the cave could've been for better lighting.

"You know there are other ways right? Have you ever been to Ogla? It's beautiful. We could travel there and sell her off!" She glanced over her shoulder to gauge Keelin's reaction. "Or if it's not to your liking…" Keelin wasn't quite sure if she meant her plan or her body… "Give the Oracle to the Queen... I am sure the Queen's power will be infinitely more valuable to you than the Oracles riddles."

He had been to Ogla. He was well aware of the Queen's obsession with the myths and legends. She wasn't young anymore, and it seemed she spent most of her years chasing after the Creators. It was one of the first places he went when he left home. Their visit was civil, but awkward. The Queen seemed threatened by Keelin's resolve. She offered to hire him to find the Sky Dancer temple on behalf of the Kingdom, but he declined.

"The Queen and I have met, though there are others who would pay even more." What was he saying? The games were over. His eyes continued to be entranced by the tattoos on her body. He did his best to keep his resolve. "But none would pay what I already have. She's not for sale. The Oracle though... That may work." Nodiah was not going to like that idea, but he smiled as he thought of the possibilities. They could get what they needed, and it left everyone happy.

Jaz clasped her hands together, seeming quite pleased with herself. "Ah! See I knew you could be reasoned with!" She turned back towards him. "But you see, you seem to be pretty fond of your little pet there. If she was telling the truth when she said she served in the temple then she's not going to be very fond of our little plan, and I'm betting she's our only way in. So for the meantime, I say we keep this amongst ourselves. That is, unless you think you can control her completely?" She waited a breath before continuing. "No... you can't."

She approached before he could respond, drawing out her words in a low, intimate whisper. "That's not all. That's not quite good enough for me. I have other... needs." She pressed up against him once more, licking her lips. "You're going to help me with them, and do you know why? Because I can tell you how to take down my brother." Without hesitation she kissed him.

Every inch of Keelin wanted to resist. He pulled back harshly. *Brother... Damn...* A mix of anger and passion flooded his mind. "I can control her." He wanted to tell Nodi. He had to tell her. "But it's better this way. As for Nahko I don't need any help taking him down. What is it you're actually helping me with?"

He saw the lust in Jaz's eyes. She wouldn't take a no. Could he really do this to Nodiah? It was for their good. For her good. "Not here. Can't we go somewhere a little more discrete?" He smiled playfully. He was unsure of how far he'd go, but he wasn't doing anything in front of Nodiah. That was too much.

Nodiah sat in front of the fire she had built on her own, knowing that the Captain was whispering lies into Keelin's ear, and he was eating them up for some stupid reason. It made her wonder the last time he had met a woman that was not completely under his control. A brief silence raised the tension. Hairs stood on her neck. She turned just in time to see Jaz kiss Keelin, the Captain's eye meeting hers. Her fists clenched, she was burning with anger. Then she was cold.

Jaz looked into Keelin's eyes, returning the smile. "Aw, and he has a heart too! Sure pretty boy, lead the way." She tossed Nodiah one last smirk as she followed Keelin out of the cave. Keelin couldn't help but feel used. Is this what Nodiah felt? He had to shake it off for now. This was for their benefit.

They walked down the trail a bit, and beyond the ridge of a hill. A flat spot opened up about ten feet in diameter. The rain had lightened up to a refreshing drizzle. "Before we begin friend, I've yet to hear what it is you're bringing to this deal, so I have a couple questions." He pulled the bone dagger from his pocket. As soon as he did, the intensity returned to Jaz's face. This item was special. "Care to explain this?" He grinned, now firmly back in control.

"Next, I find it hard to believe the Queen is your concern. You owe someone. You're working for someone. You're chasing something. Which is it? Or who?" It seemed an odd time to bring this up, but he needed to ask without Nodiah looking over their shoulder. Was there more people for Keelin to worry about?

"Don't presume to know anything about me... friend. You want to find out who destroyed your home? Well I've already found the one who destroyed mine. I captain his ship, and I carry his sword." Keelin's eyes widened. It made sense, but it was unexpected all the same.

"As for the Queen, I like Ogla. She is crazy and tyrannical at best, but she rules Ogla with an iron fist and bows to no one. That suits me. I respect her even if I don't particularly like her. You want to know what I bring to this deal?" She ran at him, charging him with her arms crossed over her chest. The collision caught Keelin off balance, sending him back to the ground with a hard impact. "I can give you a quick, safe, and direct passage to Ogla. I can tell you who, if anyone you have left to trust in your little pack. I can offer you the manpower you need to reclaim your home, and I promise that I might not separate your head from your neck when this is all over. Now… my patience is wearing thin. Take off your clothes."

She still avoided the question about the dagger. As he gathered his senses, he grabbed both her ankles and flung them out from under her. Her head smashed the ground, immediately causing her to reach up to her previous wound. He pounced on top of her, doing his best to pin her down. "You are strong, cunning, passionate, skilled, but by the Creators are you cocky." He smiled, sliding the dagger into his back pocket. "All of this for a payday?" He laughed, pressing his body against her a bit more. "You make sure you keep your end of the deal. Keep your Hawks off of us, and no one touches Nodiah, and I won't peel those pretty little markings off your skin piece by piece."

It was back. That animalistic wild possession. She was drawing it out, and he wasn't sure he could control it. It was scary and empowering and thrilling all at the same time. The next few moments mattered. He had to keep control.

She laughed deeply, "Cocky? Are you kidding me? You? You who took a Sky Dancer and made her your slave. You who justifies owning her so… so what? So you can protect her? Are you really so delusional that you can't see how sick you are? Taking this innocent girl and making her a murderer? Taking her back to a place of torment, where a fate worse than death awaited her if caught? Let me ask you this Keelin. How long? How long do you think it will take before she stops blindly following you and turns on you?"

He raised up at the mention of his fears. He knew she was right. "Your precious Nodiah will be your downfall, and all the while you think you are in control. You think you're using her for your gain, but she will finish you." How did she know? No… she didn't. Was it that obvious?

As Keelin debated these thoughts, Jaz wriggled an arm out from underneath him, and then smashed her elbow up into his jaw. As he flailed back, she rolled on top of him. She sat up, straddling his hips smiling at her ability to flip the situation.

"And if you think you are worth more than her, you're even cockier than

I thought. But I will hold up my end. It's you I'm worried about." Keelin was now physically and mentally reeling. He had to maintain control. Jaz seemed to be his match in every way. He had to remember who he was, and why he was doing this.

"Enough! You are jealous! Jealous of a slave! You think you can force your way into anything. Never met resistance you couldn't crack one way or another. You know what Nodiah is capable of, you felt it." He began unfastening his pants and sliding them down as he continued. "She and I are a threat. Not a bounty. And you know it."

The sudden realization of their position sent a wave of guilt crashing over Keelin. Is this what Nodiah had been feeling? Is this what he put her through? Jaz had him right where she wanted him, and all he wanted was Nodiah.

Keelin wasn't proud of what followed. It was wave after wave of self anguish and regret as Jaz smiled at her victory. She took a moment to lean forward and bite down on his neck, hard. As she pulled away he could see the blood on her lips. Then just as suddenly as it started, it was over. Jaz rose to her feet and started walking back. "If you think I'm jealous of something so fragile, you are in a world of trouble friend. I just see you both as useful."

He had to get back to Nodiah. There was so much he needed to tell her. As she made her way back to the cave, Keelin sprinted to catch up. As soon as he saw Nodiah, he approached with open arms. He needed her embrace. Her eyes told him that wasn't going to happen, something was wrong. "What? What is it? The blood?" He needed an answer quickly, and he had one.

Nodi's reaction was even quicker however. She had curled herself into the corner of the cave, warm and numb to whatever was happening. As they returned she saw the dirt, and leaves. Their hair was a mess, their bodies covered in sweat, and the bite on his neck made it pretty obvious to anyone what had happened. She recoiled from him as if she had been struck, squeezing herself into a ball that took up as little room as possible.

Keelin needed help. He needed someone on his side. This was Jaz's fault. He had to play along. Jaz would help. Right? "Nodiah, it's not what you think. She attacked me. Nodiah you have to trust me." No she didn't. She had no reason to. Keelin stormed in Jaz's direction, getting right into her face until their foreheads pressed together. "You will pay for this." He let out a low growl, and stomped his way towards the opening. He needed distance, but neither of them would leave his sight again.

For a moment, just a moment, she had thought she was something more. Every chance she gave him, he let her down. This wasn't a charade anymore. It had been so easy to overlook Keelin's cruelty thanks to those moments of kindness, but no longer. It all ran like a montage through her mind. That first open palmed slap. The long perilous ride across the desert. Him trying to choke her to death on the mountaintop. Now this.

And I will prove it to you... Exhale ... He had proven enough.

She wouldn't respond. She wouldn't fight him. She would give him whatever he wanted, not because she wanted to. Not because she saw what it could make of her. Because it was her place. She was his slave. A fact she would never forget again.

Matthew Oakley

Chapter 14

Things could not have gone worse for Keelin. He paced the cave muttering profanities and otherwise derogatory phrases under his breath. He had to figure out something. They out maneuvered him at every turn. He wasn't used to being outplayed. Dealing with Nodiah was difficult. Dealing with them both was impossible.

Jaz approached Nodiah, palms out to show she meant no harm. "Hey now…" her tone was so different, soft, motherly. "I know. I know you want to kill me, but I had to do it. I had to show you." Slowly she knelt down beside Nodiah, but she didn't deserve a reaction either. "I know it hurts. He made you feel and believe things you had never experienced before, but he is using you sweet…" She sat, running a hand along her leg. "Listen to me. I know it's hard right now, but I can show you how to take that strength, and use it for yourself. You don't have to be someone's pawn. In my village, the women rule everything. They are the strength. They are controlled by no one. They are their own masters. I know it will take time, but when you're ready to see what real freedom feels like, I will be here to show you."

Nodiah should have wanted to rip Jaz's throat out, but she didn't Jaz wasn't trying to take Keelin from her. She was trying to show Nodiah exactly what she was to him. It's exactly what she said she would do. She had truly believed he wanted to protect her, teach her, and free her, but no. She was just his weapon to wield. She needed contact. She needed to feel something other than this. Jaz guided Nodiah's head into her lap, stroking her hair. She murmured soft nothings as a mother does to a child, until eventually Nodiah fell asleep.

Keelin looked back, completely in disbelief as he saw Nodiah asleep in Jaz's lap. This made even less sense. There was no way he could sleep.

He'd wake up dismembered like the King, or chained and thrown in the ocean, or who knows what other horrible fate these two could come up with.

He watched on, shifting to the sand just outside the front of the cave and leaning his head back on a rock. The rain had let up, but things were still uncomfortably wet. As he sat, he felt a slight poke in his leg. He pulled out the dagger that was still in his pocket, looking it over carefully. Whatever it was, it was the only leverage he had now. He had to keep it. He clutched it tight to his chest, and laid his head back on the rock trying all he could to stay awake, but eventually he lost the fight.

Nodiah's eyes popped open as she realized Jaz had moved. She pushed herself up quickly and swung her head around as her vision adjusted to the darkness. Near the entrance was Jaz, standing over Keelin with the dagger in her hands. She was conflicted. He deserved it. Not like this though. Not by her. In a few light strides, Nodiah propelled herself forward and collided into Jaz with everything she had. She began flailing, scratching, hitting and doing all she could to inflict damage quickly. "Stop! STOP!" Jaz screamed from under Nodiah. Jaz was stronger, but every shift she made Nodiah countered. "I wasn't" Nodiah's nails raked down on her cheek, drawing blood.

Keelin woke up and immediately scurried back from the fray. He watched as Nodiah savagely beat on Jaz. She was doing everything to protect herself, but it was having very little effect. The blows to Jaz's head seemed to stun her, but Nodiah just kept going. Keelin had to decide how to intervene without furthering the rifts between them. "Nodiah... NODIAH! I'm okay... thank you." Keelin walked over, grabbing the dagger back from Jaz's hand. He was unsure if she would actually stop, but that weapon was important.

Jaz laid there for a moment, angry, hurt, and gasping. "It's nothing," she snarled between breaths. "It's mine. A reminder of my past. I wasn't trying to kill you. We have a deal. If I were trying to kill you I wouldn't use that thing." Her words were separated by heavy breaths as she tried to recover, but they seemed honest.

"Well then you won't mind if Nodiah hangs onto it." He handed the dagger back to Nodiah. "If it really means nothing why are you trying so hard to get it back?" He knew he wouldn't get an answer. Nodiah took it in her hand, smiling at Jaz's displeasure over her having it. Why did it mean so much? It seemed old, but not particularly sharp or practical.

She moved back towards the fire, when they all heard noises approaching the entrance of the cave. Jaz took the opportunity to snatch up her belt and her blow darts. Birds took flight, trees bent, and the noise grew. Whatever was coming was doing so quickly. "Your crew found us." Keelin's gut reaction. It didn't feel right though. It didn't sound right. Someone was running. So Keelin ran out to meet it.

As soon as he made his way into the treeline, he became aware of what was coming. A large grey creature with fangs extending down past it's jaw, with a massive neck and shoulders was barreling in his direction. It was canine in nature, but much larger than even his own wolves. Its body was broad like a bear. A scruffy thick lion-like mane extended from its neck to its front shoulders. He backed slowly as the creature slowed and began sizing him up. They stood eye to eye. He had no chance fighting this thing alone.

Something moved in the bushes causing the creature to turn its head, and Keelin took his chances. He ran full sprint back towards the others. "GET TO THE BACK OF THE CAVE! NOW!" There was nowhere else to go.

Nodiah froze, clutching the dagger, which suddenly felt very small. Jaz must have seen the hesitation in her eyes. She grabbed her by the shoulders and forced her behind a rock farther back in the cave. Nodiah could still hear the beast approaching. She watched as Jaz grabbed her pistol, and the chain that had bound her. Maybe Jaz armed would be a bigger help against whatever this was.

Jaz left Nodiah and approached Keelin slowly. "What the hell is that thing?" She asked in a low voice, never taking her eyes off of the creature. "They're fast, and they go after anything that moves, we should name it a Jaz," he snickered. "Striders. I didn't know any were left." As the creature stared them down, it seemed to be planning, thinking... Keelin continued moving slowly farther into the cave until he finally felt something brush against the back of his thigh.

"Now isn't the time Nodi, come on." He immediately felt another firm push up against his rear. This was not the time to play games. "Seriously? I'm glad you're ok but..." He reached his hand back and was shocked to feel a coarse coat of fur. "Nodi, don't move." He glanced back slowly. Behind him stood a much smaller version of the strider that was in front of them. They were in their cave.

A second cub made its presence known from a crevice higher up in the cave wall. It seemed that with all of the exhaustion, fighting, and drama, they had never noticed the pair of youngling that had been hanging around watching them the whole time. Keelin did what he felt was natural, and picked up the one behind him. He pushed it out towards the open so that the presumed mother could see it. Shortly after, the second followed. They wandered towards the mouth of the cave, rubbing up against the large one. A series of quips and grunts escaped the little ones, and for the moment all seemed well.

Keelin made his presence known, moving closer. He held his hands low, and crouched as he approached the beast. It leaned back in defense, and showed its teeth, but Keelin continued. He got within a few feet, then an arms length, then extended his hand. He wasn't sure if he was about to lose an arm, but he had an unnatural sense of safety. He believed in what he was doing with all of his being. The strider leaned forward, pressing its muzzle up against his hand. He slowly pulled his hand back as he called out to the others. "It's ok… I think…"

"NOOO!" A new voice entered the picture. A young, wiry string of a man appeared from beyond the trees, blocking the line between Jaz and the strider. "Please don't hurt her." Keelin turned back with a scowl as he noticed Jaz holding her dart gun, getting ready to fire.

Attention turned back to the man in front of him. He was 18 at best, wearing some sort of camouflage that blended in rather well with the surroundings. He held a large book in one hand, and a machete on his hip. "The striders are protective, but they aren't mean. She was just protecting her young. I'm sorry if my friend startled you." He calmly approached the strider, and stroked its side. It began to pant and turn into the man's touch happily. "We have gone a long way to protect them. They are very rare creatures." The mom laid on the ground in front of him as the man turned back to the three outsiders.

"My name is Aeroaunt, but most call me Aero, and I have to ask... what are you all doing out here?" It wasn't a threat. More inquisitive than anything. Nodiah put on her White Wolf attire and made her way out towards Keelin, but Jaz responded before she could get there.

"None of your business what we are doing out here boy. But I'd look after this pet of yours more closely. It was almost the end of her." Nodiah quickly cut her off.

"Peace… We are just traveling, Aero is it? Your friend gave us quite a scare is all. Have you had any run-ins with anyone else tonight?" She asked, thinking of the Sea Hawks.

Aero took in the trio, now a bit more out in the open. A small smile began creeping up the corners of his mouth, and then a full on laugh bellowed out. "I....I'm sorry. Did I miss a Spirit Festival or something? What are you all supposed to be dressed as?" Nodiah took in their group as a whole, and realized that to anyone else they must have looked like quite the odd bunch. She returned the laugh a little, but let him continue. Everyone finally relaxed a bit.

"My people have roamed this area for decades, protecting the circle of life here. It is important, though we aren't even sure why. We were just told to protect it. I was out wandering, and came across a fire out on the lookout, and numerous things, when my friend here showed up. I asked her to take me to you by using your scent, and here we are!

You can imagine her surprise when the invaders we were chasing wound up being in her home. You would be a bit angry as well." Keelin ducked his head, a little embarrassed he didn't inspect the cave more carefully. "If you need a place to sleep tonight you can join us. It's not far." The offer seemed sincere. He couldn't help but think that any kind of settlement would be better than the cave. Engagement with other people, food, and a proper fire sounded amazing.

Aero ran back into the trees, and came out with a large sack. He set it down in front of them, and unrolled it to reveal all of Nodiah and Keelin's things. They both were truly relieved to see their possessions. Keelin marveled at the tracking ability of the beast. Especially considering the detour to the Vendetta, and the rain that was falling before. Following them would've been nearly impossible.

"Ladies? Shall we join him?" Keelin wasn't making this decision alone. He wouldn't be blamed for whatever trouble it brought. He wasn't sure what to make of the young man, but something still didn't sit right.

Nodiah immediately moved towards her things, particularly her bow which she grabbed off the ground and inspected. As soon as she did, Jaz swiped it from her. The anger instantly re-ignited as they stared each other down. "What are you doing with this? You have no right. Imagine, a slave girl carrying around a relic of the Majila warriors. It's shameful!"

Nodiah stood her ground. "It was my gift. It was my right after passing the trials. Nahko gave it to me. It is *Mine*." The last word coming out in more of a snarl. She spun around to Keelin, quickly making up her mind. "Keelin, let her go with him. We need to keep moving. She has caused nothing but problems, and she will only slow us down." She trailed off as she read the hesitation in his face. He wanted, or needed, something from Jaz. Why couldn't he see they were better off on their own? Jaz shot Keelin a knowing smirk, and awaited his reply as well.

Keelin knew leaving Jaz would be a mistake. She would simply rally her crew and track them down again. They didn't need to be hunted. At the same time, he had no intention of actually letting Jaz get to the Oracle. There had to be another way. This stop could give him a chance to come up with the plan. "After all we've been through, I think some rest and some time with people other than these two would be welcome. Besides, we're running low on supplies. I'm sure your people are willing traders Aero?"

"Oh of course. It's what we specialize in!." Keelin began to wonder how he didn't know anything about Aero or his people. They weren't that far from home, and he had traveled far and wide. In spite of that, he had no idea who, or what they were.

"Then lead on friend…" He didn't look to Nodiah or Jaz for approval, instead following Aero and the strider away from the cave. Nodiah resigned herself to following Keelin, but not before grabbing her bow back from Jaz. She knew they had the advantage for now.

They walked mostly in silence, with just a bit of chat here and there to pass the time. Keelin figured they were moving away from the water, but his internal compass was off, which was odd. At one point it felt as if they had turned a circle, and yet the landscape was completely unfamiliar.

Finally, voices, laughter, and music burst through the trees. They moved into a bustling village that popped up from nowhere. Tents formed rings around a large central fire. Nodiah could feel her heart lift at the sound of music. Her hips involuntarily began to sway to the beat. It had been so long since she had danced of her own accord. Nothing could wipe the smile from her face as they followed Aero.

"Let me lead." Aero moved out in front and spoke out in a fascinating collection of noises. It was very intricate yet melodic in nature. It hardly sounded like a language at all, but it worked. In a matter of moments they were being welcomed.

Matthew Oakley

Chapter 15

A rather stout looking older man was the first to greet them. He stood a few inches taller than Keelin, and much broader in the shoulders and waist. He wore a leather hood which seemed a little out of place, but Keelin didn't think much of it. His voice was deep, but friendly. "Welcome, welcome! Aero tells us you need some supplies. You are welcome to stay as long as you'd like. Rest up, and when you're ready to start talking business, come find me. I'll be happy to show you what we have available."

Keelin studied the man for a moment. "We appreciate the hospitality… Who are you exactly?" He didn't mean to be rude, but not knowing was a feeling Keelin was not fond of.

The man smiled, and moved aside clearing the way to the fire. "Why don't you find out for yourself?" Keelin had a moment of hesitation, but they all made their way closer.

Only a few moments had passed, before they were offered exotic looking skewers of what they could only guess was bird meat of some kind, along with a mixture of vegetables. Keelin took a small bite, and then proceeded to devour the first. The flavor was better than anything he could remember having at the Den. He had to know the secret.

Aero led them to a row of logs, and motioned for them to sit. As they did, Keelin and Nodiah shared a smile. He honestly had no idea where their relationship stood, but that could wait. Something new was a welcome distraction.

"Our performance should start soon." Aero informed them.

"Performance? Is this a nightly thing Aero?" Keelin wondered out loud.

"Of course. We have to keep the Creators happy. Do you care to dance with us?" They were performing for the Creators? These people got more and more interesting with every new detail.

"Me?... No no... but she does." Keelin gleefully pointed to Nodiah just as the beat of two massive drums began filling the air. There was no hesitation. Nodiah's soul was glowing at the sound of the percussion. She hadn't heard music since she killed the King. That was an altogether different kind of celebration. She didn't know what Creators these people worshipped, and she honestly didn't care. She just knew that the empty space in her heart was filled by the idea of getting to dance.

She shook out her hair, dropping her bundle and her bow at Keelin's feet. She immediately moved into the throng of people who were beginning to shake and jump about, hands raised to the open sky above them. She pointed one toe, her hips cocked to the left, and spread her arms out on either side of her body. She slowly, fluidly, began moving, leaning all the way behind her until the tips of her hair nearly touched the ground. With a quick movement she leapt into the air, and sprung back, flipping and landing lightly on the balls of her feet.

The others began to circle the fire, and she moved with them, flowing like a warm current of air around the blaze. She pulled Aero towards her, moved her wrists into his hands, and began to spin. She threw her head back and let out a real laugh from somewhere deep in her belly as she turned faster and faster. Her mind shut off. This was freedom.

Jaz tore into one of the skewers, and sat down next to Keelin. "I can see why you came to get her." The Captain mused after a moment of silence. "She is something special. Beautiful... but dangerous." The last word hung in Keelins mind. Dangerous? Not now. Not like this. Watching her dance was inspiration. It came so naturally. This was his Sky Dancer.

As they continued, the pace quickened. The music got louder. Yells of excitement began rising up from the crowd. The fire itself seemed like it was dancing, pulsing up to the sky as other torches around them were lit. More wood was added, and the party continued.

Nodiah separated herself and began a solo for Aero, smiling at the overwhelmed look on his face. Eventually he spoke, "You are very skilled! It's like you're dancing on air!" He joined her in her laughter as she continued the dance. "The Golden Dragon would love to watch you I'm sure." As if on cue, a group of men in an elaborate two headed dragon costume appeared from beyond the trees. They made their way towards the fire.

Several men comprised the body, and two filled the heads. The dragon looked up to the sky, and a burst of flame shot out from one of its mouths.

Inhale...

Keelin watched on in sudden horror... Fire Breathers. He had found them. He clutched his sword, and began approaching Nodiah. He had to get her out of there.

Before he could get too far Keelin felt hand on his shoulder, pulling him back firmly. "Keelin wait. What are you going to do?" Jaz did her best to reason with him. "There are too many of them. You're going to put her in danger. We need a plan."

She was right, but he hardly heard her. "My plan... is to murder them." Keelin said through clenched teeth, his body pulsing with every breath. His eyes scanned the room. The old man, could it be? Could he be the one? No... Maybe...

He surveyed the scene and took in just how many people were around. Jaz was right. There had to be an advantage somewhere. As they continued the celebration, Keelin noticed they all had something in their hands. A small black stone of some kind. They would raise it up to their lips before blowing out streams of fire into the air. Was this the key to this ability? Maybe it was just a trick? He still made his way towards Aero and Nodiah. Keelin had to get her out.

"Careful friend. Don't wear her out. We have a long way to go tomorrow." Aero looked disappointed at the news. Nodiah glanced at Keelin irritably. Then she picked up on the anger, and worry that he was trying so desperately to hide. She felt it.

"Go? Do you have to leave so soon?" Aero cocked his head, studying Keelin carefully.

"I'm afraid so. We have a long journey ahead. Tell me though. Are there more? Of your people? Of the Fire Breathers?" Keelin asked cautiously. The question was mainly to ensure Nodiah was aware of what was happening. She was, but she wondered how these peaceful people could be the same. They couldn't be.

"A few. We are far less in number than we once had been. But we've run across a group or two." Aero was hiding something. Keelin could smell it. The situation was escalating. Others were paying attention.

"And why is it that you move around? Travel so much?" He was careful not to express too much emotion. This was not an interrogation, and Aero feeling threatened was the last thing he wanted.

"We are always being chased. In the past, the Fire Breathers did some terrible things. They hurt a lot of people. Now that we don't have the strength we once did, many people come looking for revenge." Keelin watched as Aero now turned the questioning on him. "You aren't... looking for revenge... are you?"

He didn't get the chance to answer. A loud whistle rang out through the air, cutting above the music. All eyes turned to Jaz who stood smiling confidently. Behind her, the Hawks sprung from their hiding places in the treeline and roared to life. As they poured into the camp, Keelin noted there seemed to be more than he saw on the ship.

Chaos broke free. Now it looked like Keelin had organized the whole thing however. There's no way they'd believe him. Why was Jaz helping them now? Was this even help? They had been following them the whole time.

The Fire Breathers were well organized. They didn't seem phased by the sudden attack, filing into straight lines and raining fire down on the crew. This truly wasn't the first time they had been ambushed. The crew didn't seem too bothered either, and in fact seemed excited by the challenge. All Keelin knew was that this wasn't going to end well.

He couldn't stop what had already begun. He also couldn't leave without getting the answer to the one question that wouldn't leave his mind. He charged off, searching for the large man that greeted them.

It didn't take long to find him. He almost seemed to be expecting Keelin's approach, as he stood his ground facing the Wolf. "Were you there? Do you remember her?" It was vague, but it caught his attention.

Nodiah was left to make sense of it all. She had never witnessed the atrocity of battle before. Once more, she was in shock. To make matters worse, he ran off without explanation. She had to find him. "Keelin!" She cried as he approached the Elder.

She saw the looks between the two men. Something awful was about to happen. "We… You have to stop this! This can't be what we came for." She could see he wasn't hearing her. His grip on his sword tightened, and she could swear there was smoke coming from the larger man's nostrils. She had to stop this. Defiantly, she moved herself between the two, facing Keelin. "These are not the same people. Let it go."

Nodiah now stood between Keelin and what he wanted, again. He closed his eyes, and when he opened them, all he could see was Genevieve standing before him. He grabbed her wrist, and pulled her behind him. The village burned, screams rang out, panic and confusion and pain… Wait… No… something was wrong.

He turned expecting to see the other Dragon, but there was only Nodiah. The line between past and present continued to blur until his eyes met the eyes of the man across from him. Through gritted teeth and watery eyes, he asked again. "Were you there? Northern tip of the Isle of Skye... A village called Iris. A raiding party killed a young girl, 15, burned her alive. Were... you... there?"

The older man snorted, placing his hands on his hips. "I've seen a lot of death in my day young man..." Keelin wasn't amused, but let him continue. "But no… these men though vicious and violent, are not heartless. I may know who did though. Call off your men." It was a risk. This could lead to a slaughter, but Keelin had to know.

He looked to Nodiah. "Keelin, please. These people don't have to die. This isn't why we came." She was right.

"JAZ! ENOUGH!" His roar echoed. It was not a question, or a request. The old man took a large inhale and shot out a distinct blue flame. There was no trick with his. He then let a roar of his own, and the fighting stopped.

Exhale…

Jaz approached, sizing up the Elder, her blood-lust still running hot. "Well?!?" Nodiah's eyes filled with tears, relieved that the overwhelming battle had ended. The relief faded quickly when she took a long look at the triangle that had now formed, and her stomach dropped. It felt as if they had taken a turn down the wrong path.

Keelin began explaining himself as Aero rushed towards the group. "This was not a planned ambush. Those men are not mine. They were tracking me, not you. I didn't even know they were there."

"I did find the belongings of these two. They had traveled alone. It seems the Corsair joined them later." Aero's explanation brought a smile to the assumed leader, and a few chuckles throughout.

"So it is her that is Captain," he pointed to Jaz taking a step forward.

"Answer me Dragon." Keelin's anger was loaded internally, ready to lash out at a moment's notice. "Who?"

"My name is Sparrow, and the man you are after... Tattoos on his head? A scar in his torso?"

Keelin smiled cockily, "I gave him that mark." Sparrow eyed him up and down and then let out a loud laugh.

"You?! You're the boy from his story all grown up?" Keelin gripped his sword. "My my... what a pleasant surprise. Dreugan, usually roams the Northern Glen. He is who you seek. He is my brother. Though, let me warn you boy." Sparrow closed the gap, his own intensity growing. "Dreugan is not just a Fire Breather, or an Elder Dragon, he IS a Dragon... He is merciless, careless, kills without compassion or delay. He burns, and slaughters, and takes and never thinks twice. Can you imagine what he's going to do to the boy who pierced him? He will chew you up, spit you out, and crush whatever it is you care about. He's been waiting... for you... and he will enjoy hurting you."

Keelin's eyes never wavered. He smiled in return as both men refused to flinch. He finally let out a small chuckle of his own. "He'll enjoy it. That's good. Well maybe, maybe friend, one of your men can send a message to him hm?" He locked eyes with Jaz for a moment, and then to Nodiah. "Ladies, time to go."

As he turned back to Sparrow, his sword came with. It effortlessly ran Sparrow through, and punctured out of his back. "YOU TELL HIM THAT KEELIN AND THE WOLVES ARE COMING FOR HIM! And my dear friend, I am not the hunted. I am the hunter." He pulled his sword clean, and while the others took a moment to gather what had just happened, he grabbed Nodiah and started running back towards the rest of their things.

Keelin could hear Jaz cackle and call out "Cover us boys, then meet me at the rendezvous." She then charged after Keelin and Nodiah. Nodiah's eyes rounded out in horror. These weren't the men that Keelin had been looking for. They had offered them hospitality. The trials, the Prophecy, the Black Wolf... all of it was meaningless behind Keelin's thirst for revenge. If it came down to protecting her, or getting to Dreugan, it was pretty clear what he would choose.

As they gathered their bundles, Jaz and Aero approached, though Aero didn't seem happy about it. "What now eh? You seem to have a plan, but we have a deal." Jaz rang out. They moved from the camp, and made their way into the trees nearby before stopping to have a full conversation.

"Yeah well the deal was off the moment your boys popped into camp. Your side of the deal involved us not being followed remember? You lost good men today, and you don't even care. Their blood is on your hands Jaz. Yours." He held is sword in front of him just in case. This wasn't up for discussion. "I'm sure you're used to getting what you want, but not this time. So take your deals, and your boat, and sail off." His attention turned fully to Nodiah. "Are you alright?"

Jaz didn't give her the chance to answer. "You're right. You think you're so clever don't you Keelin? Do you really think you have all the answers? You walk around like you own everything, but do you? You are alone. You have no choices... but she does." Jaz arched a brow at Nodiah. "What do you say girl? Do you still want to be his slave? You saw what he just did. Come with me and see what freedom really is."

Nodiah sensed all of the feeling draining out of her once more. Of course not. She didn't want to be a slave to anyone anymore. Jaz was the freest woman she had ever met. She was powerful, dangerous, and independent. If Nodiah went with her, would she have that? Could she? A choice.

Keelin was the first person to ever offer her a choice. A thousand images flashed through her mind. Everything that had happened. Everything that was said. One phrase stood out from it all. One thing she held onto that he said to her.

And I will set you free

"No." The word sprang from her of its own volition. "I won't go with you. I won't. Now go, please." She looked meaningfully at Aero. He didn't deserve this either. The innocent boy she had been dancing with only a few moments ago.

Jaz weighed her options, then turned to the battle which had resumed. Her men were losing. "Fine. Go. We'll cover you, but know I will come for you." She sneered directly at Keelin. "You'll realize this was a mistake. You'll need me again, and you know it. The Hawks will be watching. I will be waiting. You will be back." She approached Keelin, pressing her body against his, and tracing a finger along his neck bite. "This is not over." She attempted to take a kiss from him, but he was ready. He extended the palm of his hand against her cheek and pressed her face away. She recovered, straightened herself out, and then walked towards the battle, shouting out orders for her men to regroup. They were free of the Captain, for now.

They both looked to Aero, and were admittedly saddened. He seemed like a good person in the wrong place at the wrong time. "Thank you for defending us. I'm sorry it came to this." Nodiah wrapped her arms around him, unsure of what he'd do or say. As they broke, he smiled, and then ran back into the village.

Then they left... Just the two of them.

Chapter 16

They made a little more distance between themselves and the Fire Breathers before Keelin stopped and turned to face Nodiah. A sudden burst of energy seemed to radiate as they locked eyes, truly seeing each other for the first time in a while. The tension was almost choking as he struggled for the right words. "Nodiah, you are." His emotions were ahead of him. He just wanted to embrace her and say nothing. He wanted to forget the last two days, and go back to the Den. He wanted so much, and yet what he wanted just didn't matter.

He wiped the sweat from his brow. As he looked around, the glow of fire in the direction they came from let them know they weren't safe yet. "You are amazing." It was soft, but he knew she heard it. "We can sort this out later, kill me if you want. Lets just get away from here. Don't give them the pleasure." It was meant purely as motivation. Keelin didn't really know what to expect next, or where to go from here. They just had to get away.

More time passed until they sat for a moment to rest against some larger rocks. As he sat, she stood in front of him, placing his cheeks in her hands and making sure he looked her right in the eyes as she spoke. "I don't want to kill you Keelin." Her tone was quiet, calm, and almost eerie in its own way. "I just want to understand..." He didn't deserve death anyways. He had more people to answer to than just her, and she knew it. She glanced quickly at the bite mark on his neck, which only confirmed her line of thought.

He paused. How long until she hated him again? How long until she ran off unsure of anything? She was a portal of chaos that left devastation behind her wherever she went. The King... dead... the Wolves... infiltrated... Jaz and crew... being slaughtered by Fire Breathers most likely. But that was the way of the White Wolf. In a way, it just confirmed how important she was. The world was out to stop her, and they had continued to stay one step ahead.

He didn't respond, instead choosing the direction he thought would take them back to the castle. They made their way up to some higher ground, hoping to get a general layout of the land but still the awkward silence remained.

Finally, as they climbed the hill, he spoke. "You still dance as beautifully as ever. It makes you happy. That's what make it beautiful." As soon as the words escaped Keelin's mouth, he regretted them, though he didn't know why. He awaited a snappy reply, and continued moving.

"It does," she agreed, " When I'm not put on display. When I can dance just because, that makes me feel free. It makes me happy." She pondered his identity once more. His home, The Isle of Skye, was just one more piece of the puzzle. She took his hand, and asked honestly. "What makes you happy Keelin?"

He wasn't sure he remembered the meaning of the word. "I wish I knew Nodi. Maybe there's still a chance for me to find it out there." He bowed his head and thought a moment longer. "You. You being happy. That makes me happy." Finally they reached the hilltop, just as the sun peaked out over the mountains in the distance. He sat, and leaned back on his hands. His eyes turned up to the few stars left in the sky, and stopped thinking.

It wasn't the answer Nodiah wanted. She heaved a sigh of discontent. He was a free man who could do what he pleased, and yet he could find no happiness of his own. She sank down to her knees behind him, running a finger along his spine. It always surprised her just how much tension his body carried. "I hope I can help you find some happiness of your own. It's important." She whispered. If he had no happiness to look forward to, what was the point in any of this? Would his quests ever end? He was less free than she thought.

He gave into her touch, leaning back some, but he couldn't help but be a little worked up at her words. "The Fire Breathers took that from me. I'll be happy when I get even." He let out an exhausted yawn, and closed his eyes. "We still heading to the Oracle?" It was intended more to see where her heart was, and test her resolve. Was she still committed to seeing this through?

Her response was simple. "Yes, but we need rest don't you think?" She slid down, and they both laid back, his head cradled against her midsection as she ran fingers through his hair.

The next thing Keelin remembered was the sweat running down his nose as the sun continued to rise higher into the sky. He felt Nodiah's weight against him, and in a way that was a comfort. She was still there.

Somewhat rejuvenated, he gently sat up. They had so much to figure out. They had to rebuild the trust that was once there. For now, they had to put the past behind. "Ya know, I could get used to this. Waking up next to you I mean."

Nodiah yawned loudly before scrunching up her face and squinting in the morning light. As her eyes adjusted she found herself looking up at Keelin. "Yeah?" She inquired playfully. She reached forward, grabbing his arms and then flipping him over onto his back. She rolled through, landing on top of him, straddling his hips. She laughed, proud of herself for catching him off guard.

Her stomach grumbled loudly in discomfort, as she placed a hand over her gut. "Could we maybe wake up somewhere with a bed, and a kitchen?" She asked hopefully. She ran her fingers through her hair trying to untangle the mess of salt water, dirt, ash, blood, and smoke. "And maybe a bath?" More serious issues loomed. There were discussions to be had, like Keelin killing the Elder even though he was an innocent man... Not helping Aero... she pushed those thoughts away for the time being.

It was a beautiful day, and it was back to just her and him. There was a chance to restore things to what they were supposed to be. As soon as they found some food.

He couldn't disagree. A kitchen... a bed... even a bathroom would be a welcome sight. "I'd kill for a hot shower too..." The momentary look of horror in Nodiah's eyes made him aware of his poor wording. "You know what I meant. We definitely need to find a meal. Think we can reach Torek today?"

He wasn't sure why he thought she'd know. She seemed to have some instinct though. It distracted his mind from her, but once their eyes met, he couldn't help himself. He lunged forward, kissing with a short, passionate kiss, and then another, words stuttering out in between. "I... am.... famished..." A smile took over his face. He raised his hand to hide it, but it was no use.

She rolled her shoulders into a shrug, drawing out her answer. "Mmmaaaybe..." She bit her lip, wandering her eyes up as if deep in thought. She bounced up onto her feet, and then pulled him up locking her arms around his neck. "I can't think straight right now. Lets eat, get our bearing, and then we can figure out the plan."

Honestly, she was surprised he didn't want to make his way back to the Den. She didn't mention it however. She continued to observe, staring up at him from under her long lashes. Something about him seemed different today, almost boyish in the morning light. She wanted to remember this side of him. She stood up on her toes and pressed another kiss onto his lips.

It was all refreshing to him. He didn't need food, she gave him sustenance. The truth was, the rations in his bag were low. This trip wasn't meant to be so long. They were going to restock in the Fire Breather camp. "Well my dear, we have three choices. One, we go back to the village and see what's left, and steal some food. Two, we hunt. Three, we resort to cannibalism!!" He said with a bit of a sadistic smile.

"That seems more like Jaz's thing," she quickly retorted, pointing towards Keelin's neck. It was harsh, but one he thankfully laughed off.

He got into his things, and threw a small bag of various nuts and oats in her direction. "It's something. May not taste great, but it'll give you a boost."

Nodiah rolled her eyes, and began digging through her own possessions. "We don't have to steal anything. Our friend the Captain may have left some coin behind." She produced the small leather pouch that Jaz had on her. It clinked as she bounced it off her palm.

"Well looks like Jaz proves herself useful once more. Now we just have to find somewhere to use it." Something in her eyes looked unsatisfied with everything. She wasn't settled. "Alright, what is it? What do you want to know? I suppose I owe you an explanation?" He sat on the ground once more. "Though walking and talking may be more advantageous to us. Maybe we can find some food, sit down, and I'll answer any and every question you have. Face to face, eye to eye, honest answers. You have my word." His stomach was doing the talking, but he also just had a need to be somewhere. They had been in feels, and trees, and hills far too long. He needed culture, buildings, people, and places to hide.

She glanced towards him as she re-tied her bundle. She had many thoughts about their present situation, but in the end one feeling remained. "You don't owe me anything…" She responded quietly. She stood, dusting off her knees and slinging the bundle over her shoulder. "If you want to explain yourself, that's your choice. I'm here still. That should say enough." She began walking down the hill, taking the lead. "Come on. Can't be too far from some city can we?"

"Wait… Nodi I can't…" The words just didn't come. "What I mean is... I just… I want…"

YOU WANT WHAT? She wanted to scream. It seemed he was so close to saying what needed to be said. It never came. Finally he forcefully threw his arms around her, squeezing her tight against him. There was so far to go, but they had come so far.

She could feel his chest rising with his breaths against her. She felt safe again. The emotion radiated from him as she placed her hand over his heart. "Keelin…" she whispered. It was intended to be comforting, but it came out drenched in need.

He took his time, hanging on to that moment as long as he could. "Right, to civilization then. We should keep moving. I'm sure if we stay in one place too long, something will find us. Yet I fear we haven't yet faced the worst." It was a harrowing thought, but most likely true.

"Whenever we do, we will together." She smiled, looking up into his eyes once more.

His spirits enlightened, his heart hopeful, they began their journey back. "Tell me something. What's the best thing you've ever eaten? There must have been something in that castle you enjoyed." He was hoping to keep their minds clear for a change, but he wasn't sure how well it'd work.

Nodiah scooped his elbow into her arms and leaned against his shoulder as they walked. She bit the inside of her cheek as she thought of her answer. There was a lot. "OH! Ice cream!" She let out a small giggle at the thought. "You can imagine it's quite rare out here, but one of the only times I left the castle, we took some artifacts of the Oracle's to a shrine North in the Horuk mountains, and the monks served us ice cream." She let out a sigh of longing, wiping her mouth at the thought of the delectable cold treat. She paused, peeking up at him sidelong. "How about you?"

"Ice cream huh? I've never ha... Wait wait wait. The Oracle? You what?" His mind tried to wrap around the concept but it was failing. "Do you think maybe you could've mentioned sooner that you and the Oracle were pals? You were a Vessel?"

Nodiah gritted her teeth. "We... are... not... pals," she snarled. "She wasn't awake. I was... dismissed from her service. Deemed unworthy." The word left a bitter taste on her tongue. Her eyes flashed with the darkness of the memory once more. She could feel the cold metallic bite of the collar. She barely heard Keelin move into his answer, trying to refocus herself.

For Keelin, Nodiah being deemed unworthy seemed impossible. "Some Oracle. She may see glimpses of the future, but can't see the greatness staring her in the face. Why are we going back again?" He let out a soft chuckle. She still was clearly bothered by his latest slip up.

"I've never had ice cream, but I've heard it's wonderful." He began thinking of his own answer, trying to defuse the situation. "Our family used to make this stew, following an ancient tradition. We call it comhla. We'd use the best meats, whatever we could afford or hunt, and everyone got to pick something to add to the pot. Sometimes it was downright awful, but when it was right, it was magic. It was home.

One night in particular, it was just... perfect. My mother had brought this amazing bright blue flower. She plucked the petals and threw them in. They were just little pieces of heaven." He hadn't thought of his mom in quite some time. Or any family for that matter. The memories mostly burned with the rest of Iris. It was such a good flashback though, he couldn't help but smile.

"That sounds nice. Homely. The closest I've come to family is..." she wanted to say *you*, but couldn't bring herself to do so. "The harem wasn't the friendliest place. We were together, but always in competition. Made it hard to trust one another. Real sisters." Her mind wandered off once more as she rubbed her neck uncomfortably, just to ensure the collar wasn't there.

On the horizon, a welcome site broke their conversation. Smoke... Smoke meant people. "There! Look!" He pointed it out excitedly, hoping this village would be friendlier than the last. The idea of a shower or a bath and a drink sounded better than even ice cream or comhla at this point.

Nodiah's stomach grumbled at the site, chasing away all the dark thoughts. She laughed happily and tugged at his arm urging him forward. "I've come a long way when a place like this excites me," she said over her shoulder as they both started taking in the details of where they were running.

The rugged landscape gave away little details about their destination, but as they got closer more trails of smoke lifted up into the air. This wasn't the raging black smoke from Dragon fire. These were lines of puffy white clouds reaching up to the sky. Trees surrounded the town, creating a perfect outline. They couldn't wait to break through the trees and see what was in store.

Without warning, Keelins perspective flipped, literally. He fell hard to the ground, and was drug back, and then up into the air. Nodiah jumped, fearing for a moment that they were once again under attack. Their list of enemies was growing at every turn. Looking down at the ground, and at an upside down Nodiah, he realized he had been snared. "A hunter trap, not meant for man. These are good people Nodi, I know it."

Finally catching her breath, Nodi's fear turned to laughter. The great Keelin, hanging in the air like some sort of game animal. "Oh yes, good people. They have my blessing I'm sure. Even if they attack us, this... this is worth it."

He ignored her laughter and yelled out into the warm air. "HELLLOO!! WE MEAN YOU NO HARM!" and waited.

Nodiah stepped forward until she was right next to him, just a few inches from his face. "Shall I cut you down?" She pretended to be considering her choices. "What do I get out of it?"

Keelin was able to keep his spirits high, but he didn't like this feeling of helplessness. Her confidence was refreshing at least. She was enjoying this. "Cut me down, untie me, whatever. Just get me down please." He hoped she wouldn't leave him. She could easily dance into the village and leave him hanging, but she wouldn't do that... would she?

She thought about it. She really did. But at the end of the day their list of enemies was too long for her to leave him there. For her safety as much as his. She patted herself, and came across Jaz's dagger. She found where the snare was anchored and used the dagger to cut through it, dumping Keelin down on his head.

"Now if you're done fooling around can we please find something to eat?" Her smile showed how pleased she was with herself. It was a much needed sight. It was so light and carefree. He brushed off the dirt, and started marching towards the village, his pride clearly a little hurt. He kept waiting for the next attack, the next fight, the next obstacle, but it just didn't come.

As they reached the first row of buildings, the city revealed itself. It was large but had a very rustic feel to it. Nothing was too flashy. Everything seemed practical and efficient in design. People were wandering about, each consumed with their daily routine but smiling and happy for the most part. A few took notice of the outsiders, but none seemed bothered by them.

Keelin looked to Nodiah, and couldn't hide the excitement on his face. He wondered if this was a mirage for a moment, but it all was so refreshingly real. "I'll race ya, first one to find the Inn wins." He smiled widely. He knew he was no match for her agility, but he was as fast as anyone. This could be fun. They needed more fun.

She raised her brow at Keelin's challenge. "You're on!" She crowed, giving him a hard shove in hopes of throwing off his balance. She sprinted down the streets, her arms pumping and boots slapping the ground. She entered the market square with Keelin right on her heels.

He watched as she slipped through spaces he just couldn't. Finally his shoulder slammed into what felt like a statue. He stumbled forward, barely managing to keep his balance. "Sorry! Sorry!" he yelled back, but much to his surprise the man simply chuckled and waved him on.

She weaved and dodged her way around meandering patrons, taking in the various wares on display without slowing her pace. Two men carrying a large trunk made their way into her path, but without a second thought she slid low, gracefully gliding under the trunk so quickly they barely noticed. She laughed and tossed a glance over her shoulder to see how Keelin would handle the obstacle.

Then she slammed hard into something, stopping her in her tracks and knocking her off her feet. Something wrapped itself around her, tying her up in a jumble. Panic set in for a moment, until she realized just how soft these restraints were. Finally she popped her head back out into the daylight, and took in the display of silks and fabrics she had completely destroyed.

The furious merchant looked down at her, awaiting an explanation. "I..." She stammered before her eyes caught a deep purple dress. It looked exquisite, embroidered in gold with an intricate swirl pattern. Suddenly she wasn't worried about the merchant.

Simultaneously, Keelin turned back from his apology just in time to smash into the trunk. He flew over the top and then rolled to a stop just near Nodiah's feet. The contents of the trunk spilled out all over the ground. "We are so sorry. We are travelers, and if we damaged anything we will pay for it. This city just looks so happy, and we were just trying to have a little fun. It wasn't intentional." He was still trying to catch his breath.

The three men didn't seem particularly happy. He continued to try and untangle Nodi, and smooth things over as the crowd surrounding them began to grow. Her eyes were still focused on the purple dress as she dislodged herself from the mess. The merchant was beside himself, checking the materials for rips and stains. Nodiah tried to help him, but he just angrily shooed her away. Her hands reached out and touched the soft silk. Then she had a truly amazing thought. "How much for this?"

"Twenty tyrs" he snapped looking at her disapprovingly.

She produced the small sack of coins she took from Jaz, and put forty tyrs in his hand. The merchant suddenly smiled, and asked her if she would like it wrapped up. She bought something for herself. That was freedom.

She turned her attention back to Keelin to see how he was faring with the other two men, while thinking to herself how much she liked this place. "Here let me help you." He moved in and tried to help them, but was forcibly shoved away.

"You've done quite enough my friend." Keelin quickly smelled trouble. There was more to this.

"No, I insist. Please." He leaned down and began shuffling through the loose red fabric that the cargo had been wrapped in. His eyes quickly scanned the area as he went. There was a series of tablets. They told a story, but about what? Again he was pushed back, but as he moved he grasped the material in his fingers which uncovered more of the items.

They were… nothing. Trinkets, pictures, and old stories. Perhaps they were headed to some private collector, but they were of no importance to Keelin. Had he become that paranoid? "I'm sorry. It's been a long journey. I meant no harm." He backed away as the men gathered the rest. Maybe this town didn't have any secrets. Maybe no one was after them here. There had to be more.

His eyes finally met Nodiah's, and most of his paranoia went away. "Let's go get that drink." He smiled, and the two headed on down the street, but Keelin kept alert. He couldn't shake the feeling that something was coming… but maybe it wasn't.

Nodiah pulled him along into a low lit tavern called The Silver Eagle. The place was clouded with the bitter and sweet smell of hookah. Low-lying tables filled the center of the room, surrounded by cushions with elaborate gold and brass hookahs in the middle of each. Every area had a different animal theme to it, but much to Keelin's relief no Wolves, or Dragons, or even striders. There was a strange looking black bird he wasn't familiar with, a rabbit, a snake, a luxurious looking area marked with the tavern's trademark silver eagle, and a few others. The outer edge had some taller tables more designed for eating and drinking.

Still struggling to fully relax, Keelin allowed Nodiah to lead their way to a taller table in the corner where a waitress quickly approached. Her head was shaved, her face was friendly with a warm, inviting smile. "I don't think I've seen you two in here before! Welcome!" She was so cheerful and happy.

"Well we appreciate the hospitality. We aren't from too far away, but just kind of managed to stumble across your town, and it's quite lovely." The woman's eyes squinted a bit as she measured up the duo.

"It has its moments. Never too much going on, but its got a lot of great people. Now what can we get you?" Keelin took a moment to take in her words. Never much going on, what a strange concept. There was always something going on.

"Any specialties? I'm never afraid to try something new." A sly smirk took over the waitresses' face. It was just playful. The level of normalcy in this place was almost infuriating to Keelin.

"I have just the thing... For you hon?" She turned her attention to Nodiah. Keelin did as well, almost challenging her to make a good selection.

Nodiah looked from the waitress back to Keelin, allowing a smirk to cross her own face. "Surprise me as well, so long as it's something spicy." She didn't break contact with Keelin, answering his challenge in her own way.

"My name is Beanfeasa if you need anything. Most people call me Bean." The waitress bowed her head and retreated towards the kitchen.

Nodiah let out a long sigh, releasing the tension from her shoulders. It felt so good to let loose for a moment. Her eyes glanced over Keelin, from the daring look in his eyes, to the bite mark on his neck, to the dirt in his hair from his earlier run in with the snare.

Finally she took in the aromas of the bar. There were so many amazing complex scents, that trying to pick out what each one was almost became a game of its own. She closed her eyes, and focused in as much as she could.

Keelin's eyes shifted around the room. There was a mix of people. Keelin recognized a few insignia from a few towns, but nothing that caused any alarms. Their waitress reappeared from a back room and made her way around the room as Keelin watched. She approached a table nearby that was occupied by three rather rugged looking men. The waitress leaned in, whispered something, and then looked back in Keelin's direction. With a slight smirk she moved on. Keelin couldn't. Maybe this town had secrets after all.

Nodi was debating on a scent. It was sweet like kubli bark, but maybe a little more flowery. She opened her eyes, intending to ask Keelin but instead just watched him as his eyes flicked around the room. She thought about the last few days. How no one would believe the story that led them to being here. Something about them had created a magnetism that neither could escape. She leaned on her hand, "Keelin..." she murmured as she exhaled, almost not even realizing she said it.

Nodi's murmur snapped his attention back to the table. She broke the silence with a simple observation. "It feels so strange to be in a place this... calm... I almost feel out of place." Nodiah considered Bean, her nose crinkling slightly in distaste. Something about this woman made her itch, but she couldn't quite put a finger on it. She was too nice. "I wonder what kind of surprises she has in store for us. Something decent to eat might help a lot of things." It was general small talk, but it was enough.

"What if... Nah forget it." His idea came and passed. It sounded absurd. There's no way it could work. Something would get in the way. They couldn't stay here. They had to keep going.

His thoughts were broken up as Bean brought their food to the table. Whatever it was, smelled fantastic. Keelin's plate had pieces of a golden brown meat, alongside a bed of greens, with the whole thing smothered in a deep red sauce. "What in the world is this?" He asked the waitress.

"You wanted surprised. Eat and I'll tell ya." She chuckled playfully then strolled away as he continued to inspect his food. Nodiah's was a much brighter hue of red, almost orange, reflecting the spiciness she figured. Heat wasn't usually an issue for her though. She was truly excited. Especially for the black rice that was on the side.

"So what's the catch with this place?" Keelin started back the conversation as he debated what to try first. "Monsters? Murderers? Black magic? There has to be something right?" He picked up his first piece of meat, and took a small bite. As he did all of his thoughts faded and a small audible moan escaped his lips. His eyes closed as he allowed his taste buds to enjoy the moment.

She couldn't let the question go though. He started something for a reason. "What if what, Keelin?" She asked, staving off her roaring appetite.

He had almost forgotten he even started the question. "It's silly. We can't... I just..." He sat back and sighed, coming to terms with what he was about to say. "I was going to say what if we just stay here? I mean. I'm pretty sure that even if the Creators themselves came looking for you, you'd find a way to take them down. Let them come." He smiled and took another bite. "But we can't. We have to know, right? I mean. Something will come. It's our destiny... fate... duty. Whatever you call it, we just have to. You have to." It was almost a depressing thought. They had to, but why?

"But, wherever you go, I go. So at least we have each other." That stare, he knew she wanted this to be over as much as he did. She finally had a break from all of that stuff, and yet he had to open his mouth and bring it back. It was time to change subjects.

"What do you think this is? Bird? Hawk maybe? Quill? I've heard Quill is delicious, he smiled." Quill hardly looked edible alive, a mass of spiky black feathers and mean tempers, but supposedly they were a delicacy in some places. "You know Coille has towns that make Quill eggs, Coille Quill is hard to say, but it is rather tasty." He focused on his food, and awaited a response, still looking back to the table with the three men occasionally.

Nodiah finally sank her fork into her dish, mostly out of frustration at him bringing up everything else once more. As she took a bite, the dish exploded to life. She had to stop herself from shoveling the rest in her mouth, knowing it would likely make her sick. "Who cares what it is? It's delicious." The perfect blend of heat and sweetness caused her to let out a small moan of pleasure herself.

After a few minutes of complete concentration on their plates, she thought about what he had said. "I think" she began with a level head, "We stay for a night and see where the land lies. We don't know much yet. We get a room, a bed," her eyes rolled back in pleasure at the thought. "Maybe take a walk in the city later." Her words drifted off. She smiled to herself as she looked down at her plate.

Her response was surprisingly sensible. Nothing about Nodiah made sense. He liked seeing this in her, and yet, he didn't. It was subdued. It was logical. The wildfire in her that burned everything in its path to the ground, also left behind a beautiful, hope filled chaos. That fire was gone. It confirmed they couldn't stay. But for a night, that could be enjoyable. "I think…"

"You enjoying your meal yes? It's good!" Before he could finish, one of the men from the table interrupted. He had a huge smile on his face as he spoke. "I don't mean any trouble friends. I just thought you might need a place to stay! I can help!" Keelin's eyes moved to Nodi, unsure of their new acquaintance. Long brown hair flowed down the large man's back, and a thick set of facial hair framed his face. His figure led to Keelin to think he was a regular of the Silver Eagle as well.

Nodiah's eyes narrowed and cut towards the man, suddenly cold as ice. She gripped the fork in her hand ready to weaponize it. She didn't trust the stranger for a second. They had been through far too much to suddenly have someone shine goodwill on them for no reason. "I'm sorry, who are you?" Keelin responded softly.

"Forgive me! Where are my manners? I am Petyr. I have plenty of room." His smile seemed sincere, but Keelin just couldn't bring himself to fully trusting this man. "Your meal is on me, and when we're done you can come sleep."

"That's very kind, but I don't think my friend could... I mean... we couldn't. I don't want to impose. I just." His eyes looked to Nodiah for help. He truly wasn't sure what to say.

Nodiah forced herself to relax, the tension bleeding out of her as she pushed a seductive smile on her face. "That is, very kind of you sir. But we have been on the road for some time, and I eh," she looked towards Keelin, "I must insist we find our own, more private, lodgings elsewhere. Our journey has been quite long, and I dare say that I intend to have him for myself tonight." She let out a flirtatious laugh, holding the mans gaze hoping her forwardness would be enough for him to withdraw his invitation.

As she finished her sentence Keelin inhaled, and a piece of food became lodged in the wrong place. He began coughing loudly, trying to regain his breath. This only caused Petyr to laugh. "You are a lucky man! But I think you misunderstood. I have an inn up the road. I just come here because our food there, not so good." He said with a smile. Petyr turned back to Keelin. "Are you ok friend?"

He wasn't ok. Keelin had faced countless perils, and was about to be taken out by a piece of mystery meat. Suddenly he was yanked from his seat, wrapped tightly in Petyr's arms. His body flailed back and forth as Petyr squeezed him like a bellows. He was certain his ribs were breaking when finally Petyr swung his entire forearm down onto his spine, knocking him to the floor. As he did, the meat dislodged and shot across the table, hitting Nodiah square in the cheek.

Breath came back to Keelin and his life was restored! His back hurt, his ribs hurt, but he was alive. "Wow! Thank you!" Maybe this new stranger was ok after all? If his intent was to kill Keelin, he would have let him choke.

"That's what we do here in Portis, we help each other! Nothing to be embarrassed of. Just last week Miro over there almost choked to death on his drink. It sprayed out of his nose!" Another deep laugh escaped as Petyr threw his arms around Keelin.

He finally looked up to see Nodi, and realized where his mystery meat had landed. "Oh… Oh I am sorry. Let me…." Keelin approached with a cloth and tried to wipe the residue off her face. "Did you mention an Inn Petyr?" Keelin was going to pay for that later, and he knew it.

Her appetite was suddenly gone. Her eyes caught Keelin, letting him know that this wouldn't be soon forgotten. She still didn't trust this man. They had no reason to, but before she could say anything they were being led down the street.

Nodiah fell into step beside Keelin as Petyr led the way. "Keelin, are you sure? I mean, didn't it seem like he was listening to us?" She would follow him of course. In a way he appreciated her uncertainty. He knew she could protect herself, she was worried about him.

"I'll tell you what. Let's see what it looks like, go for a walk, and if you don't want to come back we don't have to. Deal?" It seemed like something she couldn't object to, and to his delight she didn't, just nodding in agreement.

Matthew Oakley

Chapter 17

"Here we are!" Petyr motioned towards a large cabin in front of them made out of a pristine dark red wood. Carvings were embellished all throughout the wood panels. Everything about this building stood out from what they had seen in Portis. "Wow Petyr, it's exceptional." Keelin watched as the large man smiled a humble smile.

"Come come, the inside is even better." He split Keelin and Nodiah, throwing an arm around both of them. "I know my behavior seems a bit odd, and I apologize. I just have a good feeling about you two. I was asking your waitress if she had seen you before. You have such a unique feel!" Petyr approached the front door, but Keelin's curiosity gave him pause.

"What do you mean feel?"

"I have a bit of a gift I guess you'd call it. I sense people. I sense their spirits. I have been all over this world, observing people. I used to help Kings tell if someone was about to betray them. I got a little old, and a little tired, so I opened The Sleeping Falcon. I've been here ever since. Now instead of going out and looking for people, people from all over come to me! I've heard all kinds of stories, but I bet you two have a good one!"

If only Petyr knew how true that statement was. He opened the door, giving way to an elaborate dining room that stretched the entire length of the main floor. In front of them was a huge staircase that led up to a balcony where doors lined the outer wall. The carvings on the outside were matched throughout the walls, and the tables. Everything had so much detail to it. "Petyr this is truly amazing."

"A few years back, we found a crystal mine just outside the city. A delegation from Ogla showed up led by the Queen, and she offered to buy it for a large amount of money. We took the deal, but they never came. Not until recently anyways."

"Are we in Ogla then?" Keelin genuinely had no idea. He was fairly sure they hadn't travelled long enough to make it all the way there though.

"Portis lies on the intersection of the three, Sabal, Ogla, and Coille. Because of that, we aren't technically govered by any of them, but most of the locals obviously have a favorite." The explanation made sense to Keelin at least. There was nothing out this way. No routes ran through here. It seemed self-contained, and with no authority to answer to, he had no reason to seek it out.

Petyr continued to lead the way up the stairs to a room tucked in a corner. A large gold "3" hung on the door. As he flung it open, Keelin and Nodiah took in the huge room, first noticing a massive bed with deep purple covers on it. In the far corner, a shower. On one wall a small desk sat equipped with all the necessary writing tools. Candles hung in a spiral from the ceiling giving just enough light. It was truly peaceful. Petyr handed Keelin the key and smiled. "I don't even know what to say."

"Nothing my friend. Just tell me that story sometime! Oh and if you go out, just make sure you don't ask too many questions. We are a peaceful town, but information travels quickly." Petyr gave them both a glance letting them know this was a genuine warning.

"Thanks again. We look forward to seeing what else Portis has to offer." With that Petyr took his leave, and the two were left alone. Nodi dropped her bag onto the floor, and took a deep breath in through her nose. She stretched her hands towards the ceiling, slowly reaching backwards until she was looking at Keelin upside down.

She giggled for a moment, remembering Keelin in the snare. She smiled, released her breath, and straightened out turning to face him. Her moves were feline in nature as she stretched and loosened her muscles with every step. She crossed her wrists behind his neck, standing on her toes and leaning in until her forehead pressed against his. A slow rhythmic chuckle started from deep within. "Can you believe we've made it this far, just for you to be done in on your dinner?" She flicked her head back towards the room to hide her laughter. "And now here we are. Incredible."

Playful Nodi, just another side of this beautifully complex creature. "Are you sure we survived? Maybe we died and tomorrow Petyr opens the gates to Am Blàr, the eternal battleground! I'm pretty sure this is what it would look like." Since birth, Keelin had been told the tales of the battleground. Warriors from every land spending eternity alternating between days of rest, drinking and feasting, and days of battle against those who came before.

She laughed again, turning back to run her hands down his chest. "We? Maybe you died, but I managed to eat my food just fine. The mighty Keelin departed this world choking on a wing. Or perhaps it was the conversation that did you in?" She batted her eyelashes flirtatiously, a joking smile on her face as she recalled her earlier protests to Petyr.

"But I have you to myself now," she observed, biting down on her bottom lip. Her chest pressed against his, she could feel his excitement. "You're okay? Nothing broken from the way Petyr threw you around huh?"

Nodiah's closeness brought a weakness to his knees. He turned, looking towards the door. "Come on, let's go see what Portis is hiding." A youthful exuberance rang through. As tempting as a shower and sleep seemed, he was genuinely excited to explore.

She leaned back, shaking out her hair, feeling the dust and dirt from the travel fall from her curls. She could still smell the ocean, the smoke, and the sweat. These few seconds of peace could not erase the long journey it took to get here. Maybe it was a good thing to stop here. She shouldn't forget. "Alright, lets go explore."

As she leaned back, temptation flooded in. Chances were sometime within the next few hours she would hate him again, but he didn't care. As long as she was safe.

They quietly made their way outside. Keelin took in a deep breath of the fresh air. Everything in Portis seemed better. He led the way farther into town, not really sure where he was headed, but he had ideas. "I'm thinking we should see if there's a temple, or a museum. Something that may shed some history on this place. Somehow, I've never been here before." He said with a slight smirk to hide how much that bothered him. "I don't even really recognize anyone here. A few from the north, but they aren't really of any significance. Anything stand out to you?" It was small talk, but the King had "bidders" and guests from far and wide. Maybe she had seen something.

Nodiah's eyes wandered to every last detail of the buildings around her. She took in the beauty of the sky as the sun began to set once again, turn-ing it into a canvas of pinks, purples and golds. She felt the warmth of the last evening rays on her skin. She listened to him with half an ear as they traveled further into the city, where larger, more intricately carved sandstone buildings began to emerge.

Absently, she reached out to run her fingertips along an etching in the side of a particularly large structure, but her eyes were fixed somewhere else. After a moment she finally remembered Keelin's question. She started to shake her head. Nothing in this city seemed familiar at all. It was all just perfect. Even the children that ran through the alleys seemed happy, well-fed, and full of life. There were no beggars, no one was in need. Not even Torek had this kind of stability.

Her hand continued along the etching when suddenly she was stopped in her tracks. She turned to look at the symbol her fingers had traced. Three sharp lines, a little thicker at the bottom, slanting upward and towards the middle. Above them, three small dots. All of it enclosed in a ring.

Inhale…

"Keelin… This is the symbol of the Oracle…"

He wasn't sure he heard her right at first. "Nah come on. You're seeing things. There's no way." He turned to look, only to find her completely fixated at the markings. The building itself was quite large, and quite old from the looks of it. "Maybe it's a coincidence? A translation? More than one Oracle? Are you sure?" None of his explanations moved Nodiah. She was sure of it. Just like that, all of Keelin's feelings of safety were gone.

She continued tracing the symbol. She had traced it a million times with her fingertips. She pulled up the fabric over her legs, showing Keelin her ankle, where the exact same symbol was branded. As soon as Keelin saw it, he felt stupid. Of course she knew.

Just then a small group of people exited, talking loudly and excitedly. Nodiah pulled Keelin towards her, hiding her face into his shoulder, trying to hide even her hair from view. Fear gripped her more than it ever had before. She couldn't be recognized. Keelin's grip met her fear, trying to let her know she was safe. "Are you sure? Tomorrow? That's never happened before? She's never even left Sabal before has she?" A woman in the group asked loudly, barely able to control her excitement.

"Why now? Is it because of the King's assassination? Is it for her safety?" A male asked curiously. A third voice, much stronger and confident in nature cut through the conversation. Nodiah thought it sounded familiar, but she didn't dare lift her head, clutching Keelin tight.

"She has left before, but not awake. It is because she has woken up. She seems to be quite upset about something, but no one can understand her. She's speaking in a language so ancient it has become lost. So they are bringing her here in hopes one of our priests will find a way to communicate. If they fail, I do not doubt they will take her on to the next temple. This has never happened before. It is crucial that we find out what she is trying to say…" The group rounded a corner and their voices faded away. Her head stayed tucked as her body stiffened. Tears filled her eyes and her hands clenched into Keelin tightly. "She's….awake…"

Matthew Oakley

Chapter 18

Nodiah pulled him down the street away from the temple as fast as she could. She tugged her hood up around her, looking towards the ground. Once they put some distance between themselves and the temple, she spun around and met his eye. "She's awake. Keelin, the Oracle is awake, and they're bringing her here. Something is happening." She paced with panic as she looked to him for a calm reply.

"What though? Why here? Why would she be so upset?" He tried his best to rationalize it all. "This is a good thing right? We were going to her now she's coming to us!" None of it honestly made sense to him, but he continued to search his brain for answers. "Unless... she knew we'd be here. Do you think?." That was a frightening thought. She was an Oracle after all.

"We need to go back to the Sleeping Falcon, and then we can figure out what to do from there." He did his best to calm her down, and hide his own worries. What if Jaz did something. Jaz wanted the Oracle dead. Did she already know the Oracle was coming here?

Nodiah did her best to keep her cool, but it was failing. "Yes... let's go back. I need to think." Her mind continued racing as they hurried through the streets. "I never considered there being other temples that revered the Oracle, but, obviously." She muttered, rubbing her hands together. "We have to go tomorrow. We have to see her. Oh but there will be so many people from the palace there. We will be seen for sure." At this point she was talking to herself, considering the possibilities and weighing her options.

"I have to see her for myself. I have to see her awake!" The King dead, the White Wolf discovered, and now the Oracle awakened. The Creators were demanding to be heard, and she was the one that was meant to listen.

Keelin knew she was right. They had to go. This was their chance to learn so much. At the least he hoped she could point them in the direction of the Sky temple. At best, he'd finally have his proof of his Sky Dancer.

The Oracle wouldn't be coming alone. There would be an entourage, guards, and most likely someone who would recognize them. Their path thus far had led to nothing but destruction and chaos, and for a moment he worried that Portis would suffer the same fate. They had to do this though. They had to.

"My friends! Back so soon?... Oh…" Petyr's face turned from smile to concern rather quickly as they made their way into the inn. Did he sense their emotion? "You should go shower, then come down for a drink." He offered kindly.

"That's a great idea Petyr. We'll be down in a bit." It did sound like good advice. A shower would do them good Keelin thought.

He turned back to Nodiah as they made their way to the room. "Are you sure?" This wasn't a once in a lifetime chance. It was a once ever chance. He thought back to Fulgrim, and some advice he had received from the old sage. There are no coincidences in the world, only opportunities.

She took a moment, inhaled, and responded. "I am positive. If the Oracle is awake, I have to see her for myself." She walked towards the corner of the room, dropping clothes as she went. A shower sounded like a necessity to take off the coat of grime that clung to her entire body.

She turned on the water, and took a moment to test the temperature as she looked back at Keelin. "You really think we should go back downstairs? I'm sure some of the Oracle's procession is already in town. Probably guards. Maybe it's safer to stay in?" She just wanted a few hours of nothing before the biggest day of her life.

She arched a suggestive brow and gave him a little smirk before stepping under the water. She tossed her hair back, and let it run down her body, truly getting lost in the feeling as the dirt washed away and muscles loosened up. One way or another, she hoped to entice him to stay.

His mind was elsewhere though. As tempting as she was, there was more to Petyr's request. Keelin had to know more. "Why don't you stay and finish your shower and rest. I'll go down for one drink and pop back up. It'd be rude not to." His body fought his mind, not wanting to turn away as he took in her presence. Sleeping and just hanging out without stress or pressure would be heaven, but he felt compelled to go down. She stuck out her bottom lip for a second, but finally gave him a dismissive wave.

Perhaps a moment alone wouldn't be so bad either. It had been so long since she was truly by herself. She turned back, letting the water fall through her hair and turning up the heat just a bit more. As the sound of the water continued to drown out the world, she thought of a plan for the following day. They needed a disguise, especially for her hair. Should they sneak in early and blend in? There were so many variables.

She turned off the water, the silence was suddenly deafening. She began humming a tune to herself and made her way through the room. Her thoughts continued to swirl as she approached the bed. She took in the details of the covers, tracing along the pattern of the sheets and eyeing the pillows that looked so welcoming. Something purple suddenly caught her eye. Reaching towards her bag, she pulled out the purple garments she had purchased earlier. With a smile she traced her hands along the soft, smooth fabric. Maybe she would step down for a drink after all.

As Keelin made his way to the bar, Petyr sat down a mug on the bar and began filling it with a thick black substance. He never looked up as Keelin approached, equal parts disgusted and intrigued. "Drink friend. We must talk." His tone was the most intense Keelin had heard it yet.

He picked up the mug, and examined it closer. "I'm not a big fan of tar." Petyr's eyes told him otherwise. He brought the mug to his lips, and was surprised by the aroma. It truly was wonderful. He began to lift the mug back up when Petyr pulled his arm away.

"Sips, trust me." He smiled. "Now tell me. Who is coming?" Keelin considered his options. If he lied would Petyr know? Did he know already?

"Why don't you tell me more about your gift first?" He responded. Suddenly a game was afoot.

"You are worried. The girl, she is hopeful. Rumors have it the Oracle is coming. Did you do this?" Petyr asked a bit more firmly. Keelin's response was rushed, but unsure.

"No! I mean. I don't think so. Maybe? We were looking for her." Petyr took a moment to read the statement, and then began his typical low deep laugh.

"You don't look for an Oracle. They are an Oracle. They know." He had a point. There was something more in his words.

"AN Oracle? So there's more than one?" He shot Petyr a confident smirk, but it wasn't returned.

"You may be an Alpha Wolf, but you're not as smart as you think." He knew? He knew who Keelin was all this time? Keelin wasn't sure whether to be flattered or threatened by his reputation. "You know the Wolves? How? Who? I mean. We never come this way." Suddenly Keelin's safety net was gone.

"Again, you're not as smart as you think." Petyr leaned back and eyed Keelin once more. "I like you. I like your friend. I'll make you a deal. You survive tomorrow. I will answer all your questions. Ok?"

Survive? Dying wasn't on Keelin's agenda. They were so close. "Deal!" Keelin wondered if he was a bit too loud as the room seemed to get a bit quieter the moment the words escaped.

Turning to the stairs however, he suddenly understood. Nodiah elegantly glided down the stairs in the purple outfit she had bought early. A skirt, fringed in gold that knotted at the hips, and the top draping off each shoulder, with gold swirling throughout. He could see the smile in her eyes. She knew everyone was watching, and she loved it. Purple was a royal color, and it fit her well.

Nodiah took in the bar. There was one noisy group in the center but everywhere else, pairs or lone travelers staring into their mugs and giving her quick glances. Keelin and Petyr were across the way. She could see the tension in him, but it didn't seem like anything was wrong. Maybe it was her that was causing it. She used that confidence in every step of her walk as she approached the duo, her eyes never leaving Keelin. So much for discrete...

"Becoming fast friends I see," she remarked as she took a seat. Her nose crinkled as she peered into Keelin's mug. "And what would you recommend for someone with a slightly lighter pallet?"

Petyr took a moment to consider her request. "I must say, you look quite divine my dear! For a beauty such as yourself I have something very special" Petyr turned, grabbing a loop of keys from his pocket. He took one peculiar looking key, and stuck it in a box nearby. A moment later he pulled out a small clear chalice with a golden rim, and a tall narrow bottle.

The liquid inside was in perpetual motion. It was similar to what the Alphas had shared before, but different. This was a hypnotic swirl of oranges, reds, and pinks. He carefully handled the bottle, pouring it into the chalice, and then placed a bright blue flower on top. "Comhla…" Keelin muttered under his breath as he stared on in amazement. Nodiah flicked him a quick glance, and let out a little gasp but Petyr interrupted.

"A beautiful drink for a beautiful lady…" He smiled.

"What's that say about my drink then huh?" Keelin laughed.

Petyr chuckled but then explained. "Your drink is a local favorite. We call it Porter. Dark, heavy, yet surprising. This one though… This is the Dance of the Winds." Nodiah's eyes narrowed at the name. That was frighteningly close to Sky Dancer. She supposed he may already know her secret though thanks to his gift.

She continued to watch the liquid swirl with suspicion as the innkeeper continued. "It is a mixture of ingredients from many different lands. That's why it dances. The ingredients, they don't mix. They are not the same. Incompatible you see? Each keeps hanging on to what it is, and yet each constantly wants to become more, and so they dance. They don't realize that just by being around things different from themselves, they find what we all seek… balance…"

All three stared on for a few moments, mesmerized by the swirls and colors. Finally, Keelin broke the silence. "Well, try it already!" She pondered offering it to him. She knew what that flower meant to him. His eyes and insistence however spoke that this was for her.

She took a small sip. Immediately she picked up the sweetness of honey, blending slowly into lavender. It quickly picked up in spice to cinnamon and ginger and something else. Another sip gave way to citrus. It was constantly evolving, but never too sweet or sour or strong. "It's lovely, I must say. But what makes it so special that people travel to all corners of the earth just to collect the ingredients?"

She leaned forward as if Petyr was going to tell her a secret. This wasn't just a drink. Petyr matched her lean, but it seemed to only be for his own amusement. "I told you. I have traveled all over the world. I went and found them. Just me. I only share it with those who I find unique. A unique drink for a unique person, only seems fair."

Suddenly things clicked in Keelin's head. The Wolves hadn't been to Portis. Petyr had been to the Den. At least near it. Maybe to Torek, or Ogla... Maybe he knew the King? This man suddenly became much more interesting. "So Petyr, ever been to Torek?" He asked with a bit of a grin.

"Ahh... Maybe you aren't so dumb after all." Petyr replied.

"No he is." Nodiah chimed in. She couldn't resist. All three chuckled as Keelin took another larger drink of his Porter.

"Sips friend." Petyr insisted again. "I have been many places. I have seen lots of things. I have seen your home at Dachaigh, and I have seen the mighty castle of Torek, though the King is no longer on his throne." Petyr acknowledging where this journey started made Keelin shift uneasily.

He took another gulp of his mug, which was now empty. "Such a shame..." Keelin muttered.

"A shame? He was an ass! An unrighteous, selfish ass." Petyr quickly snarked much to Keelin's relief.

"I can't argue that!" he said happily.

Nodiah's grip tightened at the mention of the King. For the first time she truly considered the weight of her actions. The King had no heir. The Queen had died years ago. Who would take the throne next? The entire region could be in full upheaval at the thought of an empty throne. "I wonder though, where are you from?" Petyr's attention turned back to Nodiah as he leaned in again. It was her turn to share a secret.

Nodiah ticked her head to the side. "Where am I from?" A silence stretched as she sipped her drink once more. "I am not from anywhere" she finally answered, her voice low as she stared into her glass. She had to change the subject.

"Enough of your questions. I have one for you. What can you tell us about the temple of the Oracle? Does it have many patrons? Any stories? Rumors?" She flashed back to the dark, dripping cell for a moment. "Have you ever spoken with any of the girls?... The Vessels?"

Petyr pulled out the jug of Porter and refilled Keelin's cup, but his eyes never left Nodiah. "Everyone is from somewhere." He said with a bit of a scoff. For the first time there seemed to be tension.

"He said if we survive, he'll answer all our questions." Keelin chimed in.

"Not true. I said if you survive tomorrow. I'll answer your questions. I was never concerned for her." Petyr took out a cup for himself, and filled it with Porter as well. He took a couple sips and then responded.

"Temple? That's not the right word. There are many who come and go. It is open to the people, but… there are places within that no one is allowed. Supposedly there is a great power source within." Petyr took another long swig, eyes scanning the bar as he drank.

"The girls? I feel badly for them. Ogla has acolytes. Girls who's job would be to cater to the Oracle, should she awaken, and the priests of course. Now that the King is gone, the Sisters of Sabal have been recruited for the same." Nodiah shuddered at the thought. "The Vessels? They know the goal, and yet their existence feels so empty. Especially since the Oracle has been asleep for so long. But now… now they must be… well it's hard to imagine what they feel." A moment of silence fell over the trio.

Petyr couldn't begin to understand the weight of his words. Keelin extended a hand to Nodi's back, gently resting it between her shoulder blades as Petyr continued. "There are lots of stories though. I still believe the one you two are writing is better than any of mine." He smiled. "You are meant for amazing things my dear." His smile was warm. The intensity was gone. It felt as if he was stating a fact.

Nodiah felt herself loosen slightly under Petyr's gaze. His words about Keelin surviving were a little unsettling, but the warmth of his smile helped her relax. Maybe she could give a little ground. "The earliest memory I have is in Torek," she conceded, still being careful with her words. She rolled her shoulders and continued. "We are just travelers. It seems we have arrived at such a great time for Portis, and perhaps great change." she added darkly.

"Change. It's not so bad. Your drink, it constantly changes. Some see chaos. I see beauty." He reached out, taking Nodiah's hand in his own. "Listen, your fears. They are unnecessary. You have made it this far, because you believed in something. That you had an appointment. If the Universe brought you this far, it wasn't so that you could fail." Keelin suddenly felt as if he was intruding on a moment. "Your friend. He has a good heart. He wants you safe. He's stubborn, a bit naive, but a good heart." Keelin took offense to that. He attempted to stand and protest, but found his legs had no interest in supporting his body.

"Hey Wha... woah..." He caught himself against the bar and shuffled back into his seat. "Wow... I ... What?" Confusion was about all that Keelin could feel.

"I told you... sips..." Nodiah and Petyr shared a laugh as Keelin tried to gather himself. Nodiah reached out a hand to his forearm to help steady him for a moment. Seeing him so tipsy was truly amusing.

"You have given me much to think about, friend. I thank you. Tomorrow seems like it will be an interesting day on all counts." They sat a bit longer as she finished her drink and formulated her final plan. She wasn't sure Keelin would like it, but this was her call. She turned away, pressing her back against the edge of the bar and staring out into the crowd. "Can you do me a favor Petyr?"

"Of course my dear. Anything for you."

"If anyone catches your eye, the way we did, would you be so kind as to let us know? Portis seems to be filled with fascinating individuals, and I have no doubt more are on the way." Petyr simply nodded in agreement, allowing Nodiah to turn back to Keelin.

Her face slid up close to his ear. "How are you feeling?" she asked, giggling slightly.

"Fine... I feel fine. Why? H... How do you feel?" He stuttered out.

"Tomorrow we finally get some answers, and that includes from you Petyr." She shot him back a playful look, but they both understood the intent. She wouldn't let anything happen to him.

The large man nodded and smiled. "I hope so."

It took Keelin a moment to process, but once he did it was enough to sober him up a little. No matter what, tomorrow would decide their course. "Shall we retire for the evening my dear?" He muttered out whimsically.

Nodiah placed her glass on the bar, took Keelin's arm in hers, and went with him up the stairs. She had a full belly, a roof over her head, and an interesting new alliance that would give them at least one safe night it seemed. Tomorrow could wait. These moments were worth enjoying.

Chapter 19

Once back in the room, they both let out a sigh of relief. Her hand reached towards his, lacing his fingers between hers. The space felt safe. They had someone watching their back. It was good… and yet… they both knew it wouldn't last.

Keelin's inability to decipher Nodiah left him all the more unsure of what to do next. His free hand reached up, gently sliding along her shoulder to her cheek, and then playfully through her hair. He stood, encaptured in the moment. In her.

Nodiah soaked it in, pressing the bridge of her nose into the nook just above his collar bone. Her hands crept up his chest. His smell was of smoke, salt, blood, and surprisingly pine, and something else that was unique all to him.

"You know I find this rough, rugged look irresistible, but you aren't going to do us any favors tomorrow looking like you've just come off the battlefield," she remarked with a smirk while pulling on his robe. She let her eyes wander over her shoulder towards the shower, and then let him go as she led the way. "It will make you feel better. The water is actually warm. It's fantastic." She said with a smirk. She turned and bent over to fumble with the knobs, knowing full well what she was doing.

He tried this best not to take the bait, but couldn't help but watch. He quickly slid his shirt off, suddenly becoming aware of just how dirty he was. He continued to strip down, and finally made his way to the shower. The water lived up to Nodiah's description. Warm, but refreshing. "We came all this way, fought countless odds, escaped countless situations, and yet we're thrilled over a shower. It's the simple things in life I suppose."

Nodiah took in the words as she watched. She didn't speak, not wanting to interrupt wherever his mind had gone. He was complicated. Somehow she still hated him, and yet needed him more than ever. She studied him closely, every muscle, every curve, every inch, as if she was looking for something, but she had no idea what. In this small act, she understood him just a little bit more.

Simple. What a concept, All of the chaos, the drama, the battles... It was all a quest for something more simple. An easier way of life. Keelin closed his eyes giving way to the sounds of the water. He focused on his breathing, and the feeling of the drops running across his body, when suddenly he was jolted back.

"You could have it you know? An Escape..." A menacing voice, but as he opened his eyes and looked around there was no one. He closed his eyes again and tried to shake it off. *"Just kill her..."* Startled, his eyes shot open once more. *Where did that come from? Who?... Nothing... It was nothing.*

Noticing his body tense, she reached out her hand towards his lower back, pressing gently. She allowed her fingers to glide softly along his back, tracing patterns in a delicate dance of momentum. Neither said a word. She focused her energy into her hand. Every thought, every emotion, every hurt, every need... channeled through her hand and straight into her soul. Her breathing quickened. She hoped to let him feel the things she didn't have the words for.

That touch took the breath from his body. He did all he could just to stay on his feet. It was beyond words. He closed his eyes once more, letting the electricity move up his spine and fill his entire body, then much to her shock, he stepped away. He didn't deserve that. This whole time he had focused on being there for her. He wanted to break her, help her, protect her, and yet through all of the torment, pain and suffering, it had been her that was there for him. A single tear was the start, but within moments he wept.

It felt good. To let go of all that he had held onto. To have a moment of weakness. To not care for just a moment. He closed his eyes, *"No one would ever know. You could go back home. They would take you back. She has always been the problem."* Keelin audibly gasped, and then gritted his teeth in frustration. Something was coming for a fight.

Nodiah felt herself gasp at the same moment he did. Something that felt like a snake coiled in the back of her consciousness. She pulled him to her as she saw the tears, and she could no longer hold back her own. Tears of pain, love, joy, and longing. His need crashed over her in a wave. It buried her. Her hands locked into the hair on the back of his head. She hiked up on her toes, pressing her body into his, and the two shared their most dynamic, passionate, emotional kiss yet.

"Keelin..." she sighed between kisses. His name danced on her lips of its own volition. It was a question, a curse, a song, and a declaration. The depth of this moment wrapped around them, and obliterated the outside world. It was everything. As she breathed his name, it destroyed Keelin's ability to think.

"You are…" He stopped himself, and held her close. He picked her up off the ground so that they would be eye to eye. He smiled through the tears, and then buried his head into her shoulder. "No matter what the Oracle says, there is only one you, and you are mine. Not because I bought you… Because I refuse to lose you." He squeezed her soul, and then set her back down staring into those amazing eyes. The ones that made everything ok.

She couldn't fully believe what he said. They had been through too much. She stared up, debating her response. "This is for us. This is our fight. Our journey. Either of us on our own could walk away, or just stay here in Portis. If we are going to stick together, then you have to know the toughest fights are ahead." She leaned herself back against the wall, her eyes now showing a bit of a challenge as she continued. "Is it worth it to you?"

"Worth?" His eyes found their way to hers. How interesting that she was asking about worth. "Worth implies that there's a pay off. That I want something from it. That there is an end goal. I don't care if it's worth it. I don't care if we get to the end, and there's nothing." His voice swelled with determination to match the fire in her eyes. He was lying a bit, and they both knew it, but it was the right thing to say.

This was about so much more than the two of them, and yet, it was only about them. "I don't care what happens. Whatever we go though, what comes after us, You… You are worth it." He nodded, content with his answer for the moment, and hoped that she would feel the same.

Who knew? All this time. It wasn't his cruelty that would break her. It was his kindness. She felt the restraints on her soul shatter. The last chains shed, the weight lifted. She buried her face in his shoulder, and heaved an ugly sob. Her body quivered and shook as she released all of it. She was free of being a possession, free of guilt, free of the blood on her hands. Her freedom came in losing control.

One more ugly sob escaped before she pulled away, and taking a breath her lips found his again. She let it linger, knowing they had all the time in the world. She wanted to reacquaint herself with Keelin in this new light. The power struggle was over. Now it was about discovering who this man really was.

He felt it. He felt her body give as he now held her weight against him. "I didn't know this could exist. This... this is everything." It was as if they were swirling balls of energy. Each feeding off the other, interacting, pushing and pulling, but without the need for word or expression. Everything was felt. Everything was powerful. He couldn't help but smile, and even laugh occasionally.

A sudden funny thought came to mind. "Do you... Do you think Petyr can feel all of this?" He said with a smile. He reached for a towel, and began drying her off, not really expecting an answer. It was the only thought he had. There was nothing else to think about. In this moment, time didn't seem to exist.

As she watched him dry her off, she considered his question playfully. "Of course..." she replied, taking the towel, and then making her way towards the bed. "He did insist on us coming here even after I told him my plans." She laughed, intertwining her hand with his and pulling him along. She fell back on the bed, bringing him down on top of her. His lips immediately found their way to her collar bone, and up along her neck. He moved back down, kissing a line down the center of her body, stopping near her stomach while resting his chin on her. "Stars have nothing on you..." he said with a smirk.

Her arms slid up to her hair as she closed her eyes and took in the sensation of his lips. Her chest rose and fell with a deep breath as he moved. She couldn't help but peak as he stopped, returning the smirk. "Oh, he's a poet now?" she teased, but could not hide the happiness from her voice.

"Oh I've always been a poet."

"Oh really?" She looked on inquisitively.

"He wanted nothing more than to set free the soul
that captured his wandering heart.
But he looked in her eyes, and to no one's surprise,
she thought he was doomed from the start…

How things have changed…" he said confidently. His lips returned to her body, working past her navel down to her right hip. Every single inch mattered. Every mark, every scar. They were as much a part of her as her hair, and now more than ever, he loved them.

She let out a small gasp as he quoted the lines from their first meeting. The dance that changed her destiny. The corner of her mouth twitched a bit. She would have to dance for him again sometime soon. She shook off the thought, choosing instead to focus on the moment they were in.

He moved lower, all the way down past her knees to her calves, to her feet. Locking eyes with her, she lifted her feet slightly and covered them with slow, soft kisses. They conveyed his heart. He accepted all of her from head to toe, and he wanted to make sure she knew that.

A shiver ran up her spine as he continued his descent. She allowed herself to cherish each caress, without any impatience. As his lips grazed her foot, she pushed herself up on an elbow to watch him. She was both fascinated and moved at the sight of him at her feet. That was a place she had been many times, for many people, but never imagined she'd experience from this side.

Her breathing quickened after watching for a few moments. She took in a deep breath then growled his name… "Keelin…" His response was a laugh, moving his lips along her feet finding all of the sensitive spots that made her react. He continued kissing and rubbing as he expanded on his earlier thought.

"The stars have nothing… to your beauty…" He made his way up to her ankle… "To your strength…" He then switched feet. "To your guidance, you've helped me find my way…" He set her feet down, and made his way back up towards her. "But most of all, they can't match your fire…" The intensity in the room had risen with the growl. They were ready, waiting for the moment that was to come… She smiled an approving smile and leaned back.

She closed her eyes…

And there was the Oracle, reaching out for her. Screaming, and yet Nodiah could not hear her. The image slowly faded to be replaced with a tall, stunning woman with long blond hair that held up a beautiful jeweled crown. She was laughing hysterically as a wall of fire blazed behind her.

Keelin closed his eyes...

Suddenly the voice returned. *"You will fail, you know? No one can protect her. What's the end of the Prophecy? Hmm?"* That voice was menacing, tormenting.... The end? Keelin didn't know there was an end.

Their eyes popped open simultaneously, staring at one another as each tried to catch their breath. Their moment was gone. The realization of what was to come was back. Neither said anything, Keelin collapsing beside her, with his arm draped across. Each trying to act like nothing happened in their own way.

"One of these days I'll write you a song, and you can do a dance to it for me." It was an awkward statement for the moment, but it was the only thing that came to mind.

He let his head wander off to that scene for a moment, rolling to his back as he stared up at the ceiling. Daylight was already beginning to break through the window. They were running out of time. "So," He thought about asking for the plan, but it didn't matter. He considered telling her about the voice in his mind, but that didn't matter either. "You're amazing." He chuckled a bit uncomfortably. "Can't the Oracle just come in here? I'm sure we could win her over."

At the mention of the Oracle, the vision returned to Nodiah's mind. Did he see it too? She considered how much to tell him, wondering why it was coming now? Was this communication from the Oracle herself? She didn't smile at his joke, but instead turned on her side, propping her head up on her elbow as she faced him.

"Someone else is coming, Keelin." She finally pushed out the words. "A Queen, or a Princess, I'm not sure who. She's coming for us. I… I think she has something to do with this place. She's why this town is the way it is, and I think she is coming for the Oracle." She fell to her back frustrated, waiting on some kind of response. Maybe Keelin already knew who she was.

"If there's one thing we don't have luck with, it's royalty." He looked her way, and saw the seriousness on her face. "On second thought, we don't really have great luck with anything." His attempt to break the mood failed.

He sat up, looking down at her and responded in a more appropriate manner. "Let her come. Let them all come. Nothing can stop us, not now. Of course the world is going to take one last swing at stopping you, at holding you back. Maybe one of the Creators doesn't want you to succeed." He reached down a hand under her chin, and lifted her face up towards his. "It can't stop you. You won't let it. I won't let it."

He leaned back, stretching out his back, and the voice returned. *"Listen to me Wolf. You will fall just like your pack."* That, he couldn't ignore. His eyes closed as he let out a low, angered growl. His fists and jaw clenched, but he quickly twisted his body and tried to pass it all off as part of his stretch. Whatever that voice was, just didn't matter anymore.

Nodiah jumped as he growled, reaching out for him out of instinct. She pulled herself against him, pressing her body into his back while draping her arms around him. "What is it Keelin?" She asked softly. "Do you feel her too?"

"N....no. I hear her. I don't think she knows everything. She's taunting me. Taunting us." He broke her embrace and stood as he came to terms with what he had to say next. "She said the Wolves are gone." Nodiah sat still, pulling the sheets up around her. Whatever he heard had really gotten under his skin. It was a truly unsettling thought. "She's playing games. That's all it is. Lies, fear, I don't know who she is. I'll know her if she speaks. I'll know that voice… but… she clearly has a part to play."

Frustration began building as he considered their course of action. "Look it doesn't matter! It doesn't matter who she thinks she is. She doesn't have what we have. She can't stop us. It's just another hidden face with a secret to hide. We are done hiding. We will get to the Oracle. You will get your answer, then I'll drink more Portis porter with Petyr by nightfall, and then, we keep going. Together. We have to." It was more of a begging plea than a statement of confidence. They had to keep going. They had come too far.

She held her tongue as he rambled on. Eventually, she stood and made her way to the window. The soft light from the rising sun gave the first look on an already busy city. She thought back to Petyr's words, that he had no fear for her safety, but it was Keelin who had to survive. Her stomach twisted at the thought. Surely the Creators would not have brought them to this point, only to take him away from her.

"We keep going," she repeated, still looking out the window. "I have to get my answer. The throne is empty. The Dragons or Fire Breathers, the Wolves, the Oracle, The King, and... the woman... and you and me..." She turned to face him. "And you and me. Today we get answers to all of it. We are the connection. We've gathered all of these things together for a reason, and the Oracle is going to tell me what that reason is." she said with more confidence than she completely felt. If no one else could understand the Oracle, why was Nodiah so sure that she could? Maybe she couldn't, but she had to try.

Her sudden surge of confidence meant something to him, even if she didn't entirely believe it. He returned to the bed, sitting down and facing towards the opposite wall. "You and me. You will get your answers. I promise. No matter what it takes." Nodiah's heart sank again thinking back to Petyr's words.

Keelin moved past her, and began getting dressed. His head drifted to what his role would be in all of this. What would she ask of him? Was he ready? Time would tell. "We should go say goodbye to Petyr. Just for now, and then maybe go do some shopping. At least try to blend in a little huh?"

His head suddenly shot back towards the window. Something was pulling him. Something wanted him to come. It wasn't... a person though. There was a thing out there. Something that he needed. "Breakfast may not be a bad idea either? We could go back to the Silver Eagle." It was harmless conversation that he knew neither of them were focused on. Anything between now and when the Oracle came was just delaying the inevitable.

She took one last look at Portis from their little den of peace, and then turned away. She gave a forlorn glance to the wet, ruined purple silk that lay on the floor. She grabbed it anyways, and began folding it back up.

He finished dressing, putting on a long sleeve black shirt that had a hood attached, and black pants to match. He then grabbed a few small things he thought may be useful. There was a small jagged rock, a few pieces of rope that were amount his arms length, and a flint. As he searched the drawers he also found a small dagger someone must have left behind. He tucked it into his pocket, and turned back to Nodiah.

He couldn't begin to imagine what she felt in that moment. "So this woman… you felt her? You've seen her? What did she look like?" An honest question. Maybe something in her appearance could give Keelin some insight. Maybe they could ask Petyr about it.

She managed to find a simple black shirt that fell to her knees, and then a white shawl she wrapped around her body. She took Fulgrim's fang, and hung it around her neck, clutching it fondly. What she wouldn't give for his advice right now. She put her bow around her shoulder, with the arrow tied to the bow, and finally, she tucked Jaz's dagger along her thigh, and tied it down with a piece of fabric.

"I saw her. She's younger, and tall, with the palest blonde hair, and a huge jeweled crown. She's quite beautiful, but there's something very… cold… about her. I think the Oracle may be trying to warn me about her? I can't be certain."

It was a fairly vague description, but in some ways it sounded familiar. His brain raced to match the details to someone from the past, but he just couldn't find them. "Warn… you?…. You're the one that others should be warned about." He smirked, but there was a bit more truth behind his words than he meant. "It's not the Queen of Ogla, she's anything but young and beautiful."

With one last look around, they reluctantly stepped out of room three, and made their way downstairs. This was it. She'd be here soon…

Inhale…

Matthew Oakley

Chapter 20

As they descended the staircase, a deep roaring laugh caught Keelin's ear. Petyr stood behind the bar, his eyes locked on them; a knowing smile on his face. He didn't say anything. He didn't have to. He just gave them a quick nod. His words once again penetrated Nodiah's mind as they walked to the door. Keelin would survive. No matter what.

The morning air was crisp and refreshing. The sky still held the oranges and pinks of dawn, giving way to streaks of blue. Plenty of people were out and about, all busily hustling along. Preparations were under way.

At this moment, the pull came to Keelin once more. Not towards the market, or the temple… a new direction. He grabbed Nodiah's hand and began leading. They ducked down a small alley separating two larger buildings as Keelin tried to focus on this gravitation. He was unable to put words to his attraction. He was sure Nodiah had said something by now, but he didn't hear it.

Nodiah did her best to keep up. The weight of his pull was something she hadn't really felt before. Whatever he was after had his full attention. "Keelin wait, this could be a trap! Where are we going? We have to be…" Her voice trailed off as she saw the look in his eyes. He was following a path she could not see.

The alley finally gave way to a small courtyard that seemed peculiar at best. Majestic flowers stood nearly as tall as he was, opening up into giant blossoms of all sorts of colors all around them. Behind them, a small building, not big enough for a house. It looked as if there was only one room inside. "There's something in there… that's… that's calling me Nodiah. I have to go…" He waited, knowing he was going in either way, but he wanted to give her the chance to prepare herself as well.

"It's... It's calling you?" She asked with some alarm. "What if she's in there? Should I follow you?" Her questions were valid, but he couldn't be stopped. He knew he couldn't stop her either.

"There's something in there we need. Come on." He approached the building, and reached his hand out to touch the ornate red door. As soon as he made contact, it cracked open. "I guess it was waiting for us." What though?

As he made his way inside, a huge candelabra came into view, hanging from the ceiling. The walls were lined with fantastically realistic paintings. Each panel had a different person on it. Warriors fought against other animals, monsters, and the darkness itself. Some of the people looked eerily similar to a few of the drawings on the ceiling of the Den. He was so focused on the walls that he nearly missed the golden pedestal towards the back center of the room.

An elegant, ornate podium stood a few feet tall, with a small piece of parchment laying on top. He looked to Nodi, wanting to share his sense of wonder at it all. Could this be a trap? It felt... safe... He walked up to the podium, and examined the paper.

Welcome Friends,

Portis is a peaceful town, but that does not mean we don't have our defenses. Many warriors have come and stored their weapons here, knowing they would be protected. A weapon is a book. It tells a story, and yet it is a companion. When properly matched with its owner, it breathes, it speaks, it has life. You are free to use this building whenever you'd like. Start by finding the warrior who speaks to you, and search for what's hidden within.

May the Oracle point to peace

Petyr

"That bastard. I knew he knew more." Keelin muttered. He handed the note to Nodiah and turned back to the walls. What did he mean? Each picture was so unique... Males, females, tall, short, royalty, knights, discoverers, peasants... which one?

Nodiah had been examining the paintings with great interest while Keelin retrieved the note. One in particular had her attention. A slender woman stood with her hand fanned out, displaying an array of small knives. Across her face was the symbol of the oracle. As Keelin handed her the note, she read it quickly and scoffed at the theatrics of it all. Why all this secrecy? He could have told them of all of this last night.

She placed her hand along the frame of the painting, and swept along the sides. Moving to the bottom, it seemed to have a bit of give. She applied a bit of pressure. It clicked, and the entire frame swung open silently as she stepped back. Inside was a display, housing several throwing knives matching the picture. They were all held together by a thick black strap. She pulled one out, inspecting it carefully, and then grabbed the strap and tied it to her leg just under Jaz's bone dagger.

Keelin began searching for his own, noticing even the size of the frames varied as he went. Finally he closed his eyes, and tried to pick up on whatever was calling out to him. His feet moved. A few steps later, he reached his hand out in front of him and continued to move until... *click*....

His eyes opened to a rather large picture of a man wearing a cloak made from a black wolf pelt. "Keelin, that painting, it's on the ceiling in Dachaigh." She was sure of it. It made him that much more anxious to see what was inside. The giant frame swung open to reveal a long black pole arm with a wide serrated edge. He looked to Nodiah with an excited smirk as he pulled it out. "Mine's bigger", he quipped. Now properly armed he felt ready. "Your lead, what's next?" he smiled as he headed for the door.

Nodiah bit her tongue as she considered the staff. The long weapon didn't exactly blend in, nor did it quite suit the plan forming in her mind. But it called to him, there must be a reason. Instead of firing back a response of her own, she gave him a peaceful smile before pushing up on her tiptoes and giving him one more slow, sweet kiss.

Exhale...

"Come on..." They left the small weapons shed behind and made their way to the city's center. The energy in the air was growing more excited, and tense. The crowds around them had gotten thicker as it became clear they were all heading towards something making its way into Portis. Nodiah and Keelin took their places in the shadows of an alley that opened up onto the city's main street.

She squinted up into the sun as trumpets burst, and the purple and gold banners of the Kingdom of Ogla came into view. It was an unexpected arrival. Keelin immediately became concerned that Jaz had made a deal.

Both of them tried to absorb as much information as they could as the procession passed them by. First came a ten by ten block of soldiers carrying Ogla's colors and coat of arms. Behind them, a troupe of dancers and performers entertained the crowd. A grand palanquin followed next, carrying a rather bored looking young woman with black hair down to the base of her spine. Keelin took particular notice of her, but wasn't sure why.

Next in the procession was a line of grandly decorated priests, accompanied by a group of acolytes. They were all young looking women with their entire bodies covered in dark purple veils. Only their eyes peered out. A perimeter of guards surrounded them. All three, the priests, acolytes, and guards, were decorated with the rune of the Oracle in some fashion. There was more coming behind this group, but this seemed as good of an opportunity as any.

Nodiah backed into Keelin, pressing against him. "That's our way in," she breathed. "You have to replace one of the guards, and I'll take care of one of the girls." No easy task, but it was far better than she could have ever hoped for. She was sure they'd have to sneak in with the Sabal procession. The Ogla procession was almost too good to be true.

Keelin's estimations of the group weren't flattering. The guards didn't look like much. Their marching was unorganized and sloppy. The priests were pompous and overconfident. The girl with the black hair… Why did she seem familiar? "What do you think? Can we cause a distraction? Or should we just pick our moment? Tough with so many people here."

He knew what he would do, but she knew the Oracle. He wrapped an arm around her, placing it calmly on her hip and awaited her instruction as he continued to look for weaknesses in the line. Distraction seemed their best option, but what could they do? If they could get to a guard, getting to the girls would be easier, so his switch had to come first.

"Ready?" Nodiah said softly.

"For what?"

"Grab me."

"What? I'm not gonna." Her eyes convinced him otherwise.

"GUARDS!! HELP! PLEASE! SOMEONE!" Her screams rang out above the crowd just as the girls walked past. A few of the girls turned their heads, as did a few of the guards, but none seemed particularly motivated to do anything about it. "Hello!? I need help." None of the guards moved, though a few of the townsfolk seemed ready to step in. Maybe this wouldn't be so easy.

She huffed, shoving him off and crossing her arms. "I'm fine. Just a little misunderstanding." It did enough to settle the crowd, but they were no closer to finding a way in. "Alright Plan B."

With little hesitation, Nodiah pushed her way towards the procession, reaching for one of her knives. She couldn't help but feel a little spark of energy run through her body as she grasped the handle. With an impressively precise throw, the dagger left her hand, and floated into the side of one of the guards. He fell to the ground with a gasp as a scream rose out from the crowd.

She ran towards the guard, with Keelin right behind. "MAKE WAY! PLEASE MOVE! Doctor coming through. Oh, Doc we need to get him back to your office. This looks bad." Her eyes urged Keelin to play along, but she could only hope he understood.

He looked around for a moment, as if searching for the doctor himself before he realized that he himself was the person he was looking for. "Oh right. Yes yes, right away. The rest of you stay here. The attacker may still be out here. We'll take care of this one." A few soldiers had circled behind them.

"Never seen a Doctor with a weapon like that before," a particularly nosy guard pointed out. Nodiah's eyes widened. That weapon was going to be a problem after all.

"It's easier for amputations. Never know when you have to chop off a leg or an arm quickly." Keelin was impressed with his own quick thinking, as was Nodiah. "Now if you want this man to live, you'll let us through." He expressed as much urgency as he could in his voice as he lifted the man up from under his arms. Nodiah quickly grabbed the man's feet, and they shuffled back through the crowd.

A few questioning voices rose "He's a doctor? Where from? I've never seen him."

"I think they're staying at the Inn."

"They don't seem like doctors."

They did their best to ignore the voices, and move quickly through the crowd, though both could no longer ignore the magnitude of what had started. This was it.

They disappeared back to the courtyard, hiding among the flowers. They set the guard down, and both were shocked to discover just how stiff he was. It seemed he was alert, but unable to move. Nodiah pulled the knife from his side, wiped it clean, and placed it back along her hip. "Looks like these weapons may have some tricks to them. We'll have to remember that." They both continued to move with a sense of urgency as they stripped the guard down.

Keelin quickly began placing on the various pieces of armor. Any moment they would surely be discovered. "Alright, how do we get you in?" They both pondered their next move when suddenly Nodiah remembered her fabric. The purple silk cloth wasn't an exact match, but it was close. It wasn't large enough to cover all of her, but it was a start. She began ripping and tearing at the fabric, trying to gain as much coverage from it as she could.

Keelin, trying to be helpful, reached for the pollen of one of the nearby flowers, and using his finger drew the symbol of the Oracle on her garments as well as he could. "This is terrible." She exclaimed.

"There's so much going on, this can work. We just have to get close." He did his best to reassure her, but this was a long shot. They made their way back to the crowd, being sure to take a different exit than the one they came in through.

Once back to the procession, they slid themselves into position as naturally as they could. A few guards shot him questioning glances, but they kept marching. "This one tried to run." He said calmly. Much to their surprise, the lie seemed to work. Why any of them would run was beyond him.

Everything about this situation felt wrong. There was too much he didn't know. He had no control. They were at the mercy of circumstance. Keelin hated it. Nodiah however, seemed much more in her element. She fought and struggled just enough to sell the lie. Her eyes showcased her anger at being caught. She was quite the actress.

"Bastard tore my clothes. Can you believe it?" The other girls shot Keelin a glance of disapproval, but no one said a word. They simply fell in line and continued marching.

Keelin's guard position allowed him to survey the crowd as they walked along, though admittedly only one side of the street. No one particularly stood out however. Things were calm for the moment.

It became clear that the procession was heading towards the temple, but what was unclear was the location of the Oracle? They had assumed the Ogla congregation were the first to arrive, but maybe the Oracle was already here.

The pair shared a glance of confidence as they approached the building, and then walked past it just a bit. Finally, everyone stopped. Keelin looked back as the black haired girl left her palanquin, and the other acolytes filed in behind her, including Nodiah.

This left Keelin among the other guards, some of whom seemed to be paying more attention to him than he was comfortable with. They did their best to stay within site of each other. Keelin tried to decipher if there was a way to follow Nodiah inside, while she still did her best to blend in, and observe all of the people around them.

Another palanquin filed in behind the first, and trumpets blasted to life once more. A crier stepped forth and announced their present company. The Kingdom of Ogla presents the High Priestess Kendra, and her sister, the Queen of Ogla, her majesty Queen Bodicea. Keelin turned, expecting to see the same rugged, stern looking Queen he had run into before. The entire congregation knelt, and bowed. Keelin and Nodiah did the same, though admittedly peeking some.

From out of the other palanquin stepped a tall, young, gorgeous blond with long hair running down her back. She placed a beautiful jeweled crown on her head. Nodiah gasped, and then buried her head staring at the ground. She did her best to control her breathing, but she could feel the panic rise. She looked back to Keelin, expressing her fear with her eyes.

They said more than enough. This was the woman she described. This was the new threat. Keelin was still trying to come to terms with the idea that this young woman was the Queen. What had happened to the old

Queen? Why hadn't he heard? Had the Wolves truly become that isolated with the world, or was this a recent event?

The time for questions quickly passed as the Queen made her way next to her sister, and the duo led the way into the temple. The procession began to make their way inside, but as soon as Keelin moved to join them he felt a hand on his shoulder. "Where do you think you're going pal?" A stern, raspy voice called out. "Do we even know you?" He called out inquisitively.

"Ogla sent out for some locals to volunteer to the guard for today. The Queen insisted on some people that knew the town to help with security." He stood before five guards that were now suddenly weighing his story.

"What about that weapon? That's not standard." A short, stubby looking bald man had taken the lead of the interrogation, but he didn't look like much of a fighter. If it wasn't for the crowd, Keelin could have taken them all quickly. It would blow his cover. What would Nodiah do?

"No, but I'm much more comfortable with it." He pulled the pole arm from his back, and began looking at the blade. "I'd rather have something in my hands that I know how to use versus a little sword I might make a mistake with." He began spinning the pole arm from one hand to another, and then inspiration struck. He picked up speed, surprised at how natural the movements felt. He quickly began turning it around his body, spinning himself as he moved until suddenly he simply became a blur of rotations. The other soldiers began shielding themselves slightly as if the twirling was letting off a bit of wind.

He threw the pole up in the air and expertly caught it on the way down with a twirl, and then extended the blade towards his questioners. "See what I mean? If I'm to protect the Queen, I need my weapon." The men nervously nodded in agreement, and backed off.

This gave Keelin the clearance to approach the rear of the group, and make his way into the temple with a few other guards at the back of the pack. Behind them, the procession from Torek began to take shape. He kept his eyes forward, and slowly they all made their way inside.

Inhale...

Chapter 21

The inner chamber was larger than one would expect from the outside. The ceiling stretched up to a massive dome with what appeared to be constellations of the night's sky running across its surface. There were several hallways in every direction leading off this main room. The lighting was dim, the atmosphere quiet for the amount of people filing in.

Nodiah followed the acolytes to the back left corner, and knelt facing the entrance, watching everyone else pour in. Ogla took up the left half of the room, lining the walls. She was thankful for the chance to make eye contact with Keelin once more, as it brought some comfort to an otherwise tense situation. Getting into the temple was the easy part of this. The Queen, the Oracle, the people from Sabal... There was danger at every turn.

Keelin returned the glance with a soft smile, and followed the guards to a position almost directly across from the Queen, near the entrance. He couldn't help but wonder what it was that made her so threatening. She seemed average at best. A typical princess, dealing with her unlikely ascension to the throne. Next to her sister, a figure with a mask and hood covering their face. They were... hiding. Why?

The Sabal delegation entered, stealing his attention. They had no King, so it was intriguing to see just who came through the door. He watched as Nodiah turned her face away, doing her best to not be recognized as the King's harem entered.

The Sisters of Sabal were dressed in deep red veils similar to the ones the Ogla girls were wearing. After the Sisters, were guards, and then two striking figures. One was an intense looking man with a snarl permanently etched on his face. He had a long grey beard, and his eyes were angry and passionate. His mannerisms were strong and powerful, but felt forced. The other, a large man with flowing black and gold robes. A hood was pulled up over his face hiding most of his features as well. The group took their places along the right half of the room, the two men taking their place next to the Queen.

Nodiah couldn't help but take a glance, but instantly wished she hadn't. The man of her nightmares. The creator of her torture. The one who gave her a fair share of her scars, was now just a few feet from her. Her blood ran cold as she instantly brought her hands to her neck, feeling the shackles clang shut once more. She did her best to control her breath, but her fear showed as some of the other girls began to check on her.

Finally, the local priests entered. A group of 10 robed figures in two lines, all bearing the symbols of the Oracle. The back two were carrying incense of some sort which quickly filled the room with smoke. Behind them, two more women. These two walked in unison, facing the ground. Each step purposeful, intentional. In a way it immediately reminded Keelin of Nodiah.

They had black paint forming thick stripes across their eyes, which intensified the nature of their entrance. Their steps of unison suddenly became a dance. Bells and drums began to fill the chamber with a familiar beat. Keelin smiled, looking in Nodiah's direction hoping to share the moment, but he instead noticed her panic. He had to try and help.

He moved along the wall, pushing his way through as the girls continued their dance. His movements were subtle, and quick, but he knew others were watching. It didn't matter. He made his way to her side, lifting her to her feet and then retreating back to the wall nearby.

As he lifted her, the tears fell. "It's him. Keelin it's Cadius. It's him... I can't. I can't do this." Cadius? From the auction? The High Priest. Things suddenly fell into place. "He did this to me. I can't." He had to calm her.

"Nodiah... Nodi. Hey. Listen. I'm here. You can. We can. You're ok." He let her face sink into his shoulder, and suddenly was aware of a new, strong presence.

"What is the meaning of this disrespect!?" Cadius now stood just a few steps from them, scowling as he growled at them. Keelin felt Nodiah dig into him even tighter, wishing she could just disappear. Whatever he did to her, he would pay.

"She's just overwhelmed. Seeing the Oracle like this isn't a daily occurance. It's a lot to deal with. I'm just calming her down." He kept his tone relaxed, and his eyes focused, doing his best to hide her hair beneath his arms.

"Well see to it that you do, or take her out of the room." He shook his head, and returned to his position. Keelin looked around the room, trying to see who else was paying attention.

One of the Sabal guards seemed to be watching a bit too closely. He was a younger man with a familiar face. Wait... Aero?! Now it was Keelin who was panicking. "You heard the High Priest, lets go." They had to regroup.

He led Nodiah away from the crowd, and through a side hallway. They ducked around another corner, and found their way down a staircase.

Once down to the next level, Nodiah lost all control. "It's too much Keelin. I can't do this. He chained me up and he beat me. My back, it's from him. He's strong too, he's magic or something Keelin. Please. We can't do this. There's no way out. I'm sorry! I'm so sorry!"

"Stop..."

"I just. I want to get answers but..."

"Stop!"

"We're so close... I ju..." without hesitation, Keelin's open hand struck Nodiah's face. She sprawled back, barely keeping on her feet. A sudden explosion of rage filled her body as she turned back to him. That was the last thing she needed.

"You've made it through everything the Creators have thrown at us so far. You aren't stopping here."

"I... am done." She scowled, ready to fight back if needed.

"No. You aren't." He wasn't ready to accept that answer this time. "Look, I saw what you did to the King. I'm scared of what you'll do to this man. I also know that we've had some pretty convenient breaks this entire time. What if the Creators aren't against us. What if they're for us? We will survive. We'll get through this. It doesn't matter that the Queen, and the Fire Breathers and this Cadius are out there."

"Wait wait... Fire Breathers? Keelin..." Suddenly she wondered if his motivation was back to being more about him than it was her. "We can't do this. People will die Keelin. I can't."

"Aero is out there. He's disguised as a Sabal guard," he reluctantly informed her. "Remember what Petyr said, if the Universe brought us this far, it wasn't for us to fail." Those words hit home. She dropped her head, and tried her best to put all of the pieces together.

"The two girls that came in last. I was one of them. They are Vessels. The Oracle uses their energy to channel the Creators, and then delivers their message. In order to prepare for that experience, the High Priest puts them through every kind of torture you can imagine."

She shook, trying to contain her emotions but failing. "It's his belief that the Oracle is actually evil. That she will do everything she can to corrupt and twist and hurt those she uses. Many Vessels don't survive being used he claimed and so this training is necessary to prepare us. He broke me Keelin, you put me back together. I don't want to be broken again. Not like that." It was a sincere plea. It made so many other moments make so much sense.

Suddenly Keelin's heart broke for her. "So we do what we do. You're a Wolf now. You aren't a Vessel. You aren't a slave. You're a Wolf. Wolves hunt. We still have control. No one knows we're here. Escaping town will be easy. We just have to find our moment." The swelling of confidence almost felt unnatural. He wasn't sure where it came from, but it felt good to be back in control of the situation.

He finally looked around to take in the surroundings. Two large stone slabs were spread out behind them. In between was a small fountain, bubbling with a bright blue liquid. Along the outer edges of the room stood statues, each possibly a different Oracle, but it was hard to say for sure. As Nodiah's eyes followed his, she suddenly wiped her tears and smiled a bit herself.

"Something went our way. This is where they'll perform the ritual." She smiled, and then began to laugh a bit. Maybe the Creators were on their side after all. It didn't last too long however, as noise began to travel down from the stairs. They needed somewhere to hide quickly, and options were limited.

They moved off to the side, wedging themselves behind a statue and making their bodies as small as possible. In walked Queen Bodicea and her sister, along with the masked guard and a few other guards from Ogla. Cadius and his counterpart followed, along with a few guards from Sabal, including Aero, and several of the Portis priests. They were followed by the two Vessels, and finally a woman whose aura and presence seemed to outweigh everyone else.

"The Oracle..." Keelin couldn't help but mutter aloud. She was extremely tall, thin and wiry. Even taller than Strom. Her skin paled from years of seclusion beneath the Castle. Her head was bald, but there was a strip of markings that ran from front to back. A narrow white bandage wrapped around her eyes. A bit of blood seemed to seep into the bottom of the fabric though it was impossible to age. Painted on her forehead was the symbol of the Oracle. A wispy white cloth clung to her skin, but it was fairly transparent. The power and intentionality in her movements made Nodiah's seem clumsy in comparison. A harrowing thought crossed Keelin's mind. *If she truly is an Oracle... she's seen this moment before. She knows we're here.*

Nodiah grasped Keelin's arm as they continued to watch, waiting for their moment. The two Vessels laid down on the slabs as the group spread out throughout the room. Cadius placed several familiar looking tablets down on the edge of the slabs, and then washed his hands in the water from the pedestal, and the Oracle moved between the girls.

Her eyes found Aero, standing out because he was awkwardly shifting his weight back and forth from one foot to the other. He looked... nervous. Why?

"Oracle, we welcome you to the inner sanctum, and we await your words." Cadius focused intently on her. The Oracle moved around the slab on the left, touching the tablets that Cadius had laid out. She then did the same with the one on the right, and finally turned back to Cadius and began to speak.

"Ashtu Thrian oh Tak Leo Pan Tat Thole... Reshan Tell a li Ko Rosu Kalo..." The Oracle turned to face Keelin, as both squeezed behind the statue as much as they could. Those words...

"Keelin... How? She?" Nodiah's face turned white as she remembered Keelin's words from the mountain top.

Exhale...

"Because she's an Oracle." He moved from his position and out towards the group, shielding Nodiah behind him. "I think I understand now." The room quickly grew tense. All eyes shot towards the shadows as Keelin approached. "I woke you up."

"Blasphemy. Who are you boy? How dare you interrupt such an important ceremony." Cadius blasted out. As Keelin came to the light, his rage only grew. "You! The Guard?!"

"Well, sort of," he replied quickly. He felt Nodiah crawl out behind him, not wanting to be alone. "I am Keelin of the Wolves. I am now the protector of the White Wolf."

"NOW!" A shout rang out, trying to take advantage of the distraction. The surprise was where it came from. The Queen... Suddenly, her masked guard charged at the Oracle. A burst of fire illuminated the room, seeming to appear out of nowhere as the large robed figure next to Cadius cut the guard off. All hell was breaking loose.

Keelin backpedaled, using the shadows to his advantage as he tried to assess the scene. "Keelin, what is this?" Nodiah shot out nervously, attempting to process it all herself for the first time. Aero and the Sabal guards in the room were on the attack, led by the man in the robes. They were in direct conflict with the soldiers from Ogla.

Nodiah stepped back, clutching two of her knives in her hands tightly. The Oracle stood calm, of course. The fire, where did it come from? Her thoughts were scattered. It was enough of a distraction that she never noticed the figure approach from her left. Suddenly a slender arm wrapped around her throat, squeezing her airway shut. *Keelin..* wheezed out.

He quickly turned to see the masked figure clutching her tightly. They spoke out to him before he could move. "That's far enough Wolf. You already know how bad my bite can be." It couldn't be... How... Jaz. "I told you I'd come for you. I also told you I liked the Queen." She removed the mask. Once again Jaz was a step ahead. He turned back to the room, and quickly recognized some of the Sea Hawks. They were here all along.

"Look we all can get out of this with what we want. We don't have to."

"Now who wants to make a deal? Nah. Deal's off. I already have an agreement. The Queen wants your girlfriend, and the Oracle, and I just brought her both. What could you possibly offer me that she couldn't? Hmm?" Her confidence was as present as always. There had to be a way to use that against her.

His eyes went to Nodiah's, looking for a plan of some sort. Hers flashed with anger more than anything. Her fists still clutched the daggers tightly, but Jaz had to know that. "Ok Jaz I'll tell..."

"No you won't tell me anything. See your friend over there? The little fire kid? He's not alone. The big guy. That's who you're looking for." Keelin scoffed at the mere idea.

"You're lying. There's no way he..." As Keelin turned, he realized the man's hood had dropped. Tattoos covered his head. Black soot circled his eyes. This was the one he remembered.

"Here's your choice. You let me and her settle this one on one, and you go deal with your own battles. It's that or I snap her pretty little neck right now." Jaz's grip tightened. Keelin watched as Nodiah's head turned from a bright red to a deep maroon color as she struggled. She did everything she could to break free, finally dropping the daggers as the energy left her body. That was his limit. "ENOUGH!"

His tone caused Jaz to let go. Nodiah collapsed to the ground, clutching at her throat and gasping for air. Jaz stepped forward and rammed a foot into her ribs for good measure, immediately taking the air back out of her body. As Keelin stepped towards Jaz, a voice called to him from behind.

"Boy... I heard you've been looking for me. My brother says I torched your little lover or something. Seems like you moved on just fine to me." The deep, booming voice carried above the chaos of the fight. Keelin took his pole arm from his back, and responded without turning.

"How's your heart Dreugan? Mine isn't the only one that never fully healed is it?" Keelin turned just as the large man pressed his hand up against his chest where he had been stabbed.

"I've been waiting for this. It's true. If only you knew what was really going on." Such a cryptic message. He was trying to get in his head. The time for talk was over however. This had to end.

Nodiah staggered to her feet, grabbing the knives from the ground nearby as Jaz approached. "I hated you from the beginning. What do you gain from this?" Nodiah gritted out from behind a clenched jaw.

"Oh I'm well aware. The feeling is mutual. That's what makes this such an enjoyable moment. I'm going to take your man, kill the Oracle, and run away to a palace in the hills of Ogla, never to worry again." Jaz's smile made Nodiah sick to her stomach. There was no truth in any of it.

"What makes you so sure the Queen will have your back?" Nodiah was buying herself a bit of time to regain her composure, and calm her breathing.

"Who do you think got rid of the old Queen my dear? Bringing the Oracle to the Queen was always the plan. Things just got reversed. As for Keelin, he doesn't love you. We talked about this. Why do you think he's over there fighting his past instead of being over here protecting you?"

She... No... She was wrong. She lied. Mind games. Nodiah was in control. Her mind wandered back to Rowan of all people. Suddenly, she understood him a whole lot better. She did note that he looked a little like Dreugan, but that thought could wait.

"Do you know what true power is Jaz?" She got to her feet, placing the throwing knives back along her left thigh, and pulling out Jaz's bone dagger from higher up. She smiled as Jaz's eyes found the dagger. "True power... is what you decide is worth fighting for. What's worth dying for. Not only convincing yourself, but those around you of the same thing. Your men, they believe in you. That gives you power. You... You believe in this dagger, and I have it. That gives me power, and I... I believe in myself. There's nothing more powerful than that."

Nodiah twirled, turning her back to Jaz for just a second, and as she spun around she extended her arm and let the dagger go. It flew through the shadows, directly at Jaz's head. Much to her shock, Jaz caught it by the handle. The Captain grinned from ear to ear as she inspected her possession. "Thanks... I..."

There was no hesitation. Nodiah charged, pulling another blade from her thigh and slashing out. Jaz narrowly bent back and dodged, managing to grab Nodiah's arm in the process and fling her forward. They both moved to a fighting stance and began to circle one another.

Dreugan's inhale turned into an exhalation of flames, shot out in Keelin's direction. He managed to dodge it fairly easily, but nearly tripped over the hiding Cadius near the slabs. The Vessels were still on them, and the Oracle, Cadius, and the priests seemed to be doing their best to carry on with the ritual as the fighting roared on around them. Cadius backed away, and the duels continued.

"Call off the guards. This doesn't have to happen like this. Lets settle this. I'm the one you came for." Keelin called out, trying to minimize the conflict.

Dreugan considered the request, and then let out a shot of blue flame, and a roar into the air. Suddenly the Sabal guards backed towards him, still defending themselves when needed. "Same with you Jaz. Call off your men. Nodi's the one you want."

"I'm gonna kill her. It doesn't matter what happens to them." She barked back.

"So there's no reason to watch them die. Let them go." She continued to circle with Nodiah, neither losing any concentration. Finally she let out a sharp whistle, and her Hawks made their way out of the room, followed by the Fire Breathers disguised as Sabal guard. Aero was the last to go, taking a final look at the duels before moving up the stairs.

Keelin moved off to the opposite side of the room from Nodiah, giving him more room to maneuver without worrying about the slabs or priests or anyone else being in the way. Speed was his ally. "It's time to face judgment Dreugan. I wonder how many others there were." Keelin's anger swelled. His control began to fade. His thoughts disappeared.

"I told you then, and I will tell you now. I am not your enemy. Look what I made you."

"You MADE ME?" Keelin screamed back.

"YES! Do you think you ever become Alpha without me? You'd be living in some cottage growing crops and milking cows. I set you free. I let you come what you were supposed to be. Isn't that exactly the same thing you tell her?"

He pointed towards Nodiah. The line had some truth to it, but all it did was enrage Keelin more. "I made you into one of the most powerful men on the continent. Even in the Northern Glen we warn our men to be careful around the Wolves of the South. I broke you, and I set you free."

Keelin walked towards Dreugan, dragging the pole arm behind him allowing the blade to scrape along the ground. The slow, haunting noise echoed through the space as he closed the gap. Dreugan braced himself, observing Keelin and picking his spot.

Dreugan inhaled, Keelin thrust the pole up from his side, pointing the tip out in front of him. At the last second, Keelin slammed the blade down into the ground and used the momentum of the pole to vault himself up into the air and over Dreugan and his blast. The Dragon turned just as Keelin unloaded a right hand to his face. He let out an unrelenting fury of blows that rocked Dreugan off balance. As he staggered back, Keelin pressed in close moving to body shots that never let him catch his breath. If he couldn't take in air, he couldn't breathe fire.

Shot after shot hit, until finally Dreugan simply wrapped his arms around Keelin and began to squeeze. His grip compressed Keelin's smaller frame. He wouldn't last long in his clutches. Desperate, Keelin took a page out of Jaz's book and slammed his head forward into the bridge of Dreugan's nose. The shock of the impact allowed Keelin to wiggle free as Dreugan brought his hands up to his face. This gave Keelin the chance to get back to his weapon.

He turned, just as Dreugan let out another blast of fire, but because Keelin had changed direction he didn't have the momentum to dodge it. Instinctively, he began to spin his weapon quickly. The resulting whirlwind fanned the flames. Some arched around him, but most were stopped in their tracks. It appeared his weapon had some tricks to it as well. Keelin sped up the spinning as Dreugan continued to fire flames in his direction, but he knew the fight had changed.

As Keelin's confidence grew, he began to spin his body with his steps. Dreugan began to back pedal away from his approach, still shooting off fire occasionally, but clearly bothered by this new defense. This took some of the strength out of his attacks. Keelin had him right where he wanted him.

He pressed in, but suddenly lost his concentration. His balance disappeared as he tripped over something. He sprawled against the ground, watching his pole arm slide away from him as well. Behind him was a smirking Cadius, holding onto a long staff. "You're gonna pay for that."

From his back, Keelin now looked up at Dreugan. "It must be so hard, to know you came this close to getting your revenge." Dreugan chuckled, and inhaled deeply. There wasn't enough time to get his weapon spinning again.

As he reached for the pole arm, a new sound rang out from the stairs. "Keelin!" The young voice shouted out. Something small flew through the air. For a moment, Keelin's mind transported back to that first encounter, and he knew exactly what it was. He gripped the pole arm, and swung with all his might, smashing the vial just inches from the Dragon. The resulting explosion instantly consumed Dreugan in flames. His screams only lasted a few seconds before his body thudded to the ground.

Keelin himself had to put a few flames out from his body, but he quickly rolled them out. He turned to the stairs, and couldn't help but smile at Aero who returned the gesture, and then disappeared back up to the floor above.

On the other side, Nodiah continued circling with Jaz. Each were opportunists. Neither was willing to give an advantage however, so it became a mental game. "Enjoy your dagger for now. I'm just going to rip it from your dead hand in a few moments." Nodiah growled towards the Captain.

"I'm only taking my time because I want to remember the look in your eyes, when I end this little fantasy." A smirk crossed Jaz's face. Nodiah had to do something.

She cocked her arm back, and flung the knife towards Jaz, running after it immediately. She grabbed another as she ran, watching as Jaz easily moved out of the way. Nodiah closed the gap, and leaped into the air flipping over Jaz's head.

Unfortunately Jaz still had enough balance to thrust her bone dagger upward, slashing it across Nodiah's thigh. She fell to the ground hard, reaching her hand towards the pain. The site of her own blood only fueled her fire as she staggered her way back to her feet.

Inhale...

Jaz was charging in. Nodiah managed to spin out of the way, swinging her blade down and behind her, using her momentum. She felt the all too satisfying resistance of Jaz's back. Nodiah turned towards Jaz, bringing her other knife towards Jaz's neck, but her arm was caught.

Jaz used her own momentum to roll Nodiah over her shoulder and to the ground once more. Jaz attempted to jump and bring her dagger down on Nodiah, but missed as she rolled out of the way.

Both were gasping for air at this point, feeling the effects of their wounds. "It's going to take more than finesse to finish this Nodiah. I'm not sure you have it in you." The intensity continued to rise. Both knew this had to end soon.

It was at this moment the explosion of the fireball caused both to pause. Nodiah suddenly became fearful. She remembered Petyr's words. She turned, expecting the worst. Thankfully, it was Dreugan who dropped to the ground. Keelin was still there. "I thought I lo-.."

Pain consumed her body from head to toe. From across the room she heard Keelin shout... "NO!..." She tried desperately to take in a breath, but couldn't. She looked down to find Jaz's bone dagger sticking out from under her ribs. Unable to find air, she fell to her hands and knees, trying to scrap together any energy she could.

The only thing she could think to do was grasp the handle, and pull the dagger out releasing some of the pressure. "It was a valiant effort." Jaz chuckled, now taking her time. The Corsair Captain stood over Nodiah victoriously as she retrieved her bone dagger.

"Have you no honor? No dignity?" Nodiah angrily asked.

"That's the difference between us." Jaz grabbed a fistful of Nodiah's hair, and pulled her back to her feet. "There is no right way or wrong way. The only thing that matters is that you get the job done." Her attention turned back to Keelin "You watching Wolf?" She mocked. "I want you to look her in the eyes as I take her life." Jaz moved behind Nodiah, placing the dagger along her neck and pulling her head back. Keelin felt helpless. This couldn't be it. Not here.

"It's okay Keelin. It's ok. We made it so far. You need your answers. It's ok. You got the one who took her from you. You brought me to the Oracle. You gave me so much. All of the gifts the Alphas gave me. They mean everything." Nodiah placed her hand up to her chest. She didn't mean those words. She couldn't have. "Do you remember what you all gave me?"

"Saying your goodbyes? How touching. Do you see it now Keelin? Do you see what real power looks like?" Jaz continued to boast. Her confidence was as annoying as ever, but Nodiah kept going. Her left hand slid down her side, grabbing her last throwing knife stealthily.

"The bow from Nahko. The arrow from King Malachi's throne from Rowan." Suddenly everything stopped. All eyes turned to Nodiah at the mention of the King. "And Fulgrim..."

In one motion she grasped the fang hanging from her neck tightly with her right hand, and raised it up towards her left shoulder. Her left hand brought the knife across the chain, cutting the fang free. Her right hand continued up, over her shoulder and her body twisted just enough to let her slam the fang into Jaz's neck.

The Captain let out a cold shriek of pain as she staggered back. Nodiah's breathing increased. She felt all of the primal nature, rage, and anger come flooding back from the encounter with the King. She was a wounded animal, ready to kill.

Jaz inspected her wound, and then saw the look in Nodiah's eyes. Nodiah dropped her head back and let out a booming howl that echoed through the room. Her smile returned. The pain faded. She was focused on one thing.

Jaz backpedaled, now desperate to end it. "Wait wait wait. We can still work together." Nodiah cocked her head to the side blankly at the pleas of the once proud Captain as she continued to close the gap. "Bodicea.. A little help." The Queen lowered her head at the mention of her name and taking a few steps away. "I made good on my word, and you're just going to...What's going to happen when the world finds out you paid me to kill the Oracle?" The room gasped for a moment as eyes turned to the Queen once more.

"That's.. That's preposterous. You are the one who murdered the former Queen, and quite possibly the King of Sabal as well. I don't have to explain myself to you. That's simply..."

Keelin stepped towards the Queen, putting himself between her and the door. "Come now. The Wolves killed the King, and you hired her to kill your mother. I'm pretty sure Jaz would happily confess if we let her live." Keelin's attention turned. She had her own price to pay. "That's why you came. You're just here to cash in on the crystal mine in Portis, but you're worried the Oracle will expose you. Something's in there."

"It's the word of a... a Corsair... and a dirty Wolf... versus a Queen. Who will they believe? This is ridiculous. This won't stand. Sister. Please." Her eyes turned to the High Priestess.

"I'm simply here as a formality. You are Queen." Keelin smiled as the Queen's eyes grew large. He hesitated for a moment however. He knew Kendra from somewhere. That statement must have meant more than he knew as well. Finally out of options, the Queen lunged forward, catching Keelin a bit off guard and driving him back.

The two wrestled for a moment, jostling until finally Keelin was able to get behind her and hold her secure. Keelin watched as finally the Oracle moved, and seemed to be heading in his direction. "Back off, or so help me she dies." Threatening an Oracle felt empty.

This left his back to Nodiah and Jaz however, who never missed an opportunity. Without hesitation, she hurled her bone dagger forward with all the force she could muster. Nodiah watched helplessly as it whizzed past her shoulder. She wasn't the target. "KEELIN!" She closed her eyes.

Keelin felt an unnatural calm as the Oracle approached, and then placed a hand on his back, pushing him forward. The dagger connected with the Oracle straight in the chest. The priests immediately surrounded her as she collapsed to the floor. Blood began to run from the corners of her mouth.

Nodiah's eyes opened, but she couldn't believe what she saw as she turned. The rage faded. Her heart broke. "No no no no...." She ran to the Oracle, hoping that somehow this being was immortal. She knew better. She shot Jaz one last glance as the Captain made her exit up the stairs. "Keelin..."

He instantly dropped the Queen, and made his way to the Oracle as well. Much to everyone's surprise, the Oracle spoke. "Leave me with the Wolves." The priests immediately rose, but the rest of the room was a little more apprehensive. Keelin and the Queen, Nodiah and Cadius were the last four.

"Remember me?" Nodiah scowled towards Cadius.

"Of course my dear. You aren't one who is easy to forget. I fall asleep to the sound of your screams in my mind." He replied equally as intense. "It's a sound I'll hear again soon. Do you really think you'll leave this place alive? I told you I would find you." It was a haunting thought, but honest.

Her eyes closed...

Her eyes tried to make out something in the darkness. Nothing came this time. She must have been blindfolded. Her body strained against the bolt holding her to the floor. They were giving. She was close! He laughed as he moved around her this time. "Would you like to know the truth my little Vessel?" He smiled... "Why now? Why do you think I need a Vessel hmm? I don't. She isn't going to wake up. Not in our lifetime, and we're all better off for it. I'm doing this to you because I need a personal servant. Someone to cater to my needs. I need to put the proper amount of fear in you before that happens..."

He was lying. All of this was just some sick selfish ploy? Why did he need a Vessel if the Oracle wouldn't awake? No... She wouldn't allow it. She pushed her body back in the opposite direction, and then rammed herself forward with every ounce of fight she had left. The bolts gave.

Her right arm brought the chain around his neck with a loud clank. He fell back, and immediately she pounced. She landed on top of him, and crossed her arms adding more pressure to the chain. "You will let me go. You will NEVER take a Vessel again. Make up whatever lie you have to. I will not serve you." She scowled.

"Where will you go? Back to the King? Fine! Have it your way. I will get my hands on you again. I will break whatever is left of you. You have nowhere on this continent you can hide you stupid little girl." His words wheezed, but it didn't lessen their impact. She wrapped the chain around her fist, and swung down hard.

Her eyes opened... She was brought back by the thought that they would be waiting for them. There was no easy escape. Finally the Queen and the High Priest made their way out. It was hard to watch. They would be difficult enemies to deal with. That didn't matter now.

Keelin and Nodiah were left alone with the Oracle. "Antha ek to insah lari neh toh Nodiah jek onias ko lari neh to Keelin... I... I'm sorry." The words started weak, and then faded to a whisper, and she was gone. The Oracle died before they could ask anything. Their journey was over. No answers. No leads to the temple.

"What... What did she say?" Nodiah asked behind tear filled eyes.

"She said she was sent to protect Nodiah, but fate told her to protect Keelin too." It brought some comfort. If she was in fact sent to protect Nodiah, then Nodiah had to be something. She had to be chosen. She had to be a Sky Dancer... but they had no way to get to the temple now. Jaz, the Queen, Cadius, the Dragons, and who knows who else were waiting upstairs.

A sudden small noise caught their attention. A cough. Someone else was in the room. From the slabs, the two Vessels began to stir. They sat up, and then instantly ran to the Oracle's side. "WHAT DID YOU DO??" One screamed at them.

"It wasn't us. It was the others, disguised as guards." The duo took in their faces, seeing the emotion and tears. Nodiah continued to try and explain. "I was one of you once. I was a Vessel. What Cadius does to you, it's not right. It's not necessary. You can escape." She pleaded with them.

"We know. But she was worth it." The girls tone was somber, but cognizant. "The Oracle actually woke up. She was not the monster he said she was."

"She stepped in the way of a blade for Keelin. She protected him." Nodiah continued to explain, hoping something would click. Both Vessels looked to her surprised at the idea that the Oracle would shield him.

"Then this is what was meant to happen." Now coming to terms with things, they stood. "Cadius will blame you. You have to leave quickly."

"How? They're waiting." Keelin chimed in.

"Do you think they'd build a room this important without a way to sneak the Oracle out when needed?" The girls moved over to the same statue the duo had been hiding behind, and pulled down on the arm. A section of the wall lurched back, and slid to the side, revealing a long tunnel. The Vessel took one of the torches from the wall, and lit a sconce on the wall. It quickly created a chain reaction that lit several more down the hall.

"Go. You can't come back. Not to Sabal, not to Portis. Just take these and go." Their words were a warning more than a threat. Each of them pulled out a small dagger made of bone. They were extremely similar to Jaz's, but with slight differences.

Once more, chaos had been left in their wake. They took one last look at the Oracle, realizing the answers they were after now laid dead.

Exhale...

They made their way into the tunnel, not sure of where it would lead. They could pop up into a trap for all they knew, but it was the only shot they had. Nodiah grabbed Keelin's hand as he led the way through the twists and turns. There was only one path at least, but that meant it had a very intentional purpose. It had to lead to a safe room somewhere.

Seconds turned to minutes as they twisted. Occasionally, they could hear shouts and panic from above. The word of the Oracle's death must have reached the crowds. "Back to being on the run." Keelin sighed.

"They deserve better. They deserve the truth," Nodiah responded. She was fearful of what the final cost of all of this would be for the people of such a great city.

"We can't tell anyone the truth if we're dead." It was a valid enough statement from Keelin. They had to make it out. They could free Portis another day.

Finally the tunnel twisted to an end. A staircase led up to what appeared to be a trap door beneath a floor. They made their way up the stairs, and crouched down just under the door, trying to see if they could make anything out from above.

It was hard to see much. There were large footsteps pacing back and forth across the beams. After a few seconds of listening, a familiar voice boomed out. "You're clear." Petyr...

They cautiously lifted the door, and Petyr helped them up the last couple steps, shutting the door behind them. They appeared to be in a room at the inn. "How did you know we were down there?" Keelin wondered out loud.

"It's so good to see you Petyr. Cadius and the Queen, they're trying to say we killed the Oracle." Nodiah did her best to explain.

"I know I know, word always comes to the Falcon first. We don't have much time." Petyr's words were more determined than panicked.

"We didn't get our answer though. We will stay. We have to show Portis the truth." Keelin stood his ground, but Petyr seemed to laugh him off.

"I told you, you aren't as smart as you think. We have to go now."

"We?" Nodiah responded quizzically.

"You won't make it out without me. I can help." Petyr began intently searching through the shelves for something. He looked through books and scrolls, unraveling them at a furious pace.

"What are you looking for? Can we help?" Nodiah asked.

"No my dear, It's here somewhere. All will be explained soon. AH! Here it is! Yes! Come come." Petyr led the way out of the room and towards the front of the Inn. There sitting behind the counter were the bags with the rest of the duo's belongings.

"Hey wait a minute. Want to explain the weapons room? And why the tunnel led here?" Keelin suddenly wasn't sure what to believe. Things were too convenient.

Petyr's response became frustrated. "I am trying to save your life. You weren't supposed to make it this far, and so there must be a reason, but if you are dead then no one will find out what that is now will they?" There were no more questions. Nodiah and Keelin grabbed their things. "Put these on." Petyr handed them oversized black robes with hoods to hide their features, and the trio quickly made their way out to the streets.

"Stay behind me. Nodiah in the middle." He used his large frame to block them out as they walked. They headed straight for the tree lines, not risking being seen on the roads. They almost made it, when a voice called out.

"Petyr! Is that you? Where are you going?" It didn't sound particularly familiar, but Petyr turned to answer cautiously.

"There is a rumor the killers escaped. We're going after them." He replied calmly.

"Then I'll join you!" Nodiah and Keelin didn't look up, instead burying themselves more in the robes.

"Head to the gate. Look for the girl with the blue hair."

"Blue? I thought it was red?"

"She changed it to try and disguise herself! Have you never dealt with assassins before?" Keelin chuckled a bit to himself beneath the robe.

"Oh... right..." The man hesitated, but then finally left towards the gate.

As soon as they hit the trees, their walk turned into a full sprint. They took one last look back at Portis. The brief amount of time they had some sense of normal was worth it. It gave them hope of what the future could be. Maybe once this was all settled, there would be another Portis out there. Maybe things would never really be settled. Now that the Oracle was dead, there was very little certainty about anything.

They continued in silence, each reflecting on what had been and what was to come. Finally, after exchanging a few glances, the silence became too much for Keelin. "Where are we going?"

"Not much farther." His answer was short and focused.

"That's not good enough Petyr. Come on." Keelin insisted, stopping in his tracks.

"Keelin, we've been through a lot ok. I get it. Not now." Nodiah's pleas radiated through her stare as she walked past him and continued. She was right. He just didn't like to wander.

Finally, the trees gave way to a small clearing roughly ten feet in diameter. Nodiah looked up first, and let out an excited shout. "Aero!" There before them was Aero with a familiar large strider by his side.

"Hello friends!" He exclaimed cheerfully. Keelin stood silent, unsure of what to say to the young man who saved his life.

"Aero... I... Thank you." He said humbly. His brain couldn't process what was happening, or what all Aero had done for them.

"Dragon... Wolf... Queen... King... They're just labels. Labels don't define us. You both are trying to do the right thing. Mistakes happen, but you're good people." The duo smiled at the profound wisdom of their friend.

"Aero has agreed to help take you to your next destination," Petyr interrupted.

Nodiah looked at him dumbfounded. "Next? Where are we going?"

"To the Hall of the Sky Dancers. You have the daggers right?" Petyr chuckled. Nodiah and Keelin looked at each other, and then back to Petyr, smiling a bit uncomfortably. Surely he was confused. They handed him the three daggers. How did he know about Jaz's?

"Petyr, we told you. We didn't get any answers from the Oracle. She's dead. We don't know how to get there." A smile crossed Petyr's face from ear to ear as he saw the confusion in their eyes.

He unrolled the scroll he had grabbed from the shop, and held it in front of them. Keelin approached first. "It's a map... Is this? How?" He looked on carefully, recognizing the top tip of the Southern Pass was on the bottom of the map.

"Petyr. What the hell is going on?" Nodiah now was demanding answers.

"I told you both, if Keelin survived I would answer all of your questions. The Oracle isn't dead."

"She survived? Enough riddles Petyr. Please!" Nodiah begged.

"The Oracle isn't dead... I am the Oracle."

Inhale...

Glossary

Dachaigh– (Dock–Eye)– Celtic word for home

Torek– Paying tribute to Vercingetorix, the Celtic King who took on Julius Caesar

Sabal-(Sah-Ball) Refers to a genus of palm trees

Coille– (Kah-Lee) Celtic word for forest

Ogla–(Oh-gla) Scandavian word for Holy.

Nodiah–(No-die-ya) Biblical word meaning Witness, or Ornament of the Lord

Keelin- Celtic name meaning fair and slender

Saiorse- (Sur-Sha) Celtic name meaning freedom.

Rowan- Irish name meaning little red one

Fulgrim- Latin for lightening

Comhla– (Ko-La) From the Celtic còmhla meaning together.

Nahko– Native American word for bear

Jashilyn Majila– No meaning

Dreugan– Scottish for dragon.

Beanfeasa- Celtic word for fortune-teller

Petyr- American name meaning stone. A nod to another particular character of fantasy genre fame.

Aeronault– Celtic word for dragon.

Cadius– Breton name meaning little fighter.

www.ingramcontent.com/pod-product-compliance
Lightning Source LLC
Chambersburg PA
CBHW071515110726
47908CB00003B/849